SHANNON'S LAND

D. B. Woodling

Copyright 2015 by Debra S. Woodling
All Rights Reserved

Woodling, D.B.
ISBN: 978-0-7443-2175-3
Shannon's Land / D.B. Woodling – 1st ed.

No part of this publication may be reproduced, except in the case of quotation for articles, reviews, or stored in any retrieval system, or transmitted in any form or by any means, electronic, mechanical, photocopying, recording or otherwise, without written permission from the publisher. For information regarding permission, contact:

SynergEbooks
948 New Hwy 7
Columbia, TN 38401
www.synergebooks.com

Cover art by Jennifer Givner

Printed in the USA

CPSIA information can be obtained
at www.ICGtesting.com
Printed in the USA
LVOW10s1414040917
547475LV00014B/1216/P

9 780744 321753

SHANNON'S LAND

This book is a work of fiction.
Names, characters, places,
and incidents are either
creations of the author's imagination
or used fictitiously.

For my Children: TaMarra and Christian
A special thanks to Ron and Liz for their frequent encouragement

ONE

Summer 1874
Leeds, Missouri

The rain pelted her face nearly as hard as he had before he knocked her to the ground and abandoned her for good. Her body battered, her heart broken long ago, this time she didn't call after him. Instead, she watched him, mounted on their best sorrel, until he disappeared over the swollen hillside, and Shannon Cook decided her long trail of regrets would finally end here.

Despite the relentless shards of rain, she sat motionless as her eyes darted from woods to range and back again. Although Shannon had little reason to believe the Comanche would travel north from Texas, she'd heard tales of Kansas settlers attacked and murdered not so many months before. What would she do if the Indians chose her homestead for their next raid?

She heard her son's cries and reluctantly attempted to stand. The brown Missouri glop staked its stubborn claim on her boots and she fell backwards twice. As she slogged through the sludge, she kept her eyes trained on a second-story window. She knew from the sound of things that Zach's plump cheeks rivaled the color of her red gingham dress, his eyelids shone purple, and his tiny lips quivered between howls. She called out to him, her long-anticipated infant, the missing element she once felt certain would resurrect her decaying marriage, and then she murmured, "Maybe Cole's right. Maybe I *am* utterly worthless."

As she neared the hitching rail, the rain came to an end, and a hazy sun began its blurry ascent over a bleak tree line. She winced with even the smallest of steps but managed to reach the porch. Her footsteps against the wooden slats echoed across the pasture. She was truly alone in this untamed wilderness and froze in the doorway, her gaze flying from the rag rug bordering the hearth, to the cook stove, then the curtains tailored by her own hands, finally settling on the oil lamp she'd looted from her father's house. The Diamond Sawtooth lamp's crystal inlays cast triangular patterns on the wall and she stood mesmerized, wishing it possible never to think about anything else. Not the husband who had abandoned her. Not the father who had forced her out. Not the son who now depended on her solely for survival.

Her left eye was swollen shut, and she knew from innumerable experiences that the bruises beginning to form would remind her of Cole for weeks to come. Shannon whimpered and grabbed hold of the baluster. Shaking, she fought the overwhelming urge to retrieve the oil lamp and pour the kerosene throughout the dreary whitewashed two-story then set everything afire.

Zach's wails intensified, and she croaked his name through guilty tears. Once upstairs, she reflexively collected him from his cradle. Her heart skipped just as it always did when she held him, and she wondered how anything so glorious could be born of such ugliness.

When the baby refused to suckle she panicked, her thoughts racing to the livestock Cole had taken with him. How would they survive without milk, meat or poultry, without suitable horses to pull the plow? At least he had left her Sara, only because the old nag was about as reliable as summer rain for crops blowing yellow and lifeless in Missouri's midsummer heat.

A chill scaled her spine as she considered patronizing the nearby precarious town. Named for her father, Mika Leeds, despite local objections, Leeds was equally corrupt as the man himself, comprised mostly of drifters, drunks, outlaws, tawdry women, thieves, and murderers. She was quite certain the small remainder wouldn't raise a hand to help her or anyone closely associated with her father and not only because he'd taken the majority of the townspeople's monies with him when he fled. She'd heard he'd gone to St. Louis, but Shannon knew even if she could finance the two-hundred mile trip by Missouri Pacific Railroad neither she nor her son would be welcome.

She rocked her hungry baby to sleep and returned him to his crib. Cringing, she sponged the mud and blood from her bruised and battered body, discarded her tattered dress, and wiggled guardedly into her only best bib and tucker. Then she trudged outside, wrestled Sara from the barn, and attempted to hitch the obstinate beast to the buckboard.

* * * *

Luke Richards rode his horse, Thunder, further into the bottomlands of his employer's vast ranch. Discovering the herd gone, he touched a spur to the black stallion's flank and the horse switched from canter to full run. He reined the Morab at the manmade break in the fence, his gray eyes hard, his face blemished by furious lines. "Jack Marsh," he hissed.

He rolled a smoke, rested a hand on the pommel, and inhaled deeply. Jack's chief tool was responsible, of that he was sure. Luke tracked the hoof prints, nonetheless, but was able to distinguish little thanks to the gully-washer. Because his employer's recently acquired Angus bore no brand, immediate recovery of the herd was crucial. Luke gnawed his mustache thoughtfully and thought it best to return to the ranch; inform his employer, Samuel Willoughby; and get a few of his more intimidating associates rounded-up.

He spun Thunder about and when but three yards shy of the fence break once again, he reined the stallion hard, grinned, and plucked a fistful of red hair from a hawthorn's sagging branch. Now he had proof of Jack's involvement and his name was Red Morton. Luke considered the inevitable clash and wondered if a few allies would be enough. Morton wore brutality like a custom-made suit.

TWO

It never occurred to Shannon that news of her husband's desertion would reach town so quickly until she felt the cold and inquisitive eyes upon her as she steered her horse and buckboard down Main Street. As she made her way past the livery stable, blacksmith shop, and The Bank of Leeds, the *clip-clop* of Sara's hooves echoed down the narrow thoroughfare. The lips of the men gathered outside Jed's Barber Shop were still, a sight as uncommon as prayer meetings inside Ruby's bawdyhouse. Moments after she passed the saloon, she knew by the shadows that fell across the street that several of the dancing girls had come out onto the balcony, some no doubt accompanied by their drunken male companions.

Shannon reined Sara at the hitching rail outside Johnston's General Store. The townswomen craned their necks, their fierce eyes effectively communicating longstanding animosity, and Shannon briefly considered returning home. Climbing from the buckboard, her horse suddenly reared. Shannon lost her balance and fell into mud and horse manure. No one offered to help. No one resisted laughter. Not even those many men once down on bended knee.

The majority of the women whispered behind gloved hands; a few volunteered their comments openly:

"My goodness, will you look at that. As I live and breathe, I do believe it's Shannon Cook!"

"Surely looks more like the gravedigger's woman!" another said.

"Looks more like the one he's diggin' the grave for if you asked me," Kate Reeds bellowed. "Whatever do you suppose happened to that beautiful red hair?"

"I declare if it don't bring to mind a sweet potato pie."

"That skin a hers looks more beet juice than cream!" Kate added.

Shannon blinked back tears and pushed past them. Zach began to cry and when he became the target of their unkind remarks, Shannon whirled around to face them. Resisting a more poignant spew of profanity, she told them all to go to hell.

Met with more of the same condemnation inside the store, Shannon kept her head high and her senses alert. Quickly navigating the barrels of onions, potatoes, and pickles, she approached the counter. "Mr. Johnson, I've made a list of things I need if you would be so kind..."

Joshua Johnston sensed his wife, Eunice, eavesdropped from the storeroom and reached up in an effort to separate his thick, dark brows determined to meet in the middle. The morning had been a long and miserable one, primarily due to his wife. She was never happy. To make matters worse, his movements hadn't been right in days and, although, she had tried to convince him it was nothing more than dysentery, he wondered if she had intentionally given him spoiled meat.

He glanced over his shoulder toward the storeroom and knew by her sneer and stiff carriage that Eunice intended to involve herself. He also knew he had little choice but to break off Mrs. Cook's words, mainly due to the prompting from his very large and imposing wife. "Mrs. Cook, it distresses me to have to tell you that I cannot extend any more credit to you at this time. Your husband has a sizable bill due and has not made the slightest attempt to make good on his word. Perhaps if he could come by..."

"Oh, Joshua, don't sugar-coat it!" Eunice bellowed, leaving the storeroom and smacking an empty flour sack and a pudgy elbow down on the counter. "Cole Cook's done spent all his money on gamblin' and whores, no doubt, down at Ruby's place. A Cook's word is 'bout as useless as confederate money!"

"Be still, woman," Joshua told her sheepishly.

"I see she still has you under her spell," Eunice hissed in a low tone and shoved him backwards. "She turned you down years ago or don't you remember!"

Johnston lowered his head then glanced over his shoulder. Once convinced Eunice had returned to the storeroom, he whispered beneath a morose mustache: "Mrs. Cook, due to your hardship and the unpaid bill being no fault of your own, I will give you what I can until you can get in touch with kin to pay your debt."

They exchanged a pitiful smile, both aware her only kin was a father who had disowned her years ago.

"Mr. Johnston, I'm much obliged to you for your kindness, and I will see that Cole's debt is paid," Shannon should have said more quietly.

"Ha!" Eunice mocked from the other room.

Joshua again tried to summon the courage necessary to stand up to his wife. Secretly he hoped that she would either leave him or die. Even before the birth of their second child, he'd had such thoughts. At first he'd experienced guilt, but the guilt had quickly turned to shame for not kicking her out or ushering her up to God. He was thankful that her true passion seemed to consist of squeezing every dime she could out of the store. At least she no longer had an interest in him intimately. The mere thought of her enormous mass beneath him nearly made him wretch, and he shook off the chill creeping up his spine.

Ignoring Eunice's intense glare, which was her promise of the punishment to come, he looked longingly at Shannon. "I'll get your goods together and have our boy bring them outside directly, Mrs. Cook." For her sake, Joshua thought it best to get her well out of Eunice's reach as quickly as possible.

"Thank you again for your kindness, Mr. Johnston." Shannon didn't acknowledge Eunice or her snarl as she closed the door and stepped out into the street.

Just as Shannon assumed, the women lay in wait. Struggling to clear a path, she recognized Jenny Saunders who elbowed her hard. "Where's that husband a yers?" she asked.

"Probably down at Ruby's between two whores and a bottle of cheap whiskey!" a woman alongside shrieked.

A third woman blocked Shannon's path and pointed to the

sign above Johnston's store. "You see that sign? It says store, not charity!"

"Ladies, ladies," Kate Reeds said, demanding the limelight. "Look at her! Charity's soon to be her only salvation." Kate closed the space between them and hovered over Shannon. "Won't be much longer men'll stop droppin' themselves at your feet."

Fearing for Zach's safety, Shannon quickened her pace and decided to seek refuge in *Emily's Finery Shoppe*.

Emily had been standing at the door watching the spectacle through the glass panes, trying to imagine what the young woman could have done that provoked such unkindness. Probably nothing, she convinced herself, as she, too, had been a victim of their volatile manners from time to time. She clutched the doorknob, fighting the urge to fetch the carbine and inspire the mob to clear out. Instead, she motioned the young woman inside. "Ma'am, won't you come in and have a look at the latest fashions? Please? You simply must! They've come all the way from St. Louis."

Emily closed the door abruptly once the young woman and her child were safely inside and pulled the shade down so vehemently that the women left standing on the other side dared not follow. Recent matters had taught them never again to cross Emily Dunsmire.

Shannon thought to explain that she had no money for such things. Instead she simply mumbled, "Thank you, ma'am."

"Good heavens! Where are my manners? I'm Emily. Emily Dunsmire."

"Pleased to make your acquaintance. I'm Shannon Cook and this here's my son, Zach."

Emily suddenly felt her knees weaken, and she sucked in a full breath and held it. Weeks had passed since she'd arrived in Leeds, all the while summoning the courage to ride out to the Cook homestead, and now Shannon Cook stood directly in front of her. She knew she had to bide her time but battled for restraint. "My, that's a lovely dress you're wearing, Mrs. Cook! Did you make it yourself?" Emily glanced out the window while waiting for Shannon's response and to her dismay the crowd had yet to dismantle. They had moved away from the front of the shop, but it was clear they were hoping to continue their sport.

Shannon recalled the day her sister grudgingly allowed her the leftover mauve taffeta and silk brocade. Without taking her eyes off the door, she said, "Yes ma'am. It's rather worn I'm afraid."

"Well, it's absolutely lovely." Emily placed an arm around Shannon's shoulder, gently steering her away from the windows. "Let's not think on those ole hens out there." Appraising Shannon's dress more closely, Emily exclaimed, "My lands, those brocade stripes are striking. And I don't know how you managed those knife and box pleats! They do so accentuate your exquisite waistline."

Shannon blushed and mumbled her gratitude.

Taking her by the hand, Emily guided her toward the far end of the shop, suddenly realizing an opportunity. She instructed Shannon to sit and brought her a cup of tea. "I'm a businesswoman and not much a one for wasting time, Mrs. Cook. I was just thinking this morning how much profit I could procure if I were able to make such grand gowns. If you would be interested, I would be willing to give you thirty percent of whatever I'm able to sell them for. Does that sound fair to you?"

Elated at the possibility of a means to an end, Shannon replied, "That sounds absolutely divine, but I don't rightly know that I can manage such finery."

Emily cupped Shannon's hand. "Never know unless you try. Besides, I'm willing to bet you can tailor a fine gown, one that could disguise even those two-legged cows yonder as queens." Shannon laughed and Zach began to kick and coo. Emily smiled at the baby and tried not to think about the past. "I'll get you your notions and you get one finished. Then come on back and I'll have a look. What do you say?"

Shannon looked into Emily's eyes and thought they were nearly as blue as the sky just before sundown and nearly as vivid a color as the auburn hair that cascaded down and around the lobes of her ears. Her scent familiar, Shannon decided it reminded her of the honeysuckle which grew indiscriminately along the lane to her land. "I'm much obliged, Miss Dunsmire. Why, it's an answer to a prayer!"

THREE

Emily kept vigil at the door once Shannon and her baby left the shop. "That a girl!" she said aloud when Shannon wouldn't allow the mob to corral her into Main Street's ankle-deep muddy ruts.

Emily had heard many a rumor about Cole Cook, but even had she not, she knew by Shannon's hollow eyes that his abuse extended far beyond the surface. "The only fault that can be said of Shannon Cook," she murmured, "is damn poor judgment when it came to picking a husband." She had once made that same mistake. Emily smiled at her reflection in the glass. She was still a breathtakingly beautiful woman. Many suitors had gone away distraught when she turned down their marriage proposals, the majority of them occurring on the East Coast.

Distracted and thinking about the task that lay ahead, Shannon neither saw nor heard the drunken rider only half-mounted on his horse. Just as the collision seemed inevitable, a hand grabbed Zach from her arms and another launched her toward the boardwalk, where Shannon found herself assuming the prayer position outside Jed's Barber Shop.

"Dammit, you fool woman! Trying to get this baby a yers killed today?"

Shannon looked over her shoulder and saw Luke Richards for the first time. Words didn't come easy. Never in all her days had she seen a man so pleasing to the eye. He was tall, she guessed nearly six-foot-two, lean but in a manner suggesting hard work as opposed to drinking his breakfast and supper. His hair was thick and dark but laced with ribbons of chestnut from too much time spent under a blazing sun and a little long for her liking. His gray eyes gleamed, but she sensed both warmth and distrust in them, eyes that had witnessed more bad than good.

"Unhand my child," she shouted, reaching for Zach. "And I

would appreciate it sir if you would not be so inclined to bash in my brains should I have the misfortune of meeting you again!" When she sensed the smirk ready to play out on his full lips, she was convinced of her initial assessment... anything that looked that good probably wasn't.

Luke placed Zach in her arms and flaunted a usually effective, infectious grin. "And what a shame it would be to bash such beautiful brains, too." He laughed outright when her green eyes flashed and she didn't return his smile. Refusing his outstretched hand, he shrugged his shoulders, left the stunning redhead on the ground, and thought how much he appreciated a woman with guts. "Since I reckon what you really intended to say, Miss, is *Much obliged*, I'll be along." As he turned to walk away, he intentionally violated her with a long and inappropriate leer.

Luke heard his associate's whistle and his eyes suddenly riveted on the saloon. When he faced Shannon again, his expression abruptly changed. "Might serve you well to get that baby back in that shop you came from. Trouble's brewin'."

Shannon eyes followed him and the five who shadowed him as they strolled across Main Street, their eyes slanting up the street then down. They carried themselves tall and determined, gun hands poised on low belts.

Luke inspected an impressive buckskin mare hitched first at the rail, recognized it as a horse belonging to Red, and signaled to the other men. Luke was the first to step stealthy between the saloon doors, however, and shouted, "Red Morton, we got some business outside!"

Red went for his gun just as Luke knew he would.

Luke had no desire for any in his party to risk a bullet, though he considered with these men's particular skills there was little possibility. In a blur of silver and walnut, Luke brought up one of two Colt Peacemakers and had Morton in his sights before the red-haired brute's six-shooter even cleared leather. "Them fists a yours only good for rustlin'?" Luke taunted.

Of course, cattle rustlers preferred to keep their supplementary occupation on the quiet, especially those thieves who'd developed an affection for the town in which they pilfered, and he figured sharing that information would spur the man into action. Luke's eyes were alert and penetrating, but he noted a kind of arrogant certainty in Red's. That might have troubled a more inexperienced man, but Luke was ready. Born into a large family in which food was often as scarce as a kind word, he'd split many a knuckle on the rock-hard jaws of his older brothers.

"Don't make no never mind to me which way I unlimber you," Morton said, sweeping a grin around the bar. "Dead is dead."

Laughter circulated... mostly anxious chuckles.

Luke planted his tongue against his upper lip and took a few steps toward him, his keen eyes narrowing. "Close your mouth and move your feet then. I got cattle to collect."

"Take it outside, boys!" Ruby, owner of the saloon and bawdyhouse, bellowed nervously.

"Shuck those gun belts, too!" ordered Lance Tucker, Foreman of Plains Paradise-Samuel Willoughby's spread-and a former notorious gunfighter himself. "Hear? On the bar!"

Lance's widely documented reputation preceded the current event, and Red Morton's crew immediately complied. Once outside, Luke quickly found himself and Morton smack dab in the middle of a circle of bloodthirsty spectators, some making bets. He faked a jab, which was his way of testing Morton's fighting technique. Just as he figured, the big man lunged for him, planning to make easy work of it and trap him between his tree-trunk-like arms.

Luke knew he had to bring him down fast and rather than retreat, as he knew Morton expected, he brought his left arm up hard, buried his boot heel in Morton's right knee, and threw him off balance, successfully blocking his advance. Then he smacked two solid rights, breaking Morton's nose. The crowd gasped their surprise, and even Luke was amazed when the Goliath head wobbled. He intended to follow with a rib punch, but Morton read his intentions and dodged clear of the blow.

This time Morton's pounce was successful and his arms encircled Luke, squeezing him and emptying his lungs. Luke swung his legs forward then back and kicked him hard, his spurs digging into the fleshy sides of Morton's calves. Red yelped a growl and instantly dropped Luke to the ground.

Luke had hardly caught his breath before Morton recovered. Fortunately, Luke was already on his feet and landed a solid uppercut to the big man's chin. Not the least bit fazed, Red Morton hit Luke brutally, the blow stamping a deep gash over his right eye. Luke's head swam and Morton got a hold of him good then, his powerful right fist delivering three evil kidney punches. Blood polka dotting his gray flannel shirt, Luke elbowed Morton fiercely in the ribs, then drove the back of his head into Red's broken nose. Not much more than a blink or two after, a scattergun persuaded the two men to dive for cover.

FOUR

"Old man Jamison says this here's about cattle rustlin'," the sheriff said, approaching Red. "That right?"

"So we was accused, lawman," Red replied and spat blood.

"I gave Red here a friendly warnin', Sheriff," Luke called out. "He contested it some in the beginnin', but in the end I believe he was open to counsel."

Laughter circulated among the crowd, and Morton's glare promised reprisal.

"I'd heed his notice," Jacob told Red, "'cause in this town, one man ropin' another man's cattle guarantees HIM a ropin' if you get my meanin'. Be on your way, both of you. Anymore fightin' in my town'll get you a night in the hoosegow."

Luke gathered his hat from the ground. Lance handed him his guns.

"Reckon she's waitin' around to thank you proper?" Lance asked Luke and gestured across the street.

Luke exaggerated a grin and tipped his hat to Shannon. Both men laughed when her nose saluted the low clouds, and she went on her way.

"She's a pretty little thing," Lance teased.

Luke scowled. "So is a cottonmouth."

* * * *

Shannon was exhausted as she neared the long lane home. The range eerily quiet, she listened hard for any movement, her eyes sweeping from one side of the lane to the other. Night was coming on fast, and she cursed herself for staying so long in town. *I'm nearly as bad as the lot of them*, she thought, *standing around keeping track of swings and misses.* Cradling her baby closer, she told him, "Weren't but one side in that fight, Zach, and that be the devil's. You best remember that when you're older."

Dusk dispersing long shadows across the porch, Shannon squinted as she tried to distinguish the object near the door. "Dear Lord, it's Duke!" The bloodhound that had always accompanied Cole must have given up trying to keep up with him and returned home. Jostling Zach, she sprinted toward the house.

* * * *

Once the supplies were unloaded, she fell into bed and hoped Zach would sleep through the night. Waking many times despite her sleeping baby, she crept out of bed with each occurrence and surveyed the land around the house from one upstairs window or another. Her final sentry ending shortly before dawn, Zach woke crying just as she had lapsed into a deep sleep.

"Mama's here," she cooed and took Zach from the crib. Quickly realizing his weren't the only cries disturbing the morning's quiet, she abruptly returned him and grabbed the rusty carbine from its position over the door. She tore down the stairs, thrust the door open, and fired into the sunrise. The pack of coyotes scattered. Duke lay motionless and bloody, his breathing labored and sporadic. Shannon fetched water from the well and did her best to cleanse his numerous rips and tears. She went back inside and returned with a jar of lard to dress the deeper wounds.

Suddenly, Duke pitched his ears skyward, his keen eyes glassy and locked on the woods. Shannon scanned the timber and instantly noticed the pack's leader. When her eyes locked on the coyote's, it charged. Shannon grabbed the rifle, planted the butt against her shoulder, aimed, and pulled the trigger. The shell jammed, and the beast drove its hind legs hard against the ground, its midair advance swift. Her eyes wide, a scream lodged in her throat, Shannon flipped the gun end-over-end. The animal landed within a foot of her, and she clubbed it until it lay bloody and lifeless. Feeling more depressed than victorious, she coaxed Duke inside, and swung the wooden crossbar into the latch.

Nearly reaching the upstairs landing, she heard the arrival of several horsemen. She listened as one dismounted, his spurs clanging across the porch floor, his fists hammering the oak door. Dishes aligned on a shelf along the outside wall crashed to the floor. "Who's out there?" she asked frightened and irritated.

"Jack Marsh. Open the door or my boys'll open it for you! We've some banking business to discuss."

Shannon flipped the crossbar up one-handed and flung the door open. The knob ricocheted off the wall. She looked from Jack to the broken dishes, her piercing green eyes settling on his indifferent squint. Jack's eyes snaked over her and she was suddenly conscious of her state of undress. She lunged for her shawl, but it disguised little of what lay beneath the thin gauze nightdress.

Jack choked on his lust. He'd spent many sleepless nights imagining Shannon Cook pinned beneath him once again as he had his way with her, setting her free only when he tired of her and only after he'd stripped her of all hope. Six years had passed, yet the shame she had caused him rekindled his hate. He wanted to reach out, witnesses or not, and crush her. He was quite sure the town had not forgotten, though neither man nor woman would dare speak of it. Jack Marsh was accustomed to getting exactly what he wanted, and Shannon Leeds had not only rejected him but for a no-account.

He heard the child cry – Cole Cook's child – and he unsuccessfully repressed his rage. Crowding her in the doorway, he shoved her backwards and plastered her face with a document. "You see what I got here?" he yelled, "the deed to this hovel! You've got thirty days to vacate this land!"

"That's not possible!" Shannon ducked under his arm and darted toward the desk. She wrenched open a drawer and, discarding paper after paper, futilely searched for the deed.

He came up behind her and forced his body against hers. "The First Bank of Leeds now owns this land outright! It seems your husband gave up his claim to it, among other things," he told her, his words blowing hot in her ear as he ripped the shawl from her shoulders.

Shannon didn't need to hear the quiet whistles of appreciation to know that Cole had left her with nothing not even her self-respect. "Get off my land," she cried. "And take those cowards with you!"

"For the time-being," Jack hissed.

FIVE

Emily couldn't help but hum one of her favorite songs, *Aura Lea*, as she steered the horse and buggy up the lane to Shannon's land. The day was hot and sticky, but a slight breeze in the air tempted her to inhale the honeysuckle and fading lilac. All morning she had looked forward to her visit with Shannon and the baby, and she soon found she could think of little else. Almost upon the house, she saw Shannon on the porch rocking the baby furiously. "Get up, Maybelle!" she called and gently switched her mare's backside.

Once she reached the house, she hitched the horse to the rail and grimaced as she stepped over the dead coyote. "My God, what's happened here?" When Shannon didn't answer Emily said, "It has to be near a-hundred-degrees out here. Darlin', please take that baby out of this heat." Uneasy when the girl still said nothing, she led her inside.

Emily took the baby, brought Shannon a glass of water, and encouraged her to drink. Then she wet the end of a cloth and encouraged the child to suckle. "Shannon, what on earth has happened?" When Shannon didn't respond, Emily put Zach down and shook her shoulders. "Please, say something!"

Shannon's haunted eyes suddenly locked on Emily's. "In less than a month I have to go!"

"Go? Go where?" Emily noticed Shannon's hands shook and quickly retrieved the glass.

"Cole cashed in the deed, and the bank says I have to get out!" Shannon began to cry.

Emily refused to indulge her. In her opinion, coddling destroyed character. "You're not going anywhere, Shannon Cook! You get some rest, and we'll sort this out afterwards."

* * * *

Shannon woke to the smell of chicken frying, the scent so deliciously powerful she eagerly left the bed and hurried downstairs.

"Well now, looks like you joined us just in time." Emily smiled and set a plate on the small, dilapidated table.

"But where'd you get..."

Emily interrupted. "Born and raised a city girl, so you might happen upon a feather or two. But as fresh a hen as you'll find. I don't care to discuss the particulars."

Shannon shivered. She had always found wringing a chicken's neck a wretched task. "Well, it smells absolutely divine! I hope Zach didn't give you too much trouble."

"Not a lick. He's quite a treasure! Aren't you?" she cooed to Zach.

Shannon smiled at her baby. Between mouthfuls, she asked, "Do you have any children?" Shannon thought Emily seemed suddenly melancholy. "I'm sorry, maybe I shouldn't have..."

"I would rather not talk about it if you don't mind." Emily left the table and began unpacking her satchel.

Shannon sensed Emily had memories possibly more horrible than her own and suddenly lost her appetite.

"What do you think of this fabric?" Emily asked, waltzing around the room swishing crimson satin.

"It's breathtaking!" Shannon exclaimed, unable to resist running her hands over it.

"And this one?" Emily asked, revealing the most beautiful green silk.

"It's the color of an emerald!"

"It shines nearly as magnificently, don't you think?"

"Indeed." Shannon's shoulders suddenly slunk and her smile faded. "I can't tell you how grateful I am for all you have done for me and Zach, but I'm afraid there's no reason for me to tailor the dresses now. In thirty days I'll have no land anyway."

Emily gripped Shannon's hand tightly. "Now, you hush that kind of talk, Shannon Cook! That's just pure nonsense. Thirty days is a long time for people like you and me. You sure don't look to me to be a quitter!"

Shannon pulled away. "Don't you see? It's no use! I wasn't able to get a real good look at it, but I reckon that deed is worth one-thousand dollars. I can't come up with that kind of money in a lifetime, let alone thirty days. I know what I have to do." Shannon's eyes settled on some place faraway.

"What would that be?" Emily asked impatiently.

Shannon hesitated. "Got no choice in this world than to swallow my pride and go on back to my pa's house if he'll allow it." Her laugh empty, she said, "Reckon living in town, you've already been apprised that once I got the wrong pig by the tail, my pa pitched me to the wind."

Emily shrugged her shoulders. "I heard some tittle-tattle around town but mostly about your husband cutting out. I also heard he wasn't exactly fine as cream gravy, the kind of man a woman could easily disremember."

Shannon snickered. "That's surely the Sunday truth."

"What's this about your Pa?" Emily asked watchfully. "Sakes alive, why wouldn't he welcome you back home?"

"I can tell you haven't been around these parts too long."

Emily sensed by Shannon's sudden silence that she expected her to volunteer some personal information of her own. "I came here from New York City, been a few months back. Reckon I missed the small town feeling I remembered as a girl. You still haven't answered my question. I can't imagine a father denying his own daughter, but a grandchild, too? He does know he has a grandson?"

Shannon stood and paced the floor in front of the large stone fireplace and realized she hadn't bothered to avoid the loose board that creaked with her every step. Cole hated noise unless he was the maker. She had never talked about her relationship with her father with anyone, but Emily, for reasons unknown to her, put her at ease. "When my father realized I was set on marrying Cole, he told me if I went ahead with it I was dead to him. He left town before the ceremony. Sold everything he owned and rode the Missouri Pacific to St. Louis."

"He didn't hold your husband in high regard?"

Shannon impersonated a laugh. "Goodness, no, they were two peas in a pod!" Turning her back, she leaned against the fireplace and pounded a fist repeatedly into the mantle. "And it didn't take me long to realize my pa was right about him." She glanced at Emily over her shoulder and debated whether to continue. Hadn't she already shared too much? After all, Emily was practically a total stranger.

Emily strolled to her side and clasped her hand. "Go on."

"I couldn't bring myself to admit it for a long time." Shannon stopped and slapped away a tear. She was through crying over Cole Cook. "Cole married me for my father's money."

"Oh, that's utter nonsense! You're a beautiful, delightful woman."

Shannon shook her head. "The day we found out Zach was coming, Cole was so happy! He stayed close, which wasn't his nature, worked the place, even brought me flowers from the field. The day after Zach came into this world, Cole sent my father a wire. When my pa didn't reply, Cole had no use for me or Zach." Shannon swept Cole's tintype from the mantle and threw it into the fireplace.

Emily fidgeted, dug her fingernails into her burgundy satin skirt, and felt the color rise in her cheeks. Cole Cook may not have been the ideal husband, but she had never met a man who was. A slight smile teased the corners of her mouth, and she thought Cole Cook most fortunate they had never come face-to-face. She'd pulled the derringer from her garter on more than one occasion and shot men less deserving. Emily grabbed Shannon's wrists before the young woman could clear every object from the mantle. "Shannon Cook, you listen to me! How many more years of your life are you going to waste on that man? It's time to claim what's yours!"

"I told you, it's impossible!"

"*Impossible* is just a word born of a coward!"

Shannon smirked. "That right? Well, I've never been one to declare sunshine in the middle of a downpour."

"Humph! And I never been one to jump from a horse for

fear he might stumble! Tomorrow you will go into town, find out just how much that deed's worth and set your sights on paying whatever you must! Then you take that passion you've wasted on that man and put it into something useful like making those dresses."

"It's no..."

"Shush!" Emily interrupted. "You sew those gowns, take your money, get your seed and cattle, and show that bank it's both a working farm and ranch. You'll get your loan then. Never in all my days have I seen a bank turn down a guaranteed venture."

Shannon nodded surrender. Anything was better than crawling back to her father.

Emily gathered her things and suddenly remembered the rotting carcass outside. "Darlin', where might I find a shovel?"

SIX

As was her dog's custom for the past few weeks, Duke laid at her feet as she sewed. Zach cooperated, too, often cooing at his reflection in the tintype suspended from a beam overhead when he wasn't chewing on the doll she'd fashioned from yarn. Shannon set the gown aside, picked Zach up, and bounced him on her knee. "You are going on a grand adventure today," she whispered, kissing the folds of his tiny neck until he giggled.

She decided the green satin gown was by far her favorite. Admiring it in the mirror, she twirled across the room, abruptly stopping when Duke thought it a game and decided she needed two partners. She swept the gown out of his reach and admired the ecru lace that covered the bodice, sleeves, and buttons. It enhanced the splendid color of the fabric just as she'd planned. In contrast, the crimson gown had a deeper bodice, therefore, certain to be the more popular among the women of Leeds, Missouri. Her brows furrowed and Shannon folded both gowns carefully. She still doubted Emily's plan. Even if she could procure a loan, her crops should have been in weeks ago.

* * * *

Zach fussed from the lane's end to town, and Shannon blamed the bumpy ride and sweltering heat. Singing to him only pacified him for a few minutes. Sweeping her sweat-drenched hair behind her shoulders, Shannon rubbed her throbbing temples. Zach finally quieted nearly halfway to town but woke howling a short time after Shannon took him from the buckboard.

"Too bad she doesn't know the first thing about takin' care of a youngen," a voice called behind her. When Shannon heard thunderous laughter, she knew her aggressor wasn't alone.

She crossed the street and stepped onto the boardwalk only to find her route blocked by three other women. "Let me pass," she blew through pursed lips. The women ignored her, and she thought their expressions even more menacing than before.

"Good afternoon, ladies." Luke Richards said as he brushed past Shannon, tipped his hat, and herded nearly all the women out of her path. Only Kate Reeds refused to budge, and Luke moved on her like wildfire to a dry prairie. "You aware if you stand out in the midday sun your skin's soon to resemble the south end of an elderly cow? Seems to me, Mrs. Reeds, it has made some measure of progress already."

Kate Reeds huffed insult and attempted to slap his face.

Luke intercepted her hand effortlessly. "If I were you, ladies, I'd move on into some shade straight away, least those husbands of yours decide to put you out to pasture."

Their response was a collective gasp. But Kate held her ground, and Luke stepped in closer yet and shoved his hat back. "Well, Mrs. Reeds, if I didn't know better, I'd think you were waitin' for a kiss." Kate repeated her attempt to cuff his cheek. Luke grabbed her wrist and chuckled when she retreated, her entourage trailing close behind.

Shannon began to giggle. When he whipped around to face her, she wished she had kept her mouth shut.

"That belly a yers truly yeller?" he admonished. "Best find your sand, woman. I got more important things to do 'sides fight your battles." He tapped the top of his hat and then pulled it down over stern eyes.

Shannon stood speechless. By the time she'd formulated a suitable retort it was too late. She watched him as his spurs rang down the walk and felt her insides boil.

Emily was in the back of the store going over the month's receipts. The shop had always done a lucrative business, and Emily often thought she would have had quite a little nest egg put away if not for the monthly visits to Doc Murphy. Emily giggled and wondered if she should have accepted his proposal. She heard the bell on the door jingle and sighed annoyance. But when she heard a baby's cries, she grinned and hurried toward the front of the shop.

Shannon eagerly stepped inside before Emily reached the

door. "I don't know what the devil's gotten into him. He hasn't stopped crying since we set out." Shannon's words trailed off, suddenly realizing that Zach had briefly calmed during her encounter with Luke Richards.

Worried, Emily took Zach from Shannon's arms. "Little fella's plumb feverish!" She noted Shannon's panic and added, "Probably just cutting his first tooth. Why don't you hang the gowns over there, and we'll try and cool him down some?" Emily poured water from the pitcher into the washbowl and wiped Zach from head to toe. Soon after, he quieted and drifted off to sleep. "Let's have a look at those gowns," she whispered to Shannon.

But Shannon wouldn't take her eyes off her baby.

"He'll be just fine. Come now, I'm on pins and needles!" Emily quipped.

Shannon giggled and spread the emerald gown across a large mahogany table.

"Shannon!" Emily gushed. "It's absolutely heavenly! I particularly admire the covered buttons! I believe it's even finer than the ones I've seen in the catalogs. Honestly, I thought of offering your gowns for much less, but now I wonder if I should charge more."

Shannon beamed. "Truly?"

"Yes. It's magnificent!"

"And here," Shannon said, spreading the crimson gown across the opposite end, "is the one will probably catch their fancy."

"That bodice is wickedly superb!" Emily squealed. "Where on earth did you learn to sew like that?"

Shannon's smile faded. "From a woman I called Lucy. I'd forgotten how much I miss her."

Emily swallowed her own emotion and laid a hand on Shannon's forearm. "She was good to you?"

"Yes… like a mother."

The pain hit her hard. Emily pressed both palms to her chest and quickly sat down. "Shannon, be a dear and run upstairs and collect the brown bottle atop my dressing table."

"What's wrong?" Shannon cried, rushing to her side.

"Please," Emily whispered. "And hurry."

Shannon tore up the stairs and returned with the vial.

Emily motioned for her to remove the cork. Steadying her hands, she took the small bottle and placed two drops on her tongue. She shivered and wondered if she'd ever become accustomed to the taste.

"What is that?" Shannon asked after Emily seemed better.

"Nitroglycerin. My heart is apparently aging much faster than the rest of me."

"Should I fetch Doc Murphy?"

"No, darlin', my little tribulation has passed. Now if you'd be so kind as to help me to my feet, I'll fetch your due. Then you go get your seed and see about some cattle."

"I believe I'll wait for my baby to wake and take him along."

"Nonsense, he'll stay here with me."

Shannon felt her forehead scrunch.

Emily laughed. "Oh for heaven's sake, don't look so down in the mouth! I'm as good as maple syrup! Now off with you!"

Shannon hesitated but noticed the color had returned to Emily's cheeks and her eyes seemed clearer. "You're certain?"

Emily nodded and pressed a stack of bills to her palm.

"I can't take all this!"

"You can and you will. Now go," Emily ordered, gently pushing her toward the door.

"Miss Emily, this is too much!"

"It's not near enough, you ask me. Now, get a move on, girl!" Emily watched as Shannon walked to the end of the row and laughed softly. The young woman had once again caught Luke Richard's eye.

Luke thought, with the exception of Amanda, Mrs. Cook was the loveliest thing he had ever seen. He'd had a beautiful wife, until the fever came and claimed her and their infant son. Though ten long years had come and gone, he could still see the fire he'd intentionally set when he closed his eyes... every time he closed his eyes.

The Tsitsistas tribe squelched his plan to die in the burning cabin with Amanda and his son, Wyatt, and Luke stayed with the Indians for two years, eventually earning the name *Fire Lover*. A smile teased the corners of his mouth. Chief Red Cloud had a peculiar sense of humor. He took one more look at Shannon Cook and kicked the dirt, determined he never again gamble his existence on another. He watched her disappear into the feed store and vowed to avoid her whenever possible.

"My, my, if it isn't Mrs. Cook," Jack Marsh suddenly barked behind her. He could see the terror in her eyes when she turned, and it warmed every part of him. "Seems good fortune is smiling on me today," he sneered, rolling his cane slowly from her right ankle to her hip.

Shannon kept quiet, the past paralyzing her.

"Aren't you the least bit curious?"

Shannon glared, gambling on the storekeeper's assistance. "Say your piece, Mr. Marsh."

Jack laughed and crowded her. "You've saved me a long ride, Mrs. Cook. Proper bank protocol dictates I inform you each week until the thirty-day eviction warning has transpired. So be advised, you now have twenty-two days to vacate. What's this?" Jack demanded, grabbing her hand.

"Most refer to them as seeds, Mr. Marsh! Leave me be."

The storekeeper reluctantly took a step forward. "Mr. Marsh, the lady's just tryin'..."

Jack shoved a leathered finger across the counter. "Mind your business, Finney, if you know what's good for you, least your own note suddenly come due. Now, why on earth would you be in need of seeds?" he asked Shannon. "Must I explain this to you again, little lady?"

Shannon held her breath. He reeked of something both new and peculiar. His eyes squinted retaliation and she knew time hadn't diminished neither the contempt nor the scar he carried over his right eye. Cole had nearly killed him once while protecting her honor. Learning of her engagement to Cole, Jack ambushed her as she rode her horse towards the back of the family's orchard one beautiful spring afternoon. She shivered, remembering the covey of quails that took flight when he snatched her from her horse and pinned her arms against the ground. Then he tore her clothes from her body. The more she resisted, the tighter his grip on her wrists, and the harder his knees dug into the tender flesh of her thighs. Shannon hadn't heard Cole ride up. Neither had Jack and Cole nearly beat him to death.

She thought about what Luke had said and tried to muster courage. "Mr. Marsh! I'm to be getting my crops in and show the bank I can make the land profit and buy back the deed to it myself!" When Jack laughed, she wished she'd let Cole kill him. "Cole had no right to sell it! No right, you hear me. It's my land, too."

Jack sucked his teeth. "Why would I expect anything less? All you seem to know how to do is waste your time."

Shannon slapped his finger away from her earlobe. "I was preparing to call on you before leaving town. It seems you've spared me the trouble." She reached into her satchel for the money. "Now, you take this as a down payment."

"We are talking about a sum of twelve-hundred dollars. This pittance here doesn't even come close." Jack suddenly grinned manically, stepped back, and tapped a forefinger against his cheek. "Now how could a little lady such as yourself come into fast fortune?"

Shannon's nostrils flared. She knew he was baiting her, so she kept quiet.

Jack pointed a finger dramatically toward the ceiling. "I believe I have the answer to such a question; I hear Ruby's looking for another whore." Jack read her intention and immobilized her wrist. "Twenty-two days, Mrs. Cook," he growled. "Then that pretty ass of yours had better be off that land." He wrestled the currency from her hand, threw it on the floor, and crushed it beneath his boot.

Mr. Finney waited until Jack Marsh not only disappeared from the store but set foot into the bank across the street before he spoke again. "He's got it in for you, Miss. Believe it! That Jack Marsh is like a wild animal when it sets its mind after prey. He clamps down and you can't shake him loose.

Shannon chewed her lower lip and squinted past tears. "Don't you worry yourself none, Mister Finney. Thanks to Mr. Marsh, it seems I find myself with unexpected fortune. I'll take those seeds and more."

SEVEN

Zach continued to cry all the way home. Shannon brushed his cheek with hers and instantly coaxed her horse toward the creek. Under different circumstances, she would have leisurely enjoyed the water's hypnotic rhythm as it cascaded over the rocks and flowed downstream. Instead, she quickly took Zach from the buckboard, ripped a piece from her petticoat and dipped it into the stream. Sponging him from head to toe, she gasped as tiny bumps erupted over his abdomen.

She panicked and considered returning to town. Since she'd once been told there wasn't a doctor in the world who could offer much, she sprinted toward the buckboard then bullied Sara into a rapid gallop. Once inside the house, she ran from window to window and slammed the shutters closed. "Please, God! Don't take my son!" she prayed until she felt sure she'd been heard.

All through the night, she routinely sponged Zach with cool water and kept a constant vigil. Each time her eyelids dipped, Duke nuzzled her awake. By sunrise, she'd only managed a few winks, but Zach's fever had finally broken.

Hopeful, she immediately dropped to her knees and whispered her gratitude. Now determined nothing would come before her son, she wondered how she would manage the role of mother, farmer, rancher, and tailor. Realizing she couldn't subject Zach to the hot temperatures while she worked the fields, she decided she had little choice but to sew by day and farm by night while he slept.

Zach dozed so much the next few days that Shannon was able to finish one entire gown with the exception of the hem. Still fussy and quieting only when rocked, Shannon found she was able to do much of the detail work on the dresses at the same time.

Zach's rash had gradually disappeared, and she was relieved when his appetite returned. He smacked his lips and sucked in his cheeks as she fed him corn mush and cooked carrots. At one point, he became so excited he squealed and bobbed his head up and down. Shannon laughed so hard she doubled over. Duke barked confusion.

She put Zach down for the night and looked longingly at her own feather mattress. From the upstairs landing, she whistled for Duke. She heard his large paws thump against each stair, his bloodshot eyes searching hers expectantly when he reached the landing. "Be some changes around here, boy," she told him apologetically as she stroked his ears and marveled over the velvety texture despite pieces missing here and there from his bouts with trespassers. "You'll be staying in tonight, boy, keeping watch over Zach." Patting the braided rug near Zach's crib, Duke sat on his haunches and groaned his disappointment. "You stay put," she whispered sternly but caressed his snout on her way to the door.

She lit two kerosene lamps and headed for the barn after slipping some of the seeds from the burlap bag into her apron skirt. Her horse whinnied surprise as Shannon led her from the stall and into the damp night air. As she struggled to hook Sara to the plow, Shannon was grateful for the full moon that illuminated her very rebellious partner, obviously determined to have no part of this night's adventure. "You're two shakes from a switching," Shannon bluffed as the horse continued to fight her bit. Having anticipated the typical rebellion, she reached into her apron and produced chunks of apple. The mare slurped the fruit from her cupped hand and aggressively nosed around for more. By the time she'd hooked her horse to the plow, Shannon was exhausted.

* * * *

When the sunrise peeked through a lavender skyline, Shannon led Sara back toward the barn. Glancing over her shoulder at the neatly plowed rows, she mopped the sweat from her body and then wiped her horse down. Leaving the mare to graze, Shannon staggered back toward the house.

The dense feather mattress engulfed exhausted muscles, but no sooner had she drifted off into a sound sleep did Zach wake crying. The sound of a rider approaching alerted Duke, and Shannon covered her ears to her dog's barks and her son's howls. Grumbling, she rubbed exhaustion from her eyes, collected Zach, strolled to the window, and strained to identify the visitor. Stumbling toward the stairs with Duke following closely behind, she quickened her pace, anxious to end the loud rapping. "Who's there?"

"Mornin' ma'am," a voice called from the other side of the door. "I just got into town and heard you might be able to use a hand 'round your place here. My name's... Ben. I just been let go off a place up north due to the folks there losin' their deed."

"You heard wrong, mister."

"Could I trouble you for some water? It's mighty hot out here, and I come a fer ways."

"Help yourself, plenty of water in the well." Shannon heard a loud thump and peered out the window. "Mercy's sake," she muttered when she saw him lying on the porch. She flung the door open and immediately realized her poor judgment. He lunged for her but she bolted inside. "Take your foot out of my door if you know what's good for you!"

The intruder jammed a rifle barrel through the small gap. "You best step away from the door if you know what's good for you, little lady."

Shannon screamed when he breached the barrier between them. She kept her eyes on him and backed toward the fireplace. Holding Zach tightly with one arm, she swept the other behind her and tried to locate the poker.

His bird-like-eyes became smaller, and he smiled a nearly toothless grin. "I see what you got planned there, misses. You best rethink that plan!"

"What do you want? I don't have much to spare."

"I'm sure we can work out somethin'," he said, snaring her around the waist.

"Let go of me! Please, you're scaring my son!"

"You best let go of your son, lessen you want something

bad to befall the little bastard."

He reached for Zach, and Shannon knew she had little choice but to set the baby down.

"That's better," he grunted, sliding a filthy hand down her cheek. When she resisted, he pulled a knife from his belt. "You see what I got here?" he warned, placing the blade against her throat. "You best be real still and this here will be over before you know it."

Duke attacked him, the dog's massive jaws clamping down hard on Ben's hand. Shannon freed herself and smashed the poker over his head. She claimed Zach as she attempted to call Duke off, then ran outside and hid in the woods. The dog joined her, a short time after, and together they watched the cabin onto noon when Ben staggered out cursing and cradling the back of his head. He successfully mounted his horse after a few attempts, but the horse didn't seem to take to him much either and eventually bucked him off. Enraged, he began to whip the horse. When it reared, he shot it.

Shannon covered her gasp and wished she'd killed him. Her regret turned to panic when he headed for the barn. She watched helplessly as he led Sara out and began transferring his pack. Keeping a tight hold on Duke, she jostled Zach to keep him quiet. Then she heard something that sounded like distant thunder. As the single rider galloped closer, tall in the saddle and imposing, Shannon immediately recognized Luke Richards.

"They hang horse thieves in these parts," he called as he advanced on Ben. "You aware?"

Wincing as he swiped a wad of Luke's tobacco spittle from his head wound, Ben didn't answer.

"If I were you, and sittin' here lookin' down on such a pitiful, ugly, smelly varmint like yourself, I'll thank God the rest of today that I ain't, I would take that saddle off that horse, throw it over my shoulder, and move on."

Ben went for his gun. But before it cleared his holster, Luke shot him in the leg, dismounted his horse, spit again, and claimed the weapon.

"Damn fella! I'm real sorry about the leg," Luke said, a tight grin stretching his lips. "I was aimin' for your privates." He ground his heel into the bullet wound, and Ben's screams echoed across the pasture. "Now, you're a man that needs to listen better. And that hole in your britches is proof."

Duke barked. Shannon cursed. Luke turned, mounted his horse, and galloped toward her hideout. He dropped to the ground when he reached the woods and immediately discovered all three. "This here seems kind of a strange place for woman's work if you ask me."

"Don't believe I did, Mr. Richards! Although I must say I am mighty glad someone happened by, even if it be you, as I seem to be in a bit of a fix." Was that relief she saw in his eyes?

Luke moved in closer to get a better look at her face. He spit on his bandana and told her to stop wiggling as he wiped the dried blood from her nose and mouth. "Good God, woman! What in tarnation went on here today?"

Remembering the heathen on top of her, Shannon burst into tears. When she could, she attempted to explain her poor judgment. "He said he was looking for work."

Luke's sneer suggested disproval.

"After that, the feller just hit the porch like a sack of potatoes. Seeing as I'm a Christian, despite what folks say, I thought to give him aid."

"That same God give you a brain?"

Seething, Shannon had a few words for him but nothing other than sobs came out.

Luke lowered his head and stuck his hands in his pocket. He'd started her waterworks all over again. Using his church voice, he told her, "Soon as I'm gone, take that baby of yours into the house. I've got some manure to spread." Luke climbed into the saddle and drove the stallion hard toward the house.

Ben saw Luke coming and, hobbling on one leg, attempted to mount Sara again. Luke swept Thunder close, certain Sara would jump sideways and wreck the varmint's effort. "Ever hear of the Pony Express?"

Ben was stoic and nodded hesitantly.

"That's real good, 'cause you're about to witness it firsthand." Luke lassoed Ben's feet, tying the rope off at his saddle horn and rode off at an accelerated pace.

EIGHT

Luke slowed Thunder when Shannon's land was nearly out of view and rolled a cigarette. "Still drawin' a breath?" he called over his shoulder and laughed when Ben chose to verbalize the saddest string of profanity he'd yet to hear.

Once in town, Luke shrugged off the contempt of the churchgoing ladies and wondered if they would feel such almighty compassion for the son-of-a-bitch had he the desire to explain the situation. Considering the wrongdoing had been done to Shannon Cook, he figured they still wouldn't come around to his way of thinking. He hitched Thunder to the rail and realized the women intended more righteous suggestions. Rather than bring Ben to his feet, Luke drug him into the sheriff's office by his boots, his grin swelling each time his prisoner's head rebounded against a step.

Kate Reeds was the first to rush him. "Mr. Richards! What makes you think you can treat this man like an animal?"

Luke scratched his head and only pretended confusion. "I reckon 'cause he is one."

"And just what gives you the right to judge this poor creature?"

"Well, Mrs. Reeds, we can sit here all day and discuss it if you'd like. Meanwhile, this *poor creature* gonna be bleedin' to death, which is just fine by me. And don't think I haven't noticed that I can't get anywhere near town without you makin' good and sure we cross paths. How you s'pose that's sittin' with Mr. Reeds?"

"You're a heathen!" Kate blasted. "And you best think about repentin' before it's too late,"

* * * *

Inside, Sheriff Jacob Conner straightened the crude but sentimental painting of Abraham Lincoln on the wall behind his desk and took to his chair with the intention of peacefully spending the remainder of a hot afternoon. He heard the commotion outside and grudgingly abandoned the idea. He flung the door open, saw Mrs. Reeds scurrying off in a tizzy, which wasn't that unusual, and found himself nose to nose with Luke Richards. "What in blazes you think you're doin', Richards?"

"Your job I'd say, Sheriff."

Jacob bristled. "Mind tellin' me just what the hell you mean by that, and why you find the need to further this man's bleedin' all over my jail?"

"The sonuvabitch tried to steal Mrs. Cook's horse after he tried to force himself on her. I shot him in self-defense. The woman can attest to that." Luke puffed out his chest, anxious to be on his way, his lips practically tasting the drink waiting for him at Ruby's Saloon. "Well, what the hell you waitin' for, Sheriff? I brought him to you, now lock him up!"

"Don't know as I can hold Toby... it just bein' your say-so and all."

Confused, Luke said, "Mrs. Cook said his name's Ben."

Jacob laughed. "Ben, is it? Guess I don't give him near enough credit."

"That's not his name?" Luke asked impatiently. "And what the hell you mean you can't hold him? I caught him red-handed tryin' to steal the woman's horse and saw with my own two eyes the way he beat her. You can either lock him up or he can take his chances with the townsfolk."

"I'd lay odds those people would cut him loose. You know as well as I do how most of them, particularly the womenfolk, feel about the Cook woman. Not to mention, this piece of horse dung is a relation of Jack Marsh. Don't have to tell you that just hearin' his name makes half of 'em mess their drawers." Jacob watched Luke pace the small room, and hoped things didn't escalate. Men like Luke Richards had their own set of rules.

Luke took a few steps toward him. "Which one of 'em you be?"

Jacob fought the urge to grab Luke by the seat of his pants and evict him from the premises. Suspecting that an extremely difficult task and not doubting Luke spoke the truth, he told him, "Take it easy, Richards. You got to understand the law. You ain't the person to whom these wrong-doin's were done. Now, if the lady was to come in and speak her piece, I'd be happy to get a judge down here and get this varmint hung. Until then, I'd be obliged if you would take your leave. And I might warn you, if you should be thinkin' you might possibly be able to gather up enough men for a lynch mob it'll be your sorry behind in here awaitin' trial."

"I'll get the woman in here! Until then, lock his sorry ass up."

* * * *

Jacob Conner hated the law sometimes and, as he looked down at Toby Rush, this day was one of those times. "Deputy," he called over his shoulder, "get in here and lock this vomit up, so I don't have to look at him anymore."

"You still gonna lock me up knowin' who my cousin is?" Toby challenged. As Deputy Saunders strong-armed him into a cell, he told Jacob, "Yer gonna pay for this. You see if I ain't right!"

Jacob ignored him, sat back in his chair, and told himself that the law was the law, black and white, sunup to sundown. He'd seen Mrs. Cook on a few occasions but always from a considerable distance. Jacob felt his lips form a sinful smile as he thought about seeing her again. It disappeared as he considered Jack Marsh's probable swift retribution and thought it best he form a plan. Twisting his mustache, he snickered when a practical one came to mind. He couldn't very well cut Rush loose, he'd tell Jack. Not until Doc Murphy felt him fit enough. Jacob put his feet on his desk and pulled the well-worn hat over his eyes. Soon after, he lapsed into a deep sleep and dreamt his favorite dream, this time singlehandedly gunning down the James brothers. He awoke to someone clacking a cane across the width of his desk.

"Why Sheriff, I do believe I scared you silly. I do so hate to disturb your afternoon nap, but it's come to my attention you've locked my dear cousin up like a common criminal." Jack suspected Toby might talk if he hadn't already and wanted him out of the sheriff's reach. He'd instructed the idiot to burn down Shannon's house once he got her outside, nothing more. "If you know what's good for you, you'll get off your tail and release him posthaste."

"That right, Jack?" Jacob asked, snagging his tobacco pouch from his vest. "Taking a lawman by surprise could get you a hole right through your middle. 'Sides, I got no intention of holdin' that man for any other reason than his own safe-keepin' and to see that he gets the proper medical attention. And just so we're clear, your insistin' may cause a lot of folk in this town to jump, but it don't make a hill of beans to me."

"I might remind you, Sheriff that your position here is an appointed one, and for some reason quite a few folks seem to favor my opinion."

"I'm certain they do," Jacob said scowling. He pushed his hat back and set the chair legs back on the ground. "But then folks tend to like a roof over their head. You know, you might be able to clear something up for me, Jack. I've been sittin' here wondering why it is that you don't seem the least bit curious as to what your dear cousin's been accused of." Jacob watched Jack's expression carefully, but, just as he figured, the banker reacted with no emotion.

"That's probably due to the fact, whatever it may be, he's no doubt been falsely accused. And why are you wasting your time, lawman?" Jack sneered. "No judge in the territory's going to find him guilty."

Jacob chuckled. "You got a long reach, Jack, that what you're sayin'?"

Jack leaned in. "I'm sayin', you wanna take a breath come mornin', you reconsider. Reckon you get my meaning."

Jack took a few steps back when he heard the click of a hammer sear, certain the sheriff had just cocked the Colt beneath his desk.

Jacob smiled. "Reckon you got mine."

NINE

Word of Shannon's mishap echoed through the town like gunfights at Ruby's, most every Saturday night. The news reached Emily, and she feverishly gathered up a few belongings, stopping only long enough to swab the perspiration from her forehead. She considered her declaration again, but each time she thought about confessing her dark secrets to Shannon it didn't seem like the right time. She clutched her chest, the sudden sharp pain making it difficult to breathe. She reached for the vial, upsetting several toiletries atop her dressing table, and lunged for it before it rolled completely under the bed. Quickly swallowing a few drops, she pushed thoughts of Shannon's assault from her mind. Once she managed to stand, she shuffled toward the staircase and slowly made her way down the steps. Placing the *CLOSED* sign on the door, she pulled the shade just as the knob turned and Luke stepped inside.

"Reckon you've heard," Luke said with a flicker of dread in his eye and a lecture on his tongue.

"Yes. The whole town's heard by this time. The only tongue looser than Deputy Saunders' be his wife's."

"And you think it right smart to head on out there?"

"That's where I'm heading, Luke," she said firmly. Reaching past him, she attempted to open the door.

"Don't think that's a real sensible idea, Miss Emily, it bein' near nightfall and all."

"I'm much obliged for your concern, Luke. Now please, let me be."

Luke took her hand and contemplated his next move. It had been his experience that when a woman made up her mind about something only God himself could change it. "Damn," Luke muttered and wished Lance Tucker was there to mind his woman. "Now, Miss Emily, a lady ain't got no business on the street alone this time of day, what with gadabouts like me on the prowl. 'Sides, Lance would have my hide if he was to find out."

Emily whirled to face him, a slight blush stamping her cheeks, an obvious smile playing across her soft lips. "He's mentioned me?"

"That's right, much to my regret. Reckon I didn't stake my claim near fast enough," he teased.

"Oh, you!"

Luke saw the smile disappear and knew she hadn't conceded to staying put.

"Oh, Luke, I can't believe what I've been hearing! Who would do such a thing? I am just so grateful that you happened along and the poor girl and that baby of hers weren't harmed. But I won't rest until I get out and see about them!"

Luke groaned. "I ain't much good with words, Miss Emily, so please spare me the need to say many." He shuffled his feet and removed his hat. On a sigh he told her, "I'm real fond of you, and I won't be havin' what nearly befell Mrs. Cook to befall you. So, I'm askin' yuh to stay put tonight and go on out tomorrow. That woman and the baby are fine. You got my word."

Emily shook her head and began to sob. "I lost her once. I couldn't bear to lose her again!"

Luke felt his brows knit together. "What in blazes are you talkin' about?"

Emily looked away. "Don't know I should be discussing it."

That was just fine with Luke, as long as she didn't leave the shop. "Sheriff Conner's got the horse dung locked up," he assured her. "Mrs. Cook's gonna be just fine. You can see about her in the mornin'."

Emily shook her head. "No, Luke. It's time I..."

Luke sighed and glanced longingly toward the saloon. "Time for what?"

"Time I behave in a way more fitting. I've kept this a secret for many years, too many. I've come across several states, seen a lot of scalping, looting and worse just to see her again. I'm taking you into my confidence, Luke." Emily hesitated.

"Shannon Cook is my daughter."

Luke nearly choked on a wad of tobacco. "Did I hear you right? You're tellin' me Shannon, that woman with the hellfire temper, is your daughter?"

Emily nodded. "I was cleared out of town, this very town, when she was just a little girl by her father. He threw me out, and I'm ashamed to say that I ran like hell itself was trying to catch me."

Luke noticed her sudden pallor and coaxed her into a chair.

"My husband nearly killed me that night."

Luke's brows arched when she laughed suddenly.

"And so many times before that I'm afraid I've lost count. He told me if I ever came back, he'd succeed. I begged him to let me take my girls, but he wouldn't hear of it. I ran, Luke. I abandoned my babies, and I ran." She broke down, sobbing uncontrollably.

Luke wanted to comfort her, but that kind of tragedy paralyzed him, so he waited for her to get a grip on her emotions.

"One summer night, been about sixteen years back, my husband was entertaining his usual guests: William Quantrill, Bill Anderson, and Pap Price. The children were rowdy that night, chasing one another up and down the stairs. A few days prior, I'd lost a baby and was confined to bed. When our oldest house slave, the children's nursemaid, was unable to settle them, I made my way downstairs. You see, I feared Lucy-the children's mammy-would suffer the consequences of their misbehavior.

After I finally got the girls into their rooms, I heard his whip. Dear God! Luke, there's no other sound on earth like it! I stumbled back downstairs and somehow managed to take it from him." Emily covered her mouth, but the terror in her eyes revealed a horror as fresh now as then. "I tried to help her as God is my witness, and he came after me like a wild animal." Emily wiped her eyes and when she was able to finish, she told him the rest. "He beat me and just kept beating me, the other men watching as if it were a parlor game. And then... little

Shannon…"

Luke took her in his arms and then he thought he heard her say, "He beat her, too."

Unsure of proper advice, he said, "Sounds to me, he didn't leave you much choice. That daughter a yours will more than likely understand your predicament. From what I hear that piece of shit… excuse me, ma'am… that man she married suffered from the same bloodthirsty, cowardly malady."

"Do you really think she could ever forgive me?"

"I'd bet my horse on it."

Emily laughed and blotted her eyes. "You'd bet that horse no matter how great the odds against you."

Luke grinned. "Yes ma'am, that's the God's truth." He lifted her chin and told her. "Now, you mind what I say. After the day she's had, the last thing that girl a yers needs is more calamity. You'll tell her when the time's right. A smarter woman I've yet to come across, and I'm not referrin' to Shannon Cook."

Emily playfully smacked his shoulder. "I reckon you're right, Luke. Thank you," she said, sprang onto her toes, and kissed his cheek.

"Promise me you'll stay right here till mornin'?"

"If you can promise me she's alright."

"Right as rain." Luke laughed. "As a matter-a-fact, I got the feelin' if I didn't get on my horse real quick-like after just tryin' to look her over, she'd a torn out my eyes and fed 'em to that dog a hers."

Emily melodic laughter ended abruptly. Startled by a sudden commotion outside, her attention flew to the window.

Luke peered out the door. "It's only my dang horse! Hope I lassoed the varmint up tight," Luke said more to himself. "Now, promise you're not gonna wait till I've gone then ride out there anyway?" Emily's eyes seemed plumb shifty to him and her silence didn't invoke a lot of trust. "Would it set your mind at ease if I promise to check on her place before I call it a night?"

Emily smiled. "Yes, and I'll return the favor by serving you dinner tomorrow night."

"That smile a yours is return enough. 'Sides, I figure that beau a yers for the jealous type." More noise drew them both to the door, and Luke whistled a warning to Thunder. "Dadgum horse has dug a damn trench! That post is near ready to topple."

Emily laughed to tears. "That horse's disposition surely compliments yours! What in the world's got into him?"

"Can't wait to get to the saloon I reckon."

TEN

Sheriff Conner didn't care two-bits for Jack Marsh and considered him the poorest excuse for a man he'd ever run across. The more dealings he had with him the more the dislike grew. "Before you get on your high-horse again, Mr. Marsh, the notion of you not being the least bit curious as to what landed your cousin in my jail has been eatin' away at me all day. That brings me to only one conclusion... you already know the reason."

Jack had already decided Sheriff Conner wasn't going to see another election. Should the townspeople have guts enough to vote their mind, he would make certain Jacob Conner was six-feet under. He might just do this one himself. That made him smile, lift his leg, and wipe the horse manure from his boot onto the edge of Jacob's desk.

Conner scowled. "You got the manners of a goddamn Billy-goat! That your way of avoidin' this discussion?"

"I don't give a tinkers-damn why my cousin is in here or if he rots where he sits, but I can't have the good people of Leeds thinking any relation of mine is a common criminal."

"God forbid!" Jacob replied with all the sarcasm he could muster. "Just for the sake of argument, Mr. Marsh and for your entertainment, allow me to relate the entire sorry event for you. From what I hear tell, you're well-acquainted with Shannon Cook." Jacob watched Jack stiffen and knew he had hit on a very sore subject. "Would that be correctly put?"

"I'm a busy man, Sheriff. You got something to say, say it," Jack spit.

"Well, it seems your fine upstandin' cousin in there paid her a visit. And when he found she wasn't in the hirin' mood, he fancied takin' her instead. When that didn't work, Mr. Marsh, he attempted to steal her only horse!"

Jacob didn't give Marsh a chance to respond.

"We do have a witness, so if it's all right with you, seein' as we have the witness and all, I think it best he stay put for a while, at least till we can get this sorted out. And if that don't sit well with you, maybe you just might like to keep him company."

"My company's a kind you don't want." Jack snarled and slammed the cane against the desk's edge, shearing it in half.

Jacob pushed his hat back, his hard eyes focused. "You best be on your way, Jack."

Jack complied, tearing the door from its upper hinges on his way out. He stood outside grappling with his indecision. In the end, he decided gunning down his cousin once the sheriff went to supper too risky. Besides, from the look they'd shared inside the jailhouse, he was confident that Toby feared him much more than any lawman or judge and would keep his mouth shut.

Shorty Wabash slid around the corner of the jailhouse and whistled softly to get Jack's attention. Jack ignored him and thought even a half-wit should comprehend no good could come of anyone seeing the two of them together. When Shorty whistled again, Jack snarled and motioned him into an alley. Jack kicked his shin hard and nearly crippled him when he rounded the corner. "You ignorant fool! I've warned you about this before. Remember?"

Shorty muffled his pain, swallowed loud, and nodded.

"This is precisely why I no longer retain your services!"

Still whimpering and rubbing his leg, Shorty said, "That's what I come to tell you, Mr. Marsh. Got some information about the Cook woman might interest you some." He stammered most of the words and snorted mucus up and down his worn sleeve.

Jack grabbed Shorty's rotted lapels. "What the hell you know about it?"

"Toby's a friend of mine, Mr. Marsh," Shorty whined. "He offered to buy me a shot of whiskey, and I asked him how he come into all that money."

Jack let go. "I should have known better," he grunted, removing his derby and cuffing his hip with the brim. "You keep your mouth shut, if you know what's good for you."

"Yes sir, Mr. Marsh. Just thought you might..."

"Get on with it. I haven't got all day!"

"As I was sayin' about Mrs. Cook, I heard that hero fella... that's what some folks are callin' him, but I guess he goes by—"

Jack gritted his teeth and again interrupted. "What part of *get on with it* do you have trouble deciphering?"

"I'm thinkin' as fast as I can, Mr. Marsh," Shorty stuttered. "The fella's name is Luke Richards. And I heard him talkin' with Mrs. Cook's mama!"

Jack stepped hard on Shorty's injured ankle. "Now, how would a piece of shit like you be privy to such parlor talk! And just as I thought, your words are as empty as that head of yours because Mrs. Cook's mother is long gone! Now, stay clear of me!"

Shorty got to his feet and limped after him. "No sir, Mr. Marsh. That's what I'm tryin' to tell you. I heard 'em talkin'."

Jack turned about, grabbed Shorty by the throat, and threw him against the building. "And where were you when this transpired? On a wall or a piece of horse shit?"

Shorty, his eyes bulging, pointed to his throat and Jack turned him loose. "I'd rather not say just yet till yuh hear me out. This certain lady told this Luke feller she had to leave when Mrs. Cook was just a youngen. She said she's been lookin' for her for a long time. It's true I tell yuh! And I was thinkin' maybe that kind of information might be worth somethin'."

"And why is that?"

Shorty's toothy grin spanned his entire face. "Maybe this lady could git Mrs. Cook to give up her place-you know being her ma and all-with a little persuadin' if you get my drift."

Jack rubbed his pocket watch and scratched his beard.

"Sounds like a right sneaky plan to me, Mr. Marsh, and I'll be happy to try and remember just who that lady is if you was to buy me a bottle of whiskey. Makes my memory sharp, it does. I reckon a nice hot bath given me by one of them purty dancin' girls down to Ruby's place might help my recollection some too. It ain't been the same since the war, you know."

Jack backhanded him. "The war! What do you know about the war? Selling the Rebs' secrets to the Yanks, and the Yanks' to the Rebs? You're going to tell me what you know," Jack said, bringing Shorty off the ground, "or we'll be placing bets on who hangs you for treason first, Billy Yank or Johnny Reb."

Shorty seemed more confused than worried. "The war's been over for a spell, Mr. Marsh."

"Fool, theirs is a disagreement can never be completely quelled! So you'd better start talking."

"The finery shop," Shorty blurted quickly, closing his eyes to Jack's fist, "at the end of the street. I reckon it belongs to her."

"Emily Dunsmire?"

"That be the one."

"If you're lying to me, you worthless piece of buzzard meat, I will hunt you down and hang you myself!"

"I ain't lying, Mr. Marsh. I swear on my dear mama's grave, I ain't."

Jack pushed his boot into Shorty's testicles, forcing him to the ground. Shorty crawled a considerable distance, found his footing, and shuffled out of sight. Jack smiled and raked his fingers through his mustache. Shorty had proposed a surprisingly resourceful solution, but Jack knew he would have to consider his next move very carefully, particularly after the mess Toby had made. He decided he would only use professionals for his new plan despite the expense. Money was no object when it came to the suffering of Shannon Cook.

He hesitated outside the Chinaman's den but eventually stomped down the boardwalk to the bank instead and threw the doors open. He surveyed his employees and sneered, thinking they all reminded him of a bunch of pathetic little mice scampering about. "Parker," Jack shouted, settling into his overstuffed chair, "get in here and bring me all the property deeds soon to be up for collection!"

ELEVEN

Shannon woke abruptly to the sounds of coyotes howling, threw back the quilt, jumped from the bed, and ran toward the window. Only half-awake, it took her a few moments and a groan from Duke to realize he was safely inside.

The full moon lit up the treetops bordering the woods, and she watched as the bats soared from tree to tree, startling a buck bedded down in a nearby meadow. Then she spotted a figure on horseback, stifled her gasp, and backed slowly from the window. Squinting into the darkness, her eyes scanned the room in search of the rifle she kept in the corner by her bed. Finding it there, she returned to the window, dropped to her knees, and peered over the sill. Her heart raced as she considered the Comanche, but only able to distinguish one silhouette, she thought an Indian raid unlikely.

When the interloper ventured closer to the house, she thought about the man who had come earlier, and raised the rife, balancing the long barrel on the windowsill. The trespasser drew close, nearly directly under the bedroom window. Realizing the full moon highlighted the barrel, Shannon quietly withdrew it. Crawling along the floor to the far wall, she stood, and then congratulated herself on the much better vantage point. She recognized Luke Richards immediately and muttered a few words not indorsed by churchgoing folk.

Luke rode back into town after keeping his promise instead of returning to Plains Paradise for the night. That way should Emily change her mind and make the trip, he'd snag her plan. When he realized he was whistling while having impure thoughts of Shannon Cook, he clamped his jaw shut tight.

Once in town, he decided a couple shots of whiskey might take the edge off and pointlessly hitched Thunder to the saloon's rail. He went inside, rested his foot contently against the kick rail, savored his first sip, and groaned when Ruby began to sing. "Must be Tuesday," he hollered to the barkeep over the discordant racket. "Now I know why it ain't crowded."

The bartender grinned and enthusiastically nodded. "Makes a lot of the horses nervous."

"Ruby, I'll pay double for my bottle a whiskey if you'll wind up the player-piano instead," an elderly man bellowed.

"Count me in," echoed from table to table along with lots of laughter.

Ruby huffed off the small makeshift stage, but the old man didn't stop there. Encouraged by her reaction and by his fellow hecklers, he called out again. "Ruby, reckon you can teach my mule the words to that one? He's already got the tune down!"

The cruel remarks continued until the inevitable happened. Armed with a bottle of whiskey, Ruby broke it over old man Jamison's head. His eyes rolled back and he collapsed against ole man McKenzie, who lost his balance and bumped Orville Stokes, who inadvertently spilled Charlie Granger's bottle of rye. Charlie landed a good right hook and within minutes flesh met flesh with exploding ramifications.

Luke found it necessary to dodge knuckles and large glass objects and took a seat near the bar. "Better give me another, barkeep, while you've still some unbroken ones back there." Irving brought him a bottle and sat down. Luke sipped his whiskey and counted more punches hitting air than anything else. "Reckon she'll call for the Sheriff?"

The bartender shook his head. "Ain't the first time, won't be the last."

"She's got a mouth on her, now don't she?" Luke joked after Ruby shouted a few words he figured only drunken cowpunchers used.

"'Bout now, she'll be puttin' more holes in the ceiling," the bartender told Luke, motioning for him to listen.

Three shots fired off, which sent the less observant ducking for cover. Things quieted but only for a few minutes.

"Since that didn't do the trick, she'll be sendin' 'em dancehall girls out," the bartender said with a wink, his grin stretching from ear to ear.

Luke watched Ruby wind the player piano and gesture to four scantily clad young women. One grandstanded and performed an attention-grabbing striptease atop the piano. Gesturing toward the nearly naked dancer, Luke told the bartender, "She ain't got much left to lose."

"That's Belle, Mr. Marsh's favored. She's off-limits, in case yuh got a notion."

Luke's eyebrows nearly touched his widow's peak. "He's sweet on her?"

The bartender laughed. "Hell! Jack Marsh's only sweet on Jack Marsh. He just don't like other fellers tossin' a line in his pond if you git my drift."

Luke thought Ruby one resourceful woman. The brawl ended and everyone was enjoying the show just fine including him until one of the girls decided to curl up in his lap. He could sometimes settle for cheap whiskey but had never acquired a taste for cheap women, although her perfumed hair, red bloomers, satin corset, and partially exposed breasts did make his heart race some. "Seat's taken," he told her and eased her off. Tossing Irving a silver dollar, he tipped his hat toward Ruby and lit for home.

TWELVE

"Zach, eat sweetheart," Shannon said after the baby pushed out his tongue and most of the creamed oats she'd thought he'd swallowed. Frustrated, she settled him on her hip and went outside to round up Sara. Expecting to find her horse munching fallen apples just inside the corral, Shannon called to her; a few minutes later, she searched the barn. Inside, Sara lay on the barn floor, her breathing labored and shallow. Shannon dropped to her knees and noted the mare's fixed, glassy stare. Seating Zach near the entrance, she collected a blanket and covered the horse. Then she scooped Zach up and bolted for a neighboring farm. Sighting Samuel Willoughby outdoors, she waved frantically and called to him until her voice gave out.

Samuel Willoughby looked up from his chores. Even at his distance, he knew by her mannerisms something wasn't right with the Cook woman and ran to meet her. "What is it, Mrs. Cook?"

"It's Sara," Shannon panted, "my horse. Something's wrong. I think she's dying!"

"I'll go fetch one of the hands. He knows an awful lot about horses."

Breathless, Shannon dropped to her knees. Zach fussed and squirmed until Mary Willoughby approached, pulled taffy from her apron, and wrapped Zach's fist around a sticky strand. "Go, child!" she told Shannon. "And leave the baby. I'll take good care of him till you return."

Samuel reined the horse and pulled the wagon alongside Shannon. "Mary'll find our hand and send him over directly. Meantime, I'll see what I can do."

Shannon took his hand and he pulled her inside.

* * * *

Luke rounded up the calf for the third time and decided it

would be the last. "You're coyote supper, you run off again!" he snarled and untied its hind legs. His horse had thrown a shoe during the ordeal and Thunder snorted his dissatisfaction. Each time Luke got a strong hold of the stallion's hoof as he attempted shod, the stubborn horse wrestled free. "What in the Sam-hell's gotten into you," Luke scolded.

"Luke, come quick!" he heard Mrs. Willoughby holler.

Verbalizing some quiet annoyance, Luke turned to see her bounding down the hillside, a baby bouncing somewhat perilously on one of her ample hips.

"Luke! Samuel needs you over at the Cook's place. That young woman got herself one sickly horse. Go on now and hurry!"

"Yes, ma'am, just as soon as I'm done with this here." Luke knew all too well, who really ruled the roost at the Willoughby farm. He expected his delay wouldn't sit well and attempted distraction. "That the Cook youngen?"

Mrs. Willoughby's demeanor changed immediately, and Luke congratulated himself. "Well, would you look at that! The little fella has surely taken a likin' to you, Luke! Haven't seen him smile until now."

Luke hammered the last beveled nail into the shoe and grunted, "I best get goin'."

* * * *

He reached the Cook place, reined Thunder to a stop, and vaulted off his horse. Rushing the barn, he knelt beside Sara, looked her over, and returned Samuel's smile.

Shannon noticed their exchange and felt her cheeks redden. "Seems you're coming to my assistance once again, Mr. Richards," she said curtly. "Mind telling me what's so dadgum amusing?"

He ignored her and told Samuel it wouldn't be long.

Confused, Shannon asked, "What won't be long?"

Luke looked at her as if she were the town simpleton. "Ain't you never seen a mare in this way before?"

"What way? What on earth are you talking about?" Shannon gasped when Luke's hand disappeared up Sara's business end. Sara's breathing quickened, and within minutes Luke delivered the foal. "Oh my, don't I feel the fool!" Shannon exclaimed. "She's been eating so lately. I figured she was gaining from that."

"No need to be so flustered, Mrs. Cook," Samuel assured her and wrapped an arm around her shoulders.

"That's right charitable," Shannon said, acknowledging Luke's never-ending grin with a glare. "Comforting to know there's still ONE gentleman around these parts."

Luke snickered and examined Sara and her foal. "Mrs. Cook, your horse had a real rough time with this one. The foal seems healthy enough, but this mare needs a lot of rest and close watchin' after. Make sure the bleeding stops and keep her quiet."

"Nothing I can't handle, Mr. Richards."

"Where's the stud?"

"I beg your pardon."

"The horse that sired this foal," Luke explained impatiently. "Looks as if the stud weren't smartly chosen. Your horse here is a smaller variety compared to most in these parts. Another foal this size could kill her. Choose your studs more wisely, Mrs. Cook."

Shannon considered choosing a fist to persuade the grin right off his face. "That kind of talk seems a trifle indelicate! Maybe the kind of women you're used to associating with find it commonplace, but I assure you I do not. Whoever heard of picking your horse's beau anyway? Why that's as ridiculous a notion as I ever heard."

"Dictatin' nature's what it is."

Samuel grinned behind his hand and covertly drew Luke's attention to Thunder. Luke arched a brow and looked as though he'd just been tarred and feathered. He glanced from the foal to his own horse and thought Samuel's assumption likely.

Samuel Willoughby hadn't seen the world in his many days but enough of it to recognize sparks flying between a man and a woman. *'Mrs. Cook's mouth might be saying one thing,'* Samuel thought, *'but her heart's singing a whole other song.'* He decided to put his deduction to the test. "Say, Luke. I haven't had the chance to ride a horse good for nothin' 'cept pullin' a plow in years. You mind if I take ole Thunder here and you and Mrs. Cook come on back in the wagon?" Before Luke could object, Samuel turned his attention to Shannon. "Mrs. Cook, I need to get back to the missus. Would it be askin' too much for you to take a few minutes and gather up some of them apples for Mary? She makes a great apple pie."

Flustered, Shannon stole a glance at Luke, which only made things worse. "No trouble at all," she lied. "We'll be along lickety-split." She intended to gather the apples in record time.

"No hurry," Samuel replied, and Shannon thought she saw him wink at Luke.

THIRTEEN

Shannon sprinted to the barn for a basket. When she returned, Luke was leaning against the wagon and rolling a cigarette. "Best be collecting those apples, Mr. Richards."

He grabbed the basket and snared fruit from the higher branches. He dropped two-dozen by his count and then knelt beside her. She flinched when he took one from a stack in the crook of her apron and cut the apple into bite-sized pieces.

"Not really a time to eat. I'd like to be on my way!"

"Think your horse deserves a treat, don't you?" he said and strolled toward the barn.

Shannon peered over her shoulder and wondered how a man could have such regard for animals and so little for his own kind.

Luke nuzzled Sara, spoke quietly to her, and then ran his hands over her foal. "Plan on keepin' this one?" he asked Shannon.

"I haven't given it much thought," Shannon replied irritably.

"Well, if you do, you might want to do this here," Luke said, caressing the foal again. "Imprintin' makes all the difference."

"Not that I don't appreciate the advice," Shannon said, figuring this just more foolish nonsense. "But I'd like to get back to my son."

"That so? Guess you reckon those apples are gonna find their own way into that basket then." Luke dropped beside her and picked the apples one by one from her apron skirt.

She felt her skin grow hot and her heart thud against her chest. Her thighs began to quiver so she stood, hoping he hadn't noticed.

Luke wanted to run his fingers through her auburn hair. He loved the way it blew behind her in the slight breeze, the smell of lavender bathing his nostrils and reminding him of happier times. "Hear tell your husband ran off?"

Shannon glared and put more distance between them. "Not really any of your business."

"Just tryin' to be neighborly."

"A good neighbor keeps his nose out of places it doesn't belong."

Luke laughed. "Hell, you must be the best of 'em then. How long you lived here?" When she didn't answer, he said, "Surely, more than a day, probably more than a week, maybe a year or three or four, yet today's the first time you met Samuel and Mary seems to me."

"That's right. Like I said, keeping my nose where it belongs. Right here at my own place."

"That ain't no kind of life."

"Life enough for me, Mr. Richards."

"That boy of yours is gonna need a man around to teach him a thing or two. Might not be so bad to get to know Samuel. That's all I'm gettin' at. 'Less you want a dandy on her hands."

Shannon sneered and felt her temper threaten proper etiquette. "There are plenty of boys being raised without a father after the war. My son will be just fine, thank you kindly." She turned her back, gathered a few more apples, and muttered, "He's already twice the man his father is."

Luke reached for her hand and pulled her back down. Tossing his hat aside, he wrapped his arms around her and kissed her slow and hard.

Shannon eventually resisted, her decision to push him away not an easy or immediate one. Cole had never kissed her like that. "I'll excuse your very ungentlemanly behavior, Mr. Richards-you helping with Sara and all-if you will take me to my son now!"

He smiled, the twinkle in his eyes feeding an appetite she never knew existed.

"Glad to ma'am, but seein' as we've become so well acquainted, maybe you should call me Luke."

"Mr. Richards will do just fine, and it'll serve you well to remember I've had enough manhandling to last me a lifetime." Straightening her skirt and communicating her annoyance over a torn sleeve, Shannon added, "You lay hands on me again, best be expecting a hide full of shot."

Luke laughed so loud the horses startled. "Yes ma'am," he told her and climbed into the wagon.

"Mr. Richards," she roared, a hand on one hip, "you expecting me to load this basket myself?"

"Any woman can rip buckshot outa a gun I expect can load a basket on her own."

Shannon grunted and attempted to push the basket into the wagon but lost her balance and fell backwards.

"Be obliged to help, Mrs. Cook," Luke taunted, peering over the wagon's edge, "but don't reckon I can manage without puttin' my hands anywhere near."

"I'm delighted you find this so almighty entertaining!"

"Nothin' wrong with acceptin' a neighbor's help, Mrs. Cook, and this here's proof. Remember that."

"There is if it be from you, Luke Richards. Why, you're as crooked as a Virginia fence!"

Luke threw his head back and felt the breeze whistle against his teeth. When he stopped laughing, he told her, "Heard tell your pa's an Irishman. That would explain the temperament."

"My father is a worthless jackass like most men, present company included." Shannon brushed the dirt from her backside, left the spilled apples for the ground varmints, and successfully loaded the half-empty basket into the wagon.

Neither spoke once Shannon seated herself beside him.

Luke thought about Amanda and berated himself, surprised that Shannon Cook had ignited much more than carnal desire.

Mary stepped out onto the porch as the wagon turned into the lane. "Heavens, child," she said to Shannon once the young woman slid from the wagon, "What in the world happened to your dress?"

"It's just an old chore dress that's seen better days, ma'am. Nothing I can't mend."

Luke decided to keep his head down. Mary Willoughby could read men about as well as Preacher McCabe, which was one of the reasons he didn't go to church. "Want those in the house?" he asked, successfully diverting her attention to the apples.

"That'd be fine, Luke," Mary said, "and thank you, Mrs. Cook." She grabbed Shannon by the arm and steered her toward the house. "That Samuel of mine has quite the sweet tooth."

Luke heard Mary tell Shannon, "Your cheeks look a little pink, dear. Best get in out of the sun." He stole a sideways glance and thought Shannon looked as apprehensive as a wild turkey around Thanksgiving.

"I'd like to be on my way."

"I just put the baby down," Mary pleaded. "Sweet thing's tuckered out. Got supper about ready. Won't you join us?"

Shannon sniffed, tempted by the delicious aromas wafting from the kitchen. "If you're sure it's no trouble."

"We'd be happy to have you," Mary told her, patting her hand.

But once she was seated across from Luke, Shannon suddenly had less appetite.

"The missus and I were in town yesterday and heard your husband ran off," Samuel said while passing Shannon the gravy boat.

"Samuel Willoughby!" Mary chided. "I doubt Mrs. Cook finds that proper conversation."

Shannon's glare reached the head of the table. "Some things are best kept private, Mr. Willoughby, if you don't mind."

"My apologies, ma'am," Samuel whispered and decided he best limit his attention to buttering a biscuit.

Shannon felt her scalp's tingle intensify. She swept the napkin from her lap and slapped it on the table. "Yes, my husband ran off, and I don't expect him to return nor do I want him to. Not much more I'd care to share."

"Of course, dear," Mrs. Willoughby said, "more potatoes?"

"That horse of yours will need tendin' to is all I was gettin' at," Samuel said striving for his kindest tone. "I'm afraid everythin' don't always come out the way I intend it."

Thinking about the kiss, Shannon squirmed in her chair, and

hoped Mr. Willoughby wasn't offering Luke's assistance. "I'll do fine on my own," she insisted, convinced Luke Richards wasn't the kind of man so easily forgotten.

Mary studied the young couple long and hard. "Nonsense child! Young William can take you back and have a look. He knows an awful lot about horses, don't he, Samuel?"

Shannon wondered who William was and noticed Mary's suggestion seemed to catch Samuel by surprise.

"I expect he does, Mary. Young ones and old ones. Helped bring two or was it three into the world since he come here?" Samuel scratched his head. "Don't you usually spit splinters if the boy's out after dark?"

Mary glared at her husband. "Our grandson cavortin' with the neighbor boys is one thing. Helpin' a neighbor is quite another, Samuel Willoughby!"

FOURTEEN

Shannon yawned and placed her sleeping baby in his crib. She looked longingly at her own bed but grudgingly returned downstairs in search of the larger lantern. "I'll be happy when all this plowing is done," she said to Duke, stopping to rub his ears. She thought about accepting William's offer to help with the farming and planned to pay the boy something come harvest time. Patting her thigh, she called to Duke. The dog seemed surprised at her invitation outside, wagged his tail, and bounded after her.

Shannon lit the lantern. Seeing her reflection in the window, she giggled, remembering William's obvious infatuation. Once she reached the barn, she stroked Sara and then her foal, reluctantly heeding Luke's advice. She reached for the tack and her hand suddenly flew to her forehead. "Don't know what I was thinking, Sara," she whispered to her horse. "Last thing you need be doing is plowing fields all night."

Shannon abandoned the barn and jumped at the sound of someone riding in fast. Duke growled and positioned himself between her and the lane. Shannon blew out the lantern and bolted for the house, the dog yards ahead. Pouncing onto the porch, Duke began to snarl.

"Mrs. Cook! It's Sheriff Conner," Jacob called over the dog's disenchantment. He tied his horse to the hitching post and cautiously approached the porch. "Down, boy," he said, backing down the steps when Duke bared sharp teeth. The dog crept forward and Jacob went for his gun.

Shannon saw the glint of metal and yelled, "Don't you dare shoot my dog, Sheriff!"

Jacob stepped back and impatiently waited for her to call off her brute. "I'm sorry to bother you Mrs. Cook at this late hour and all. I'm only here at the insistence of Miss Emily. She's mighty worried about you and your boy. She said she rode all the way out here today, stayed pretty near two hours, and saw neither hide nor hair of either of you. What with the calamity that went on here before, she's mighty upset."

Jacob noticed how the mere mention of that ordeal had unnerved her and wished he were the kind of man to take advantage. "Mrs. Cook, the man who attacked you is sitting in my jail right now, so no need to be afraid. Some folks would like to see him hang for what he done, but the only way that's gonna happen is if you'll swear out a complaint. After that, ain't a judge in these parts would likely let him off scot-free."

"I just want to forget the whole sorry tale. Please get word to Miss Emily I'm right as rain. Good night, Sheriff."

Jacob couldn't take his eyes off of her. He'd heard the men talk about Shannon Cook, but he figured, like most everything else, they had exaggerated. They had not. "Just so there's no misunderstandin, ma'am, you do realize that if you don't make the complaint he'll likely be released?"

Shannon sighed. She planned to be ready for the mudsill if he did return. "I've got bigger things on my mind, Sheriff. Besides, I wouldn't think he'd show his fool head around here again."

"Not with that dog a yers," Jacob teased.

Shannon lips formed a tiny smile. "Thank you kindly for stopping by, Sheriff. Now, I best check on my son."

"Evenin' then, ma'am," Jacob said, tipping his hat. "I'll be lookin' in on you now and then if that's alright."

"No need to trouble yourself, Sheriff."

Jacob watched her go inside and felt an emptiness he'd never felt before.

* * * *

Finding Zach sound asleep, Shannon peered out the window and watched Jacob's appaloosa gallop out of sight. Then she slipped back outside and relit the lantern. Walking over the field, she noted tiny shoots springing from the earth. "Glory be, Duke," she exclaimed, dropping to her knees and hugging the dog. "It may be only an acre or so but it'll be enough to feed a few head come winter."

   Duke suddenly broke free and ran toward the hill separating Shannon's land from Plains Paradise. The quarter-moon offered only a sliver of illumination, and Shannon could barely make out the tree line. Instinctively, she smothered the lantern's flame and called Duke back. Because he returned right away, she assumed the trespasser likely four-footed and harmless.

FIFTEEN

William sat down at the breakfast table and examined his hands. Satisfied they would pass his grandmother's close inspection he removed his hat and vigorously plastered golden curls behind his ears. Experience had taught him nothing infuriated her quicker than dirty hands at her table, unkempt hair, or oftentimes even chewing too loudly. The last thing he wanted was to have her at odds with him, especially this particular morning. "Mrs. Cook says I can work for her real soon when I'm not needed around here. Says she'll pay me too," William announced excitedly after Mary finished the prayer.

Samuel glanced at his wife and wished the boy had picked a better time. Mary hated her men to have anything but food on their minds when they seated themselves at her table. "Got your eye on the McKenzie's Arabian, don't you, boy? Well, don't be gettin' your hopes up. A fine horse like that one won't be around long. Somebody's bound to buy him before you can get the money up." Samuel watched the joy drain out of the boy's face and wished he'd kept his mouth shut. "Me and your grandma wanted to get him for you and we woulda but with last year's crops doin' so poorly we weren't able."

"In case it's slipped your mind, William, we've yet to recover from all that cattle rustled before Luke and Lance hired on here. And I wouldn't get your hopes up on working for Mrs. Cook, neither. If there's any truth to the tattle in town, she's due to have her place taken by the bank." Mary set the tin of muffins down hard on the cook stove. "Last thing you need anyway is something to help you break your fool neck!"

William bolted from the table, headed outside, helped the screen door slam, and yelled over his shoulder. "I'm gonna have me that horse, you wait and see if I don't!"

"Since you seem to have your head set on leavin' my kitchen, how about bringin' in that bucket of milk I asked you for near an hour ago?" Mary shouted after him.

Samuel sighed and set his napkin on the table. "You're too hard on that boy, Mary. Can't be easy for him having lost both his ma and pa." When her shoulders slumped, he knew she hadn't intended to be so gruff. He laid a hand on her forearm and said, "I best go see about 'im."

Samuel waved at Luke as he started down the hill towards the barn. He watched William pick up the milk bucket and shoo Molly and her kittens away.

"Dag blame cats! Go milk your own cow!" William scolded, glaring when Samuel and Luke chuckled.

Samuel decided it best to give the boy a little space and started back up the hill. "Going into town, Luke? Mary's got some breakfast ready, unless you got somethin' more important to do." Samuel grinned and cocked his head in the direction of the Cook farm. "What went on over there yesterday?"

"That woman's trouble which is somethin' I don't need," Luke answered, although he'd been unable to think of much of anything but Shannon Cook all morning.

"Got my own kind of trouble inside," Samuel said, gesturing toward the house. "And I wouldn't trade it for anything in this world."

Luke covertly cocked an eyebrow. Mary Willoughby was a little too bossy in his opinion. He finished loading his pack and said, "I reckon you know to town is where I'm headin' Sam. Last night that trouble a yours gave me a list longer than both our arms of things she's needin' from Johnston's Store."

Samuel chuckled and smacked Luke's back playfully. "Fine by me you want to keep it to yourself." He cinched up the other side of Luke's saddle and finally caught his eye. "Just wonderin' why in tarnation a woman would prefer a young boy tendin' her place when she could have a more experienced fella like yourself?"

Thunder broke wind and Luke jumped back as the horse relieved himself. "Must a been this miserable horse!"

Samuel's laugh broke off and he suddenly turned an ear toward Shannon's land. "You hear somethin'?"

Luke shook his head.

"Sounds like a woman screamin'," Samuel said anxiously. Both men listened closely. "And it sounds like it's comin' from the Cook place."

Luke threw a foot in the saddle and before securing the other spurred Thunder over the hillside.

SIXTEEN

Shannon clung to the edge of the old well and called for help again. Her legs dangling, she tried again to shove her toes into the rock ledge and clawed at the soft earth above her. Her fingers tingled, most sensation nearly gone, but she felt something press against her hands. Tempted to lean her head back for a better view, common sense told her the less movement the better. Duke whined and she realized he'd planted his paws on her hands. A hot, wet sensation streamed through her fingers, and she considered he'd licked them. "Go for help, boy!" she begged. Instead, Duke began to bark.

"For pity's sake," she heard Luke Richards say as he grabbed her wrists and yanked her from the well.

She tried to stand but immediately fell to her knees.

"Just sit tight!" Luke scolded and scratched his head. "How you managed to grab hold of somethin' is beyond me. By all rights you should be lyin' at the bottom."

"No need to remind me, Mr. Richards," Shannon muttered, rubbing her wrists. "Just glad you happened by."

"No happenin' to it. Samuel heard you over here wailin'."

"Wouldn't exactly call it wailing," Shannon mumbled. "And this here could've happened to anybody. It's not like I was dancing through the meadow, hell-bent on testing the laws of gravity."

Grinning, Luke told her: "I'd give a week's wages to see that."

"I'm sure you would," Shannon sneered. "Reckon you'll have to satisfy your primitive urges over to Ruby's. There won't be any horizontal refreshments served around here."

Luke held his sides and laughed long enough for her to count most of his teeth. "You got a peculiar way of showin' gratitude. Pull in them horns a yers, Mrs. Cook. Fella'd have to be a fool to mistake you for a fancy lady."

Shannon latched her hands to her hips and squinted.

"Anyone makes that mistake will more than likely find himself in a bone orchard."

"Prob'ly the bottom of a dern well," Luke muttered. His expression gradually soured and he warned her, "These old wells are risky business, particularly with a baby about. Somebody should've filled that one in or at least put a proper barrier over it."

Shannon winced as he tried to help her to her feet. "Must've wrenched my back and good. I don't think I can walk."

"Best get you on inside," Luke said, picking her up and expecting her to protest. He carried her into the house and placed her on a tattered, green, diamond-patterned fainting couch. He got her a drink and watched her gulp nearly the entire glass.

"I'd best check on Zach," Shannon insisted and set the glass aside.

"Lie back," Luke scolded. "The boy's sound asleep up there or he'd be lettin' you know different. How's that horse a yers?"

"Better than me," Shannon groaned. "'Especially now she's not sharing space with a bunch of rattlers."

Luke whistled. "Find some of them, did you?"

Shannon nodded. "I heard Sara raising a fuss and thought maybe that foal of hers was in trouble. Seeing as I ran out of the house without a gun and Sara was bent on trampling everything including her foal, grabbed me a burlap bag, some kerosene and threw that burning mess on top of them coiled varmints."

"Lucky you didn't burn down that barn a yers in the process."

Shannon's eyes narrowed. "Mighty big shame I don't have you around telling me how to breathe," she said, cinching her arms across her chest. "I don't know how in the world I manage."

"Don't be too hard on yourself. You managed to get that fire out before you fell in the well." Luke grinned and arched an eyebrow.

"Don't get my back up, Luke Richards! Could've happened

to anybody."

"Wouldn't be too sure. Ain't seen nobody can kick up a row like you can."

Shannon's lips twisted into a smirk. "God willing, you won't need to involve yourself in anymore of my future disturbances!"

Luke slapped his hat against his thigh. "If there's no more peril I can rescue you from, I got cattle to brand."

"Best get a wiggle on then by all means!"

"Oh, you ain't seen the last of me. I'll be by to check on you directly... for the baby's sake. Seems to me a woman like you, trouble follows like buzzards to a carcass."

"Reckon that's true because here you be!"

Luke chewed the inside of one cheek. "Always found the more invitin' women be the ones don't use too many words. Aside from that, you're not entirely objectionable."

"In that case, Mr. Richards, I'll just point the way to the door."

Luke suddenly turned on his heels, stooped, and peered out a window. "Looks like you got company."

"That a fact?"

Luke nodded. "Miss Emily." Then Shannon thought she heard him whisper, "That there is one fine woman."

Luke disappeared through the doorway, his spurs clanking briskly across the porch. Shannon was surprised when she felt a scowl form. It seemed to her that Luke Richards was in one almighty hurry to welcome Miss Emily.

SEVENTEEN

Shannon knew, by the sound of Emily's footsteps, she'd taken the porch steps two at a time. She barged through the doorway, flustered and out of breath. "My God, Shannon, are you alright?"

Shannon described her ordeal with the snakes. Apparently, Luke failed to mention that particular calamity.

Horrified, Emily held her daughter close. She thought again of all the years missed and felt the emotion lodge in her throat. But she still wasn't convinced Shannon would understand how a mother could abandon her child and clamped her jaw tight.

"Sounds like Zach's awake," Shannon announced, motioning toward the second floor. "Best go collect him." She stood and the pain immediately drove her to the floor.

"What is it?" Emily shrieked.

"My back," Shannon managed through staccato breaths. "Been giving me trouble ever since Zach came along."

Emily sprang to her feet. "I'll go into town and send Doc Murphy along." Wringing her hands, she reconsidered. "No, I can't bear to leave you like this for such a time. I'll take Zach, ride over to your neighbors, and send someone else to fetch him."

Shannon managed a nod and heard her race upstairs then down. Zach was still fussing when Emily loaded him in her buggy. Shannon thought about the seeds she'd yet to plant and the gowns she'd yet to sew. Duke took his place beside her on the floor and whined. "This here's done yanked a spoke from the wheel," she told the dog and felt the tears spill down her cheeks. "I'm played out, boy."

* * * *

Luke, saddle in hand, tried to decipher Emily's words. *Women,* he thought, *waste precious time on explanations.* "Get on back there," he commanded, reining in most of his impatience. "I'll go for the doc." On Luke's third whistle and with a switch in his hand, his horse complied and abandoned the coolness of the barn. Luke threw the sweat-drenched saddle back on the horse and decided only minutes would be lost should he stop at the Cook place first and scoop Shannon from the floor. Thunder's hooves grooving hard ground and kicking up dust in his wake, Luke arrived within minutes. "Miss Emily will be here directly," he told Shannon as he stepped inside, "but I thought I'd see you somewhere proper before I go for Doc Murphy."

"Don't much give a continental where I be," Shannon muttered.

Luke's jaw dropped. "Why Mrs. Cook, that's some shoddy talk for a lady."

"Hobble your lip, Mr. Richards. Not like I said *damn.*"

"Not like you didn't," Luke said smirking. Then he picked her up gently and sat her on the couch.

Shannon yelped and squeezed her eyes closed.

"Got something in my saddlebag might help the pain," Luke said, clearing the door before she could respond. Returning with a half-empty flask, he uncorked it and pressed it to her lips.

"Trying to get me soaked, Luke Richards?" Shannon wrinkled her nose and pushed the flask away. "Enough scuttlebutt going around town now as it is."

"Make you right as a trivet," Luke argued, shoving it back her way. "'Sides, why would you give a tinker's damn what comes out of some blowhard's bazoo?"

Shannon reluctantly took a sip and grimaced. "Mercy, that's downright awful!"

"It does fire up your innards." Luke's eyes fell on her muddy boots. "It don't make much sense to spread that mess all over everything," he said and began unbuttoning them.

"What in tarnation you think you're doing?" Shannon asked, her words already beginning to slur.

"Can't you just be still?" Luke studied several festering

blisters and planned to draw them to Doc's attention. Then the memory came out of nowhere: he was at the foot of a bed shared with Amanda kissing each of her toes after a night of lovemaking. Luke bolted for the door and pushed Thunder hard toward town.

EIGHTEEN

Luke, with no intention of returning to the Cook place, waved Doc Murphy in the general direction. When he passed the largest oak tree, Luke barely missed his head on a long, low limb. Instead of going back to Plains Paradise, he allowed Thunder the path of his choice and let the Morab run full out. The last thing he wanted was company or Mary Willoughby's questions and drove his horse hard for the better part of an hour.

"Supper's on the table," he heard Mary bellow as he dried and stabled his horse. Knowing she would soon clang the dinner bell her usual four times should all available ranch hands turn a deaf ear to her call, Luke picked up his pace toward the house.

Mary acknowledged Lance as he strode into the kitchen, made an obvious inspection of his hands, and shook her head in disgust at the empty chairs. "Darn Fools! Even a coyote or mountain lion has sense enough to eat their supper warm!"

"Now, calm down, Mary," Samuel said. "Maybe they've a mind to eat dinner in town tonight. And Luke might still be at the Cook place for all we know." Mary started in again and Samuel slapped his hand on the table's edge. "Mary, they're grown men with lives of their own! Reckon if they wanted someone they had to answer to, they wouldn't be driftin' through this world like they do."

Following some prompting from Mary, the men bent their heads in prayer. As a collective *Amen* sounded, Luke came in. Mary's expression revealed her aggravation. Samuel's revealed just plain weariness.

Luke immediately apologized for his tardiness, mostly with Samuel's welfare in mind. For good measure, he told Mary she looked lovely. "Smells mighty good, Mrs. Willoughby. Is that the ole chicken gave you so much trouble this morning?"

"You know it is, Mr. Richards and don't be a wastin' that

charm on me!"

"Sweet potatoes, Luke?" Samuel asked with an apologetic undertone.

Luke shook his head. "But wouldn't say no to some of them fine green beans or a corn muffin."

"You've really outdone yourself tonight, Mrs. Willoughby," Lance said, squinting Luke's way.

Mary allowed a smile to form on her pursed lips. "Well, I had to cook up something special! Reckon young William here won't be calling it a day well into dark from here on out, 'less of course his school work starts to suffer."

Luke eagerly switched his attention to the boy. "That right?"

"Grandma and Grandpa said it would be alright for me to work out at Mrs. Cook's place. Miss Emily's the one hired me on accounta Mrs. Cook feeling so poorly. Miss Emily says she'll pay me two dollars a week!"

Luke whistled. "Two dollars! That's a king's ransom, boy."

William's eyes sparkled. "I'll be headin' over there now as a matter-a-fact!"

Mary's hand clacked against the tabletop. "William Willoughby," she hollered over her shoulder, "you haven't as much as touched your green beans!"

"Might as well save your breath, Mary," Samuel told her. "The boy's already on his horse."

"Don't be frettin' over leftovers tonight, Mrs. Willoughby," Lance said. "Luke and me don't plan on leavin' this table till every scrap is gone."

Mary served them all a sneer and began clearing the table. "Oh, the lot of you think you're such sly foxes, but I'm not some chicken in the henhouse."

Certain her back was turned, Samuel rolled his eyes. "It's good to see the boy so eager, Mary," he sternly reminded her.

Mary sighed and reclaimed the seat next to his. "I wasn't too set on the idea in the beginnin', but I'm just happy to see that poor young woman get some help. If I had me a man take out on me and my little one, I'd hunt him down like an old bear and skin him alive, I would!"

Samuel grinned at Luke and Lance. "Now you know why I ain't left yet."

Mary swatted him softly with her apron. "Well, if you ask me, William's interest don't just lie in gettin' that horse. I think he's kinda sweet on Mrs. Cook. She's a pretty, young thing, no one can argue that. Don't you think so, boys?" she asked, specifically studying Luke's reaction.

"Thanks ma'am for a fine meal," Luke and Lance said in near unison. "'Spect we best finish 'em chores before nightfall," Lance offered hastily, but Luke grabbed his hat first along with a corn muffin for Thunder and hightailed it.

"Well, now," Mary said to Samuel, "ain't that a getaway even Jesse James would be proud of!"

Samuel grabbed hold of her and pulled her into his lap.

"Why, Samuel," she said giggling. "You're full of the dickens tonight." Mary pinned her hair back into place and kissed him firmly on the forehead. Together they hurriedly cleared the table and retired to bed early.

NINETEEN

Visualizing himself riding into town on the stallion he wanted more than anything he had ever wanted in his life, William grinned from ear to ear. He thought he was sure to be such a grand sight every girl would have her eyes trained on him. He whistled softly and thought about Erza Young. In fact, lately he caught himself thinking about her a lot. More than a few times, he even found himself fantasizing what lie beneath her pinafore.

Suddenly, his skin felt on fire and he shifted in his saddle deciding it best to think about anything else. It turned out Shannon Cook wasn't a good choice. *If only I was older,* he thought, deciding Erza paled in comparison. He stopped at the entrance to the Cook's dirt lane, his heart still thumping against his chest, his palms forever sweating. He found reciting arithmetic sometimes quelled such impure thoughts and began reciting frantically: "Sixteen and fifty-three makes sixty-nine." But even resorting to fractions didn't stop visions of Mrs. Cook in a corset.

William brought his horse to a halt and began to pray: *Dear Jesus, please, please, please dispatch these unclean thoughts outa my head. Amen.* He took a breath, so deep he could have swam clear across McKenzie's pond, and waited. Realizing the good Lord wouldn't be coming to his rescue nearly quick enough, William minimized his predicament by placing his hat over his lap.

He drew his horse to the hitching post, his hat strategically pressed against the front of his trousers, and nearly jumped out of his skin when the sheriff rode up behind him. Relieved he didn't need the hat any more, William thought the almighty had a funny way of answering his prayers. "Howdy, Sheriff," he managed, hoping lawmen really couldn't see inside a person's soul. "I scarcely heard you comin'."

Anticipating being alone with Shannon Cook, Jacob glared.

"I'm lookin' for Toby Rush, boy. He knocked my deputy over the head and broke outa jail. Seen any strangers on your way over here?"

"No sir, not a one. Would that be the man that hurt Mrs. Cook?"

"That would be him," Jacob answered impatiently. "Mrs. Cook at home?" As he waited for a reply, Jacob thought it times like this he was glad to be a bachelor. He never had much patience for stupid questions or youngens in general.

William thought how Grandma Willoughby would take a switch to him if he greeted folks the way Sheriff Conner did. "How would I know?" he answered defiantly. "I just rode up."

Jacob grumbled inaudibly, tapped his knuckles against the door and waited. Impatient, he shifted his weight, and drummed the door.

"Might take her awhile to answer," William piped up. "She's down in the back. That's why I'm here to help out. She said I should just let myself in."

"Why didn't you say so?" Jacob growled. "Well, what are you waitin' for?"

"This Rush fella," William stammered, motioning toward the house, "what if he's in there?"

Jacob drew his Colt. "That's what this here's for, boy. Now, open the door. I'll be right alongside."

"They're sleepin'," William whispered as he drew Jacob's attention to the window. From there, they saw Shannon and Zach in the rocking chair.

"I got eyes. You the Willoughby's grandson?"

William nodded.

Jacob motioned the boy further from the house. "Stay put on the porch while I have a look in the barn." Returning a few minutes later, Jacob told William, "Might as well get started with the chores. No one's about." Jacob thought the kid looked as apprehensive as a horse thief headed for the gallows. "No one's about, boy," he repeated more emphatically. "Go on now."

Jacob returned to the house and heard Shannon singing and

her baby giggling inside. He peered through the window and witnessed Shannon tickling her pudgy infant. "Mrs. Cook, it's Sheriff Conner," he hollered. "I'll just let myself in if that suits yuh."

Shannon rolled her eyes but managed civil words. "That'll be fine, Sheriff."

"Nice looking youngen you got there, ma'am. He's a plump little thing, ain't he?"

Annoyed, Shannon said, "Expect he'll grow into HIS, Sheriff. Mind tellin' me what brings you all the way out here?"

Disappointed she didn't appear happy to see him again, Jacob said, "Toby Rush. Regretfully, he's escaped."

"He's what?"

"Practically caved the back of my deputy's skull in and got away."

Shannon glared. "Where were you, Sheriff... if you don't mind me asking?"

Jacob knew what she was getting at. "Some folks have the impression a sheriff lives in the jailhouse, ma'am, but that ain't the case."

"Maybe it should be, Sheriff."

"Now, hold on, Mrs. Cook. That's why I come out here. I've already had a looksee in your barn and everything's as it should be. Matter fact, the neighbor boy's out there now. He said you were expectin' him. That so?"

"Why would the boy tell you any different, Sheriff!"

Jacob stared at his feet and brushed his hat across his thighs. "Now, that I seen for myself that you're not in any danger, reckon I'll be headed back."

Shannon bit her lip, somewhat regretted her inhospitality, and wondered why he irritated her so. "It was very kind of you to come by, Sheriff. Been feeling poorly and got an attitude to match it seems."

Jacob managed an obligatory smile. "The varmint's more than likely left town, Mrs. Cook. Prob'ly headed out in the opposite direction and is miles away by now. Just the same, it'd make me feel a whole lot better if you'd come back on into town and stay with Miss Emily for the time being. I know she'd dance a jig to have you and the youngen stay on."

"I can't make a trip to town, Sheriff. I can barely upright myself! Being tossed around in that wagon would be the end to beat all."

"Whatever you say, ma'am," Jacob said and shuffled toward the door.

"But Sheriff, I'd be much obliged if you would take my boy back to her. High hopes don't always do the deed, and he's gonna need more than a good suckle. Besides, I'd feel a whole lot better knowing he's safe." She held Zach close and swiped a tear from her eye. "You're going for a ride, little Zach, with an honest to goodness lawman."

"You want me to take him?" Jacob asked in disbelief. "I don't know, Mrs. Cook. Ain't never had a youngen and don't know the first thing..."

Shannon laughed. "You're not exactly inspiring a lot of confidence, Sheriff. Goodness, he's just a baby. Not like solving the wonders of the universe!" Jacob started to protest again and she told him, "You'll find everything you need upstairs in the basket beside his crib, Sheriff." Deciding the Sheriff needed a little persuasion, she taunted him. "But I reckon if the task's too big, I'm quite certain Luke Richards wouldn't object."

Jacob felt the veins in his forehead throb. "That won't be necessary, ma'am," he said and took the stairs two at a time.

Shannon looked over the pack when Jacob returned and nodded her acceptance. "See, Sheriff, nothing to it."

Jacob awkwardly took Zach from Shannon's arms just as William came through the door. "Reckon I'll be on my way, Mrs. Cook," the boy said. "Got everything done just like you asked."

"Not so fast!" Jacob barked, staring William down. "As Sheriff of Leeds, Missouri, I'm within my rights to sequester you to stay on here to look after Mrs. Cook."

William looked from Shannon to Jacob. "Be my pleasure," William said blushing, "but my grandma ain't gonna like that one bit."

"Well, your grandma ain't the sheriff, now is she? Come here, boy and raise your right hand."

Confused, William shuffled over and did as Jacob asked.

"As Sheriff of Leeds, Missouri, I deputize you till I say different. Got a rifle in that pack out there?"

"No sir," William said excitedly.

"How about a toad sticker?"

William shook his head. "My grandpa took my knife on account..."

"Don't have time for your chin music," Jacob barked as he repositioned Zach. "Mrs. Cook, that husband a yours leave you a rifle?"

Shannon motioned to the floor beside her chair.

"There it be, boy," Jacob said, "but only lever it in dire straits, hear?"

William nodded and took a shaky stand beside Shannon.

"I'll make your grandma aware before I head back to town," Jacob promised William and tipped his hat to Shannon. On the way to his horse, Jacob briefly regretted deputizing William but quickly decided the boy could do no worse than the two dimwits wearing badges back at the jail. He began to load the baby's trappings on his appaloosa when he heard a rider approaching. Jacob spun, gun drawn in one swift, experienced motion. "Who you be? Identify yourself, rider!"

Luke had just left the Willoughby's barn when he saw a tall man's silhouette grace the hillside, and his gut told him to check on William. Now, spotting the appaloosa's hindquarters, his gun hand relaxed.

"I said, who you be, stranger?" Jacob asked and cocked his Colt.

"Simmer down, Sheriff," Luke called from around the house. "It's Luke Richards here to check on the boy."

"Out where I can see you! I'm not gonna tell you again!" Jacob's demand echoed across the pasture.

Luke persuaded Thunder around the corner. "What's all the commotion, Sheriff? And you mind aimin' that hand cannon elsewheres?"

"Don't never slide up on me like that again, Richards, 'less you want your horse goin' on home alone," Jacob growled, returning his gun to leather. "Not that it's any business of yers, but there's no trouble to speak of. Toby Rush broke himself out of jail after he assaulted one of my deputies. I'm just not takin' any chances is all."

Luke chuckled. "Seems to me them boys a yers got brains the size of peas, and that's being mighty generous."

Jacob glared. "What other words a wisdom you got to share?"

"Looks like yer in a hurry, Sheriff. That there could take all day. Toby Rush, you say?" Luke whistled and slapped his hat against his thigh. "Now that there ain't exactly good news for Mrs. Cook. Bet she's sittin' in there scared to death and prob'ly plenty riled at you, what with the piece of hog dung slippin' through yer fingers." Luke grinned when every muscle in Jacob's face flexed and twitched.

"Like I told Mrs. Cook, I don't expect even the likes of Toby Rush is dumb enough to stick around these parts, but the boy's to stay put for the night."

"William? The hell he is! And where do you think you're goin' with that baby?"

"Mind your place, Luke. You're interferin' with the law and that ain't looked upon lightly in my town!"

"Better your wrath than Mary Willoughby's, Sheriff, and that's a fact. Ever met the woman? Send the boy on home and I'll bunk here tonight." Luke tugged a cigar from a leather pouch Amanda had stitched for him years before and lit it.

"You'd like that, wouldn't you?" Jacob hissed. "You just on the shoot tonight?"

Luke laughed and hitched a boot against a porch step. "No, I ain't lookin' for trouble, Sheriff, but the boy ain't stayin' here in case that sonuvabitch decides to show his ugly hide." Luke gestured toward Zach. "Takin' that baby on to Miss Emily I reckon?"

Jacob considered any other alternative.

Luke grinned. "You look about as comfortable with that idea as a rabbit in a bobcat den."

Jacob bristled. Luke was a little too intuitive for his own good. "For the Willoughby's peace-a-mind, I'll let the boy go on home, but I'll be watchin' you, Luke Richards." Jacob's horse trotted down the lane, its pace slowing when Zach began to wail.

Luke leaned across the threshold. "Best skedaddle, boy," he told William. "That grandma a yers is prob'ly cuttin' her a thorny switch 'bout now."

"But Sheriff Conner..."

"Change a plans."

William told Shannon goodbye, stepped outside, scuffed his toes across the dirt, and looked about nervously.

"You afraid, boy?" Luke asked.

"No, I ain't afraid," William barked. "Just never rode by myself after dark is all."

Luke pointed toward Plains Paradise and suggested wryly, "Head straight over that hill. You can't miss it." When the boy sauntered along, repetitively looking over one shoulder, Luke knew William was frightened despite what he said. He went inside and told Shannon he'd return after seeing William home.

Luke threw a leg over Thunder and easily caught up to William. "Damn the luck! Wouldn't you know I forgot my tobacco?" He noticed the corners of William's mouth turn upwards but pretended he didn't. Happy, William spurred his horse into a gallop. Luke easily passed him and chuckled as William struggled to keep up. The Willoughby's homestead within view, Luke pulled back on the reins, tapped his saddlebag, and told the boy, "Well, I'll be, had the pouch with me all along! Get that horse of yours stabled, and I'll see you in the mornin'."

"Whatever you say." William grinned, waved him off, and led his horse toward the barn. As he hung up the bridle, he noticed Samuel's Palomino missing. Further inspection of the stalls convinced him Mary's quarter horse was also absent. William scratched his head and assumed the couple, for whatever reason, had joined the cowpunchers on their evening roundup in the bottomlands. On his way to the house, he noticed the chickens milling about. He shrugged his shoulders and persuaded the brood into the coop. Then he heard gunshots.

TWENTY

When lead ripped past his ear a split-second before he heard the shot, Luke dropped to his knees and shouted a warning. "Mrs. Cook, hug that hearth and stay clear of the window."

Shannon winced but managed to slide to the floor. Remembering William had moved her rifle, her eyes scanned the room's perimeter until she spotted it leaning against the doorframe. She heard several distant gunshots and then a few much closer. Soon after, bullets splintered the house's clapboard, and she assumed by the louder shots that followed Luke returned fire. A loud thump caused her to jump and the gunfire ended. She froze and assumed Luke was dead.

Toby Rush flung the door wide open. Grinning like a rabid dog, tobacco juice oozed from the corners of his mouth. His vile-smelling-hair hung limp to his shoulders. "What say you and me take up where we left off?" He grabbed a fistful of her hair and tore at her clothes.

Shannon screamed, partly from pain, mostly from fear.

"Take your hands off her," Luke growled, snaking his body around the doorframe. "I'm not going to tell you again you piece of shit." When Rush didn't, Luke struggled to raise his gun hand but managed to shoot him in the foot. Toby went for his weapon, and Shannon instinctively lurched sideways. Luke transferred the Colt to his left hand and fired. The bullet penetrated Rush's forehead and he fell dead.

Bleeding puddles of his own, Luke collapsed in the doorway.

Shannon crawled to his side, tears swelling her eyes. "Please don't die on me, Luke Richards!" With both hands, she ripped his flannel shirt open, launching buttons in every direction. She inspected the wound and determined the bullet had narrowly missed his heart. The bleeding was profuse, gushing from a large hole adjacent to his shoulder. She tore a section of her petticoat and applied pressure to the flowing abyss. The solution short-term, she considered her options: watch him slowly bleed to death or attempt to go for help. "Luke, can you hear me?"

Luke moaned and briefly opened his eyes.

She took his hand and placed it over the rudimentary bandage. "Keep pressing! I'll be back with the doc as quick as I can." She pitched her body toward the rifle. Using it as a cane, she managed to stand. She glanced over her shoulder on her way to the door and repeated her earlier instruction. She heard a rider approach, steadied herself against the doorframe, and raised the rifle. Relieved when she saw William, she dropped her hand to her side. "Luke's been shot!" she screamed. "Fetch Doc Murphy! And hurry!" She watched the boy vault onto his horse and sobbing she whispered, "I don't think he's going to make it."

* * * *

Within the hour, William returned with both the doctor and the sheriff. Stepping over Luke's legs, Doc Murphy told Shannon she could release her hand. "You done a good job, Mrs. Cook. Probably saved this young feller's life. Sheriff, take her over yonder," Murphy said, gesturing to the opposite end of the room.

Jacob carried her over to a chair and listened sympathetically as she described every detail. He noted she never once took her eyes off Luke. Jacob looked toward Rush's body and snarled. "I never expected the fool to return." An uncomfortable silence followed and he asked doc, "Where'd the boy run off to?"

"Wanted to save his hide and get back to that grandmother of his, I reckon," Murphy said irritably. "Sheriff, get on over here and give me a hand. This one here's the one in need of the attention right now! I'll never get this bullet out with him flailing about."

Shannon couldn't see much but winced when Luke screamed and the extracted bullet clanked against a bowl. "Is he going to die, Doc?" she asked reluctantly.

"Can't say for sure," Doc began, "but he'll need some close watching-over. I'd take him back with me but don't think he'd survive the journey. The bandage will need changin' on a regular basis, and somebody's going to have to monitor his fever and be on the lookout for excessive bleedin'. The Willoughby boy coming back to stay?"

"Not that I'm aware," Shannon said, her voice cracking as she thought about the night's events.

"S'pose you can't remain?" Doc asked Jacob.

Jacob shook his head. "I'll drag Rush's sorry carcass back to town, stop at the Willoughby farm on the way and tell the boy to hightail it back here. Don't s'pose we can put Luke in the back of your wagon and take him just over the hill?"

Shannon got the impression it wasn't Luke's best interest that inspired Jacob's suggestion, and she gnawed the inside of her cheeks.

"No doubt his grandmother would prefer it, but I wouldn't advise it," Doc said. "Besides, Mrs. Cook needs some looking after herself."

"Best be on my way then," Jacob said annoyed. "Don't fret, Mrs. Cook. I'll be by to look in on you every chance I get. That little one of yers is enjoyin' Miss Emily's company nearly as much as she is his."

"Much obliged for your help, Sheriff."

Jacob tipped his hat to her and told Doc to have a safe journey.

Murphy waved him off and packed a cool cloth against Luke's forehead. "Your back still ailing you?" he asked Shannon.

"It hurts something awful every time I move." Shannon blushed suddenly and averted her eyes. "Matter-of-fact, I could sure use a hand to the outhouse when you get a chance."

Doc chuckled. "Reckon you could. How's that going to sit with you... having the boy help you with such delicate matters till you're well?"

"I hadn't given it much thought," Shannon murmured.

Doc scratched his head. "Suppose a chamber pot might prove even more unsavory for such a young lad."

Shannon agreed and felt the color rise in her cheeks again.

"Let's get you up," Doc said, throwing an arm around Shannon's waist. "I doubt Mrs. Willoughby would mind staying on a couple of days for such duties, I surely don't. She'd most likely be more help with Luke than the boy would anyhow. I'll stop in on my way back and make the request."

As she finished her business in the outhouse, Shannon heard more than one rider ride in. "Doc!" she cried.

"I'm right here, Mrs. Cook. No need for worry. Looks to be William and the sheriff. Done with your duty?"

Shannon whispered yes and wondered why they'd returned.

TWENTY-ONE

"Don't shoot, Sheriff!" Doc called out as he assisted Shannon back to the house.

Jacob slid off the appaloosa immediately, sprinted toward them, and looped Shannon's arm around his neck. "More bad news," he told them in a low tone.

"Cut to it, Sheriff," Doc ordered impatiently.

Jacob lowered his voice further, his eyes slanting toward William. "Rush ain't the only one shot dead around here tonight. My guess is that snake decided to loot the Willoughby place before he came here. If I know Samuel and Mary, they resisted so he shot them both dead."

Shannon felt her knees give way. "Oh! Dear Lord, this is all my doing."

"Don't speak such nonsense," she thought she heard Jacob say.

Her gaze flew to William and she told Jacob to take her to him. She leaned against the mare and searched the boy's eyes. "William, dear, sweet William," was all she managed as her tears spilled into his stirrup. William stared straight ahead, his gaze fixed. Shannon gaped and she looked to Murphy for advice.

Doc pulled her aside. "The boy's most likely in shock. Leave him be. Your pity won't do him an ounce of good." Luke's sudden outburst caused Doc to abandon them and rush the house. "Sheriff," he called from the door moments later. Jacob cursed under his breath, asked Shannon to look after William, and found the old Doc struggling to restrain Luke. "Dammit, Sheriff, hold him!"

Jacob was nearly Luke's size, but it took every ounce of strength he had to keep Luke down. When Luke blacked out again, both the doctor and Jacob went back outside.

"William," Doc told him, "you stay put now, hear? These folks need you. Climb down off that horse and come on over here so I can give you instruction." William mindlessly obeyed.

* * * *

"I'll come by tomorrow," Jacob assured William once Doc Murphy had finished with him. Then he carried Shannon inside. "I'll send the undertaker over to the Willoughby's come daybreak," Jacob told her. "Be best if the boy stayed clear of there until the funeral."

Shannon bit her lip but managed a nod.

"You comin', Doc?" she heard Jacob ask once he stepped outside. "Lots of no-accounts about this time a night."

Doc nodded. "Much obliged, Sheriff. I'm a much better aim with a scalpel than that old Winchester rifle."

After they rode off, William came inside. Shannon held out her arms, and when he finally came to her, she cradled his shoulders, pulled him close, and held him there.

* * * *

William tended to the ranch over the next several days, looked in on Sara and her foal, and even managed to get the rest of Shannon's crops in. He did most of the cooking, though Shannon provided systematic instructions.

Luke took a bite from a biscuit and teased William, "Only one thing these are good for and that's target practice. I think I chipped a tooth."

"Mr. Richards!" Shannon reprimanded. "Show some appreciation!"

William seemed unscathed and vigorously tore a piece from the offensive disk. "I believe you're right, Luke. Either that or skippin' stones."

Relieved William seemed a bit more like the boy he'd been before, Shannon figured Luke knew exactly what he was doing. She listened to their friendly banter and grinned. "You both have the table manners of a savage."

"That right, Mrs. Cook?" Luke asked. "And how many of them savages invited you to supper lately?"

"I'm in no mood for your tomfoolery. It'd serve you well to eat what's given you and be thankful for it."

"It'd serve you well to put a little less starch in your bloomers."

Shannon saw William's attempt to hide a huge grin behind a hand too small to conceal it, and she wagged a finger in his direction then Luke's. "If I could leave this room, Luke Richards, I would. Kindly refrain from your saloon talk and remember your manners in the presence of a lady and an impressionable boy."

"Yes, ma'am," Luke said and winked at William.

* * * *

Luke slept most of the time as the Doc had told them he would. He said that a man like Luke would be hard to keep down and he was right about that, too. If not for the medication, which smelt suspiciously like very good liquor, Shannon felt sure all three of them would lose their minds. Thankfully, William's lost stare completely disappeared... until the day of his grandparents' funeral.

Calling William over, before he left the house to attend, Shannon told him, "If only I could manage the ride and Luke wouldn't be left alone, I'd be right by your side. You know that, don't you, William?"

William nodded, slowly pulling his hand from hers. "Just gave Luke the medicine, so he'll sleep till I get back."

"Reckon you'll be back before evening?"

"Don't see no reason I can't."

"It's likely to be a difficult day," she said, staring out the window so he wouldn't see her tears. "but I expect most of the townspeople will be there. I'm quite certain Samuel and Mary touched many folks."

"Yes ma'am. If there ain't a place in heaven for them, none of us has a chance."

TWENTY-TWO

On the fifth day, Shannon was able to walk unassisted and anxious to collect her son. When she led Sara from the barn and prepared to hitch her to the wagon, William called out. "Mrs. Cook, I'll fetch Zach for yuh. Gonna be a long, bumpy ride."

Fighting Sara, she found his offer tempting,
"Don't make much sense to take a risk like that, if you don't mind me sayin' so. That ride to town could set you back."

"You're right, William," she finally decided. "When'd you get so smart?" She smiled at him and smothered a chuckle when he shuffled his feet. "You wait here. I got some apple pie you can take along and some jerky. Got your canteen?"

Grinning, William nodded. "Don't really need all that. It's not like I'm goin' out to Californie to do some prospectin'."

Shannon gasped, pretending offense. "I believe Mr. Richards is having an untoward effect on your manners, William Willoughby!"

"Just funnin', ma'am. I'll walk back to the house with yuh. Don't make much sense for you to trudge back this way again."

Shannon put a hand on her hip. "Now, just when are you planning on calling me Shannon?"

William shrugged his shoulders. "Just don't seem right, ma'am."

Shannon looked at her feet. "There's nothing much right about none of this, William, which makes such familiarity right as rain."

"Yes, ma'am. I mean Shannon, ma'am."

Shannon chuckled. "Well that's a start."

Shannon sent William on his way and started upstairs to make ready for Zach's homecoming. Luke's cries startled her, and she made her way back down.

"No! Leave me be!" he screamed again as she reached the bottom stair.

"Luke, it's only a dream!" she bellowed over his ranting. When he continued, she clapped his cheeks until he calmed. Shortly after, he seemed to sleep peacefully. She studied him for a few minutes and whispered, "You're looking quite the ragamuffin!" Deciding to take advantage of his slumber, she sponged his forehead, beard and mustache. His eyes sprang open and she immediately distanced herself. He reached her easily and he suddenly smiled and said, "I've been gone so long, Amanda. How I've missed you." Then he pulled Shannon on top of him and kissed her until she nearly turned blue.

She managed to wrestle out of his grasp and opened her mouth to give him what for, but he'd fallen asleep again. Still half-sprawled across his body with only one foot on the floor, she froze in aroused disbelief. She pressed her fingers against her lips, his mouth covering hers not something easily forgotten and thought Amanda a very fortunate woman. She also thought it wise to get Luke Richards out of her life once and for all.

* * * *

As the days passed, Luke became stronger and, although, he still found the need to sleep a lot of the time, he often became restless. He inquired about William mostly, then clenched his fists and drove them into the mattress beneath him. Shannon was up to doing most of the chores now, but even though William had Plains Paradise to look after, he would often grab his hat after supper and leave the house to finish anything she hadn't accomplished. She assumed Luke pitied William, the boy who not so long ago only wanted a Stallion, that he hated lying there while William worked himself as hard as two grown men. Most of all, she suspected disturbing memories easily trespassed idle time. She eyed him cautiously. Wanting to help him as much as satisfy her growing curiosity, she eventually asked, "Who is Amanda?"

His eyes, wild and accusing, locked on hers. "Don't ever say her name again."

"You've been crying out in your sleep," Shannon explained. When he didn't respond, she felt rejected. "Doc's coming by tomorrow. Hopefully, he'll find you fit as a fiddle, and you can be on your way." She backed away, anxiously awaiting the cover of dark.

* * * *

After supper the following evening, just like the many nights before, Shannon quickly washed the dishes and emptied the ashes from the cook stove. Anxious to get Zach off to bed, she dutifully read to him quietly while sprawled across the braided rug, the lamplight casting their shadows on the wall opposite the hearth.

Luke had finally come to realize those shadows were real. Surprisingly, it brought him great comfort. Earlier in the day when Doc Murphy told him he could soon end his convalescence and return to the Willoughby homestead, the old man remarked on Luke's indifferent demeanor.

Shannon lay Zach in his bed and kissed him goodnight. Glancing at the empty spot always reserved for Duke, her irritation surrounding the dog preferring Luke's company began to swell. She licked her lips subconsciously, eager to take the bottle from its hiding spot in the small pantry and finish it off.

Avoiding nearly every splinter on the stair rail, she hurried to the cupboard, wrapped her hands tightly around the bottle, and quietly stole out the door to the porch. She sipped the amber-colored liquid at first and then took long swigs until she'd completely emptied the bottle. Her small world seemed to spin, her temples ached, and everything proved humorous, even William as he stood over her beckoning Luke's assistance.

"Somethin's wrong with Mrs. Cook, Luke. Come quick! She musta been snake bit!"

Luke stumbled out, immediately spying the bottle. "What in blazes?"

"Her words are all jumbled and she can't keep her head up. Sounds like snake poisonin' to me! Should I go for the Doc?"

"Only kind of venom Mrs. Cook's got in her come from a whiskey barrel. And judgin' from this bottle," Luke told him as he bent over to retrieve the glass container, "it ain't been in that barrel near long enough. Yup," Luke added, "that's some rotgut mess is what that is."

"What should we do?" William asked.

Luke sighed. "Let's get her on into the house. Pick her up slow, boy, and stand back if she starts spewin'."

Luke's face twisted into a grimace as he carried his share of the weight. By the time they reached the top stair and put her to bed, Luke was nearly white, and his hand flew to the bandage.

Zach began to fuss and reach for William. The boy picked the baby up, and then suggested Luke lie down.

"I'm really gonna miss that little tyke," Luke said after they'd come downstairs. "Maybe somebody ought to stay on and make sure the little fella is minded after proper."

"Ain't never seen her like this before," William said, defending Shannon.

"Once is one time too many. Got half a mind to send this boy a hers back to Miss Emily."

William shuffled his feet. He knew Shannon and Luke needed one another. If only he could make them see that. He offered to make breakfast. Luke didn't argue and assured him he could handle the baby.

Luke played with Zach for nearly an hour, the baby content to pull his beard, coo, and giggle. His frustration grew when Zach began to cry and, despite his best efforts, wouldn't stop. "What in tarnation's the matter with him?" he asked William in desperation. Confused, they both stared at the baby and finally decided Zach was either hungry or didn't like wet britches.

"Got breakfast near done," William announced optimistically.

"You ain't thinkin' 'bout givin' him one a yer biscuits, I hope."

William wrinkled his nose. "Heck no, he's only got a couple

of teeth!"

"Boy, a mouthful ain't near enough for them biscuits a yers."

"I'm aware!" William fired back and returned with a small piece of side meat.

"Good thinkin', boy!" Luke told him when Zach eagerly claimed it and began to slobber it soft. "What about his britches?" Luke asked, holding the baby over the floor. "He's startin' to leak like a thatch roof."

"Ain't had a lot of learnin' 'bout that," William muttered, scanning the room. "Here," he said, tossing Luke a flour sack. "Patch him with that till I think of somethin' better."

Luke blotted his own lap with the burlap sack. "Damn almighty! If I wanted a bath, I'd a headed for the creek."

"Dadgum it, Luke," William scolded, snatching the flour sack. "That was meant for his behind and now you've gone and soiled it good!"

Luke looked helplessly around the room. His eyes lit up when he spotted a doily on a corner table. "Always knew these frilly things were good for somethin'," he said and grabbed Zach by both ankles. Luke suddenly jerked backwards, managing to dodge most of Zach's stream. "The boy's got good aim, I'll give 'em that."

William laughed until his sides ached. Luke joined in, which inspired Zach to mimic them both.

"How in the world you suppose his ma can sleep through all this commotion?" William asked.

"Don't you worry 'bout Mrs. Cook, boy. She's feeling no pain, I can assure you."

"Don't be so hard on her."

It was a few minutes before Luke said anything. "You're right. I'd lay odds a woman like that one would no more bring whiskey to her lips than harm to this baby a hers 'less something was eatin' away at her good. I expect she puts all the bad things happened of late on her own self, probably thinks that we're blamin' her for it all, too."

William looked at his feet, and Luke knew the kid was near

tears.

"You mean she blames herself for my Grandpa and Grandma dyin'?"

"That ain't the half of it. Haven't you noticed her heart turnin' inside out when you can't even bring yourself to speak half the time and you go on and work yourself till you nearly drop?"

William shrugged his shoulders but swiped at his eyes.

"Well, I seen it. I seen her cryin' for us all. Samuel, Mary, you, and even me, believe it or not. I seen her wishin' she'd a kilt that sonuvabitch herself the first time he came to call so that none of these terrible things woulda happened. It's tearin' her up inside."

TWENTY-THREE

It wasn't until later in the day that Luke and William heard the sound of unsteady footsteps overhead. Shannon made her way to the top of the stairs and shielded her eyes from the afternoon sun. Her head throbbed with each step she took and her stomach churned. Shortly after she'd reached the bottom, she bolted outside and vomited.

Luke followed, taunting her. "The boy made supper. But 'spect yours will keep until later. No sense in wastin' good grub."

Shannon grasped the porch rail and eased her backside onto the top step. "Please, Mr. Richards," she murmured, "Let's not speak of food."

"Serves you right, you know. Carryin' on like some fast trick."

Shannon whipped her head in his direction and quickly regretted it. "How dare you compare me to your saloon trash!" she scolded and winced at the timbre of her own voice.

"Reckon you're right... my apologies to them. Mosta them have sense enough not to put away the likes of the fire water you threw down your gullet."

Shannon squeezed her eyes shut and thought she tasted sand. "I have half a mind to fist you good," she wished she could say louder.

"Them strong words for a woman can't even stand on her own two feet. Best get yourself right. That boy a yours got nobody else to depend on," he said, flinging the remaining coffee from his tin cup off the porch.

"She'll be alright, boy," she heard Luke tell William and assumed the boy had come out to the porch.

"I hope you'll pardon my shoddy deed, William," she said, ashamed to face him.

"None of this was no fault a yers," William muttered as he placed a hand on her shoulder. "No more than you'd be to blame if yer horse's foal was stillborn or a nest of baby birds in one of yer trees over yonder found themselves a snake's supper."

"I should have done things differently," Shannon whispered and she covered his hand with hers.

"I reckon God has his own plans sometimes whether they make sense or not."

Luke nudged William and handed him a steaming tin cup. William understood and wrapped Shannon's hand around it.

She sat the coffee down and Luke said, "Drink that, then come see about your boy. Prob'ly gettin' a might tired of honey water."

Shannon buried her head in her hands.

"Luke's only funnin'. Near every time Zach had him a swallow, he just cooed and smiled like an idiot," William assured her.

Shannon hiccoughed a laugh. "You're not saying that just to make me feel better, referring to my son as an idiot notwithstanding."

William blushed. "Heck no and didn't mean nothin' by the other."

She heard Zach winding up and attempted to stand.

"If it wouldn't be too much trouble," Luke called over Zach's wails, "this baby's fit to be tied."

William helped her to her feet. She took Zach from Luke and he asked her if she'd finished her coffee. Shannon shook her head.

"You reckon I got nothin' better to do than play nursemaid?"

"Can't abide much on my stomach right now. And it may be a good time to remind you that you're only a guest here, Luke Richards!"

"That so? Never in all my days been in a hotel I was expected to do chores."

Shannon stiffened. "I can't imagine the likes of you seeing the inside of a hotel. A cave's more like it."

Luke laughed until he winced. "Oh, is that right, Stormy

Sue? You best sit that behind of yours down before you fall flat on that pretty nose a yers."

Close enough to admire his gray-blue eyes and the full lips peeking out from under a mustache in need of trimming, Shannon thought about that kiss again and felt fire surge through her. "Tell me this, Amanda ever pull a cork?" She watched a storm wash over him. His eyes glazed over and he thundered past. Shannon sucked in a breath and held it. She had definitely underestimated Luke's loyalty to and his love for the mysterious Amanda.

William gaped and looked as though he might cry.

Luke began gathering the few belongings he had. Shannon froze as his spurs clanked across the wood floor to the door. "Don't be too long, William," he called over his shoulder. "I'll take care of the milkin' and such but get on back before night's light."

"Seein' as I've finished the chores 'round here, I'll be along now," William replied and left without a goodbye.

TWENTY-FOUR

The next morning William thought Luke more quiet than usual. He wanted to talk over events from the preceding day but didn't know how without making things worse.

"Hope you weren't expectin' 'em over-easy," Luke told him, flipping the eggs like they'd done him some wrong.

"Reckon I'll take what I can get," William muttered and approached the stove apprehensively. "Luke, mind if I ask you somethin'?"

Luke stiffened and kept his eyes fixed on the pan. "Suppose I won't know the answer to that till I hear the question." Luke gestured impatiently toward the table and told William to take a seat. "Let's just eat, boy. This chow ain't gonna taste any better cold."

William squirmed in his chair and thought breakfast a pitiful sight. "Ain't never had black sow belly before," he whispered under his breath.

"Bacon ain't burnt, just crisp."

"Eggs crisp too?"

"That your question, boy?"

William shook his head and blurted it out. "What makes women act the way they do? I mean... plumb crazy, like that there with Mrs. Cook yesterday?"

Luke choked and sprung from his chair. Once he'd managed to bring up a partially lodged chunk, he laughed long and loud.

William's fork clanked to his plate. "Well, just never you mind!"

Luke intercepted him before he reached the door. "Come on, boy. It ain't you askin' the question I find amusin'. It's the question itself. Because there ain't no man alive or dead has the answer to it 'cept maybe the good Lord himself." He attempted to redirect William to the table and failed.

"Why did Mrs. Cook get so blamed mad when all you were tryin' to do was help her? Can yuh answer me that?"

Luke cocked an eyebrow and ran his fingers through his mustache. "Wish I could, but I've been askin' myself that same thing over and over all mornin'. Reckon she was in a huff due to makin' a fool of herself."

William took his seat. "You mean 'cause of her drinkin'?"

Luke nodded. Then he grinned. "That's a relief! Thought I was in for a talk about the birds and the bees."

William blushed. "Shoot, I already know all there is to know 'bout that." William picked up his fork. Someday, he planned to find out who Amanda was.

* * * *

Shannon finished drawing her horses' water from the well and hung her head when she saw William coming up the lane. "Morning, William," she called without looking up again.

"Mornin' ma'am," William said, sweeping a leg back across an aging Belgian mare.

"I'd be pleased if you'd call me Shannon," she reminded him softly. "Truth is there isn't that many years between us."

William played it safe and only nodded. Luke hadn't been much help to his surprise. He'd assumed Luke would be an expert when it came to women. He'd seen, with his own eyes, women practically trip over their tongues when Luke passed.

"Is everything alright?"

"Yes ma'am, I mean Shannon. Can I ask you somethin'?"

"What is it, William?" When he didn't respond, she took his arm in hers. "Let's pretend yesterday never happened."

"Weren't your fault, you know."

Shannon began to cry. William wiped his palms on his jeans and clumsily embraced her.

"It is," she sobbed.

"No, it ain't. None of it. You and me have to find a way to bury this ugliness somewhere deep before it buries us."

Shannon raised her head, looked at him thoughtfully, and kissed his cheek. "You are possibly the smartest man I've yet to meet, William Willoughby."

William blushed and wasn't sure how to respond. He hadn't uttered more than twenty words to any girl, aside from his ma and his Grandma Willoughby, all his years. And he knew if he went and said the wrong thing, Shannon might just start her crying all over again. He figured a smile a safer bet.

"There's an ornery critter up at the house been anxiously awaiting your visit."

"Somethin' else I got to say," William said firmly and planted his feet.

"Well, go on, William," she said softly.

"Why do you hate Mr. Richards so? I know he's got his ways, but all he was tryin' to do was help. I guess you and him are all I got right about now, and I don't reckon I can stand the thought of the two of you always fussin' at each other."

"I haven't anything against Mr. Richards, William," Shannon crooned. "It's hard to put into words."

Shannon stared at the blue skies overhead, and William considered telling her she wouldn't find the answer there. He knew all too well.

"We just don't mix well is all. Hasn't there ever been someone in your life that you cared for, didn't wish ill, yet having them around got your back up?"

William nodded and curled a lip. "Charlie Fenwick."

Shannon hid her grin. "Well, that's the way it is between Luke and me. We do care about each other, but it would suit us just fine to lead our lives separately. There's nothing wrong with that."

"There's a whole world wrong with it!" William shot back.

"Oh, how's that?" Shannon asked, failing to conceal her irritation.

"A man like Luke ain't easy, but neither is this land you 'bout near died over. Neither is gettin' that horse I got my sights set on. Didn't figure you for someone who'd run from a little hard work."

"Not every woman needs a man about her, William," Shannon countered. "But I'll make you a promise." She waited for the boy to take his eyes off his toes. "If ever I change my mind, it's safe to say Luke Richards might very well be the first to know about it."

"You're not foolin'?"

Shannon shook her head. "Promise to keep that to yourself?"

Before he could answer, they both turned their attention to the loud commotion coming from the house. William beat her to the door.

"Oh, my heavens!" Shannon exclaimed, laughing as she peeked over William's shoulder. "That dog does look pathetic, now doesn't he?"

William laughed until he was blue. "Never seen a dog wear oatmeal before."

"See why I need you around here?" Shannon asked and hugged him. "To remind me never ever to let that boy of mine feed his own self again."

TWENTY-FIVE

Shannon hitched Sara to the wagon, again deliberated over her attire, and chuckled as she imagined the townspeople's reaction. She was surprised how comfortable she felt in the jeans William had given her. She found if she tucked the bottom of the trousers into her boots, her skin was practically inaccessible to chiggers and mosquitos just as he'd told her. When he'd also offered, 'Not much chance of a snake creepin' up between your legs in britches neither,' she was the last one who'd argue that kind of logic. She giggled, remembering William's blush as he looked at her calf-eyed and told her he'd 'never seen a pair of britches filled out proper'. Her thoughts soon ran to Luke the way they usually did. Willing him off her mind, she thought it appropriate a bank of clouds suddenly trailed across the sky.

She returned to the house to collect Zach, took her bonnet from the bedpost, and just as quickly tossed it aside. She opened the old trunk Cole had left behind and retrieved a hat, surprised that the Stetson fit nearly perfectly.

Before placing Zach in the wagon, she coaxed her horse to drink, but Sara liked the hat much more than her baby seemed to and nibbled on it instead. "Zach, look there," Shannon said excitedly as they neared the end of the lane. "See the squirrels playing tag near that tree trunk!" When he cooed, she knew he had seen them. "Take a sniff," Shannon instructed. Immediately, he imitated her. He seemed to enjoy the scents of lilac and honeysuckle as much as she did.

Once in town, Shannon shrugged off the expected snickers and offensive remarks. The boots William had outgrown and given her somehow empowered her. She felt taller, her gait stronger. She stepped onto the boardwalk with a new determination, the satchel of gowns in one arm, Zach in the other.

Emily Dunsmire ran her hands along the gowns displayed

near the store window. Shannon had done a marvelous job, and Emily felt sure with so many late-summer birthdays coming that her investment was a good one. As each day passed, keeping the truth from Shannon weighed more heavily on her conscience. She thought about what Luke had said and once again considered his advice. The bells on the door announced a visitor and she gasped when she saw Shannon. "I scarcely recognize you! I've never seen your hair down, and where on earth did you get that hat and those britches?"

"The same place I got these boots," Shannon said, hitching a foot off the ground, a wide grin stretching her face. She gestured toward the window. "I thought I'd give them something new to talk about."

"For both our sakes, you'd better hope you haven't started a new fashion!"

Shannon laughed. "Don't expect there's enough canvas or denim in these entire Great Plains to outfit those backsides!"

"Shannon Cook! Old Scratch got a hold of you this morning?"

Shannon shook her head. "It seems the devil's busy enough with them out there without bothering with the likes of me."

"My goodness, more gowns?"

Shannon nodded enthusiastically. "This is the last of them."

"You finished them all?"

"Yes ma'am."

"Why, that means..."

"Once I put my wages toward the deed, a good part of my land will be free and clear."

Emily squealed and hugged her. "Hallelujah girl! There was no doubt in my mind you could do it. Well, what in tarnation are we waiting for?" Emily asked, eagerly crossing the room to the cash register. "I'll give you the money due and after you return from the bank we'll celebrate! I have some sherry tucked away for just such an occasion!"

A few minutes later, as Shannon started down the walk, a sudden gust of wind came out of nowhere, and she caught her hat before it sailed across the street. She passed the general store where she came face-to-face with the usual barricade. Refusing to detour, she raised the brim of her hat and communicated a silent warning. To her surprise, the women immediately dispersed.

Travis Parker watched Shannon intently as she crossed the street and approached the bank. His fingers trembled and he gave up counting the bills in his charge. When she approached his counter, he dropped the bank ledger.

"I've a payment here toward my deed."

He picked up the ledger, and Shannon heard him swallow.

"That will have to involve Mr. Marsh, I'm afraid," Parker said, his gaze nervously shifting from her to Jack's office and back again.

Shannon waited but the clerk stood motionless. "What seems to be the delay, Mr. Parker?"

Travis leaned across the counter. "He's not going to like this," he whispered. "Not one bit."

"I don't much give a tinker's damn," Shannon whispered back.

Parker's jaw dropped, and he once again fumbled the ledger. Shannon heard him yelp shortly after and assumed he'd bumped into something on his way around the tall counter. Hesitating outside Jack's door, he tapped his knuckles lightly against the glass. Shannon heard Jack growl something and Travis disappeared inside. A loud commotion ensued, and Travis sheepishly reappeared empty-handed. He smacked a cowlick back in place and straightened his tie. "He won't accept a partial payment," Parker whispered. "This is most unprecedented, I assure you."

"Well, we'll just see about that!" Shannon said and threw Jack's door open. "Hear me clear, Jack Marsh! I was expecting such underhanded trickery, so I asked Sheriff Conner to send a wire to Governor Bradley. I'm gonna keep what's rightfully mine, so you best be smart and take this."

Jack thumped his heels on top of the desk, crossed his legs, and lit a cigar. He inhaled deeply and slowly, blowing smoke rings in her direction.

Choking, she waved the billowy fog away. "And I'll be expecting a receipt."

He didn't speak. His eyes violated her repeatedly, and he grinned when she looked away. He dropped his feet to the floor abruptly and she jumped. After that, he swiveled his chair and faced the wall.

"Turn your back all you want. I'm not leaving! Not until you take this money and give me a receipt."

He stood slowly, quite aware his six-feet, three-inches had always been a most effective intimidation strategy. He strolled over, reached above her head, pushed the door closed, and left his arm in that position. Now he had her cornered just as planned, and his erection grew when she shivered fear.

Nothing could scare her quite like Jack Marsh. "Well, get your man in here," she bluffed, her voice quaking. "I haven't got all day."

Jack grinned crooked before he laughed outright, a sound more reminiscent of a victory shriek. "Where you gonna run now?" he whispered, his hot breath ricocheting back in his face. She attempted to squirm out of his trap, but he pressed her hard against the door. "By now, I'd think you'd have learned not to get on my bad side." He knew, by the blurred images he saw through the glass door, he had far too many witnesses and once again reconsidered his timing. "Take your chicken scratch and get while you can." Then he opened the door and shoved her into the lobby.

Shannon stood outside his door for several minutes. Her hands shaking, she struggled with the knob but eventually managed to turn it. But this time she intended to stay in the lobby, and she spoke her mind from there. "I'm not leaving until you've done as I've asked, Mr. Marsh!" When Jack ignored her, she waved the currency in the air and addressed anyone who would listen. "You all will bear witness; two-hundred, fifty dollars to go toward my deed."

Jack went for her. Without a word, he grabbed her shirt collar, dragged her across the bank, and tossed her into the street. Travis stealthily exited and scampered toward the sheriff's office, but Jacob was already halfway to the bank. Jack saw Conner coming, took long strides in the opposite direction, and skidded into the Chinaman's den.

Jacob spotted Marsh but decided to help Shannon collect the scattered bills instead. Apprehending Jack was a losing proposition anyway. "What in tarnation's goin' on?" he asked Shannon, capturing several notes before the wind carried them away.

Travis eagerly recanted the details first.

Shannon clutched Jacob's arm and he felt a few fingernails sink in. "Sheriff, Mr. Marsh is determined to take my land and refuses to accept anything but full payment!"

Jacob released her grip and said nothing.

"Do you understand that my husband had no right to relinquish it in the first place?"

"I got no say in the bank's business. That's a federal matter."

"Damn you then!"

"Now hold on! The governor's yet to make a rulin'. Until that happens, I'll bear witness to what's transpired here today." Jacob motioned to Travis. "You tell Jack that deed better not be sold or magically disappear until this here's settled!" He took Shannon by the arm and escorted her away from the bank. "I'll hold the money for safekeepin', if that sits well with you. Don't trust that man any more than you do."

They were halfway to Emily's when they ran up against Kate Reeds. "Well, will you look here! No man will have her so she's takin' to dressin' like one."

Jacob didn't grab Shannon in time. Kate Reed's nose bounced off Shannon's knuckles before he could blink.

"Don't just stand there, Sheriff! Do your duty!" Kate yelled, pressing her palm to a bloody nose.

"Sun was in my eyes, Mrs. Reed," he lied. "Afraid I didn't see a thing." Grasping Shannon's bicep so firmly she yelped, he quickly ushered her away. "I haven't the slightest notion what's gotten into you," he admonished. "Ain't no way for a lady to act."

"Unhand me, Sheriff." The stinging retorts she'd planned to add quickly dissipated when the clapping began. By the time she'd rebuffed Conner's escort and reached Emily's, the cheers and applause grew. Apparently, several of the townspeople appreciated her no nonsense approach to the town's busybody.

Luke Richards wasn't one of them she soon discovered when they nearly collided outside Emily's door. He took one look at her, wrinkled his nose, and she heard him say, "Don't expect me to fight your battles from here on out what with cuttin' a figure like a common cowhand! I reckon you'll deserve all the unkind words comin' your way."

"I can fight my own battles," Shannon fired back and gestured over her shoulder. "Just ask around."

"Suit yourself."

She chewed her lip reflectively as he walked away and eventually ran after him. "I reckon I owe you an apology," she said, finding it difficult to keep his brisk pace, "for what I said about Amanda. It was unkind and not my place to..."

Luke stopped walking and dropped his head. When he looked up, his stare was fixed and unsympathetic.

"Let's just keep her name outa everythin' from here on out. Now, if you don't mind, I got somewhere to be."

Shannon watched him continue down the boardwalk and felt a mixture of anger and angst. And she still didn't know a thing more about Amanda.

"Apology accepted," she heard him call over his shoulder.

TWENTY-SIX

"Glory be! I can't rightly decide if this town's bringing out the best or worst in you," Emily told Shannon and pulled her inside.

"Of late, it's been my experience the two often intertwine." Shannon wrinkled her nose. "But it's not likely it's the town that's influenced me," she muttered so quietly Emily didn't hear.

"Do you suppose it was that get-up that incensed Kate so?"

"You saw that from here?"

Emily nodded and palmed a grin.

"We both know it doesn't take much where that ole biddy's concerned. If it wasn't the britches, it'd be something else."

"So she finally rankled your feathers good?"

Shannon nodded. "Reckon I don't much like being referred to as a man."

Emily closed the barrier between them and hugged her close. "Between you and me, I've had a notion to put hands on that busybody for quite some time. That woman thinks she runs this town."

"Bet Jack Marsh would advise her different. He refused to take a partial payment."

"What?" Emily shrieked.

"Sheriff Conner said he'd see what he could do."

"He didn't hold Jack accountable?"

Shannon shook her head. "He said it was federal business."

"That doesn't surprise me on either account. Jack Marsh is a horse's behind." Emily grinned suddenly. "But I'm certain Jacob Conner done all he could, because from what I've witnessed he'd do just about anything for you short of dying."

Shannon's mouth flew open. "Well what do you know," she said, the words tumbling thoughtfully from her lips. "I had no idea, but now that you mention it that man does buzz around me like a stubborn fly at a picnic. If he'd seen Jack pitch me to the street, that banker might no longer be a problem."

Emily felt her veins throb. "Jack Marsh laid hands on you?"

"It's nothing I haven't come to expect."

Emily turned her back and wrung her hands. "Jack Marsh worries me like no other. You stay clear of him, Shannon Cook. Promise me! I got some business east, and I don't want to be worrying myself sick."

Shannon wanted to know the nature of Emily's business but didn't intend to pry. "How long will you be gone?"

"A few weeks provided the train doesn't entertain uninvited passengers."

Shannon cringed as she thought about the likes of The Jesse James Gang.

"Reckon you can keep that promise until then?"

"I won't tell you a tale. No man's going to mark or block my path from now on, though should Jack Marsh keep his distance I have no plans to seek him out."

Emily cupped Shannon's shoulders. "A smart woman chooses her path, makes her foe think it was his idea and then patiently waits for him to successfully navigate her down that path in a carriage of gold."

Shannon grinned. "Is that how you got all this?"

"The shop?"

Shannon nodded.

"Husband number five," Emily told her. "He often told me he'd never have finished the railroad if it weren't for me. So I guess you could say we helped each other."

"What happened to him?"

Emily sighed, folded her arms, and bowed her head. "Dead, been almost a year now."

"I'm sorry," Shannon mumbled, finally breaking the heavy silence. "And husbands one, two, three, and four?"

Emily sighed. "That's a story for a much longer day."

She opened the bottle of sherry and handed Shannon a glass. "Mind what I say now. An intelligent and successful woman has to outthink her male counterparts... and without becoming one of them."

"Are you referring to the britches?"

Emily laughed. "Not entirely. Are you as strong as a man?"

"Can't say that I am."

"Then what makes you think you can whoop one by joining the group?"

Shannon stared blankly.

"A woman can't overpower a man, so she has little recourse but to outsmart him."

Shannon chuckled. "You saying we should use our feminine wiles?"

"Some do, mostly the lazy ones desiring to take the easy route. Trouble is feminine wiles have an expiration date."

"So does brute."

"Yes, but a man's power isn't limited to his fists. Some of the most powerful men I ever met could be blown down by a strong wind."

Shannon's head swam. "I reckon this might possibly be one of your stories requiring a much longer day."

Emily's laugh echoed through the shop. "You and Zach stay put tonight and go on back tomorrow," she said, kissing Shannon's forehead and leading her toward the chaise lounge. "I think that sherry's got a hold on you."

Shannon nodded and quickly fell asleep.

TWENTY-SEVEN

Emily told no one the entire scope of her plans. Not even Lance or Luke. She packed only the mere essentials but carrying the bag proved a challenge anyway, and she drug it behind her most of the way. How in the world would she ever manage two? The train leaving for St. Louis was a few minutes late. She ached to set the bag on the ground beside her, but she didn't dare relinquish possession, fearful someone might discover the Colt pistol tucked away at the bottom below the empty second satchel. Determined to sequester the fortune due herself and Shannon, nothing-including robbery or murder if it came to it-would detour her.

* * * *

When the train arrived in St. Louis, Emily wondered how she would ever find Mika. She knew from a letter her sister had written that he had bought a beautiful house in town. '*It is grand,*' Katherine had penned, '*with spectacular gardens and a carriage house that is larger than most of the dwellings in town.*'

Emily dabbed her eyes with the lavender-scented, embroidered handkerchief. She missed her younger sister, who had once taken her in and hidden her from a group of confederate outlaws. She remembered clearly the night the men rode in, nearly ten of them, stinking of whiskey and days shy of a bath, and donning red border shirts with pockets large enough to conceal the belly gun typically stowed beneath.

Oftentimes, these men, pure cowards in Emily's opinion, would wear shirts of blue so that they could creep up on their enemy and union sympathizers alike. But that night they openly boasted their true colors, because they had a specific mission in mind. A very personal vendetta.

Emily recognized Bloody Bill. Though she knew him to be

a murderous bastard, she was relieved neither William Quantrill nor Coleman Younger was a part of the group. Mika had always referred to Quantrill as "The Captain", and Emily remembered him as a frequent and frightening houseguest. Quantrill's appearance never failed to astound her, such womanly features and a remarkably small frame for a man so feared. She never knew why he was at the house, as Mika forbid her anywhere near his study or within earshot of the suspected surreptitious exchange. It was no surprise to her that Mika supported the regulators and would call on the more dishonorable to do his bidding, using the war as an excuse to free himself from competition of one sort or another.

That particular night in 1863, while she lay huddled in the dank, dark corner of the barn with Katherine's largest and less timid Palomino pulled in close, she shook as Bill repeatedly threatened her sister.

"Fetch the traitor whore on out here or I'll burn her out!"

Emily assumed news of her involvement with a Union General had reached Mika. Apparently, he was infuriated that everyone knew his wife shared the enemy's bed and wanted her shot, her head severed from her body, put atop a pole, and then paraded through town for all to see.

Mika hadn't counted on Katherine. She was a beautiful and very resourceful woman. Emily was thankful that her sister loved her as much or more than the finer things she was determined surround her in life regardless of her station. Denying Emily's presence and pretending loyalty to the Confederate Army and Mika Leeds, Katherine filled the outlaws with her finest whiskey while initiating toasts to the Rebels, Quantrill, and Sterling Price. Quickly realizing these men had developed a very high tolerance to drink and not all were totally convinced of her devotion, she seduced the leader and provided a most essential distraction. Emily easily escaped that night and remained forever in her sister's debt.

Murdered by her husband, a jealous and wealthy senator, a few years after, Emily was determined to avenge her sister's death. In the end, Emily settled for frontier justice and shot him dead one wintry night. Because of her third husband's important connections, both within and outside the law, Emily never appeared before judge or jury.

"Can I be of any service, ma'am?" the young train station clerk asked, jolting her back to the present.

"If you would be so kind and direct me to the Leeds' House."

He grinned like a caged monkey at the circus. "Reckon I don't need to tell you the Leeds House is St. Louie's most popular attraction," he said with sincere enthusiasm. "Folks come from miles around just to have a look."

Directed to a magnificent house, clearly the largest in the city, Emily stood across the street gaping at the gargantuan structure. No stranger to grand dwellings, she still found the architecture most impressive. Thinking about Shannon's present and past adversities, she felt a scowl form and her hostility intensify. Trimmed in gold, the ornament atop the roof in itself surpassed the value of Shannon's land. She counted five groundskeepers tending the glorious and fragrant rose gardens at the front of the property and assumed more servants minded the back.

Clouds raced overhead and drew her attention upward. Taking in the gargoyles effectively spaced six to eight feet apart along the third story fascia, a figure seated inside a window caught her sweeping gaze. She assumed the figure a man, his hair white, billowy, and reminiscent of goose feathers, his posture discordantly stately and commanding. Could he be Mika? Because of the twenty-year gap between them, she entertained the notion.

He didn't break his stare, and her plan to breach the house undetected now seemed impossible. Even had her presence gone unnoticed, the house surely would prove a fortress; an iron fence surrounded the entire property. She considered the pistol and wondered what lengths his servants would attempt to protect him.

According to the clerk at the station, curiosity seekers were commonplace outside the Leeds House, but Emily's appearance had changed little since Mika saw her last. She assumed his vantage point was equally as good as hers, possibly better, and she wondered if he'd already guessed her identity. She began to perspire and cuffed her hat tightly around her face.

"Yuh come fer da housekeepin' position, Miss?" a Negro asked, his upper body nearly bare, his dark skin beautiful and glistening, his demeanor and cadence warmly familiar.

Emily's smile formed naturally. He seemed surprised and immediately returned it. "Why yes, as a matter of fact I have."

"Ah'll fetch Miss Lucy," he said, his gleaming brown eyes whipping to the house. His joy suddenly abandoned somewhere between the ground and the second story, he told her, "She be da one doin' da hirin'. Yuh waits right here, Miss."

Good heavens! Lucy? And alive after all this time? Emily felt both happiness and fear of discovery sweep through her. "No, no. That won't be necessary," she assured him. "Worse thing a person wanting a position can do is interfere with other folks' chores. I'll announce myself around back as is surely expected."

"Yas'm, reckon that'd be best," he told her solemnly after stealing another glance toward the house.

Emily's rage flourished as she wrestled past dozens of trellises overflowing with Rugosa, Musk, and China roses of every color imaginable. The garden furniture arranged nearby was far more elegant than most indoor furnishings. Though marrying into wealth and power many times over, she had certainly never enjoyed such luxuries. She thought of Shannon's meagre existence again, and by the time she reached the back door nothing could have stopped her from pummeling her fists against the heavy oak.

"Mercy me! Lawdy, ah be comin'!" A portly, elderly woman whipped the door open and flung a towel over one shoulder.

Emily suffocated a gasp. Lucy's hair, once as rich a color as mahogany, was now riddled with gray. Her deep brown eyes no longer sparkled and loose skin hooded thin eyelids.

"Wud yuh be poundin' on da man's door fer, Miss?" she asked impatiently.

"I've come to inquire about the housekeeping position."

"Well, git on in here wid yuh. Lawd knows id don't pay anuf ta be beatin' a door down."

Emily choked on her swelling emotion. Her fondness for Lucy was timeless and she had always hoped such a beautiful soul had somehow escaped Mika Leeds. Katherine had written about Mika's threat to the slaves after the war ended. Most were afraid to leave. Mika ordered ones that tried hung and left to hang for days as an effective deterrent to the others. Politicians and lawmen alike turned a blind eye, fearful of losing either their own lives, their jobs, or generous donations.

Lucy led Emily into the drawing room. Emily pressed a gloved hand to a sad smile, fondly remembering her daughters' imitation of their mammy's waddle. "Yuh waits here. Got me a pot in da kitchen needs tendin'."

Emily didn't know how much time had passed before the old woman returned. She quickly restored Polly's tintype to its original position on the Duncan-Phyfe mahogany table and whisked mounting tears from her cheeks.

"One thing yuh need to learn right dis very minute," Lucy said, wagging a finger, "is never ever ta lay a hand on dat dare. Dat mean more to Mistuh Mika den just 'bout anythin' da man owns."

"I'm sorry," Emily muttered. "I didn't intend any harm."

"Yuh cryin', Miss?" Lucy asked, twirling Emily ninety degrees. "What in da wor'd got yuh all worked up?"

Emily didn't answer and fought to compose herself.

"Oh, child, didn't mean ta upset yuh so. Lawd-a-mercy, pickin' dat ol photograph up gonna stay tween yuh and me. 'Sides, all dat's come before yuh been drinkers and jus plain trash. Yuh be da kind da Mistuh want 'round here. Yuh wait and see if ah ain't right. Stay put and ah'll fetch 'im directly."

Emily stole another glance at the photograph and wondered how old Polly had been at the time. Lost in the past, Emily recalled a typical morning when it took all her conviction and the enlistment of Lucy to wrestle the child still enough to dress her. Clearly Mika's favorite, she accompanied him nearly everywhere. The rare occasions he left her behind, Polly sat near an upstairs window with a clear view of the lane, springing from the window seat upon his return, bounding down the stairs and out the door to greet him. Usually stern and impatient, Mika didn't seem the least bit annoyed by it. As time went by, Polly was the only one that brought him joy.

No one could resist Polly, particularly Shannon. By the time Shannon was two, Polly preferred Shannon's company to anyone else's. Mika resented it and, as a result, never had a kind word for his youngest. Emily was certain if it had not been for Polly's attachment, Mika would have thrown Shannon out, too. Because Mika was particularly hard on Shannon when he drank, Emily instructed Lucy to water down his whiskey. When he caught her one evening, he beat her with a riding crop. Lucy returned and Emily noted she still bore the scar over her right eye.

"Mister Mika say he be dis way directly. Ah's got work to do, so ah be along. Meantime, don't yuh be worryin' none, Miss. Ain't no reason yuh not be gettin' on here." Lucy raised a finger and shortened the distance between them. "Na, don't be scared off. Poe thang suffered a stroke a while back and lawdy he's a sight ta be sure! Mighty hard for 'im to git his lips ta do his mind's biddin' deeze days, too."

Emily could hear him shuffling about above her. Her heart thumping against her chest, she rummaged through drawers and put anything of value into her bag. Satisfied she had confiscated anything worth her trouble in the drawing room, she bustled through the dining room, claiming every piece of silverware including the candlesticks, a gift, she remembered, from Captain Nathaniel Lyon.

She crept up the long staircase and hugged the wall once she reached the landing. Peering covertly into the upstairs parlor and finding it empty, she located large sums of coin and valuable pieces of jewelry hidden within a masterfully carved cabinet. Tiptoeing across the dense Persian rug and back into the hallway, she located his study and riffled through desk drawers. Coming across a false bottom, she discovered more gold and a tray of silver dollars. Snickering over the irony when she came across the deed to the St. Louis property, she stuffed it into the bulging bag, too.

The floorboards creaked behind her. "Thief! Somebody help!"

Emily whirled around and came face to face with a young Negro boy. They struggled briefly and he fell.

Assisted by Lucy, Mika reached the study. Their eyes met and he lowered the gun and collapsed against the doorframe. "Victoria," he uttered. The rest of his dialogue was indecipherable. His eyes expressed his regret; hers expressed her detestation.

Lucy clutched her chest. "Sweet Jesus! Missus, Id truly be yuh!"

Emily's eyes searched Lucy's and tear droplets trickled down both women's cheeks. "Why have you stayed all these years?" When Lucy didn't answer, Emily pressed.

Lucy shrugged her shoulders and stared at the floor. "Dis man here done been punished ta hell. Ain't no fight in 'im no moe. Please, Missus, come sit awhile."

Emily laughed sarcastically and brushed past her. Face-to-face with Mika, she said, "Been punished enough, has he? Maybe you've forgotten the atrocities he's orchestrated! He burned down my father's barn when the sweet old man objected to our betrothal. He not only took a whip to you, me, but Shannon, too! He ordered the hanging and," Emily choked, "gutting of innocent men!"

Lucy came up behind her. "Please, stop, missus! Ain't gonna change nuttin'."

Emily shook her off. "Worse than all those dreadful things put together, this bastard allowed the butchering of my firstborn, most likely to destroy his own perversity!"

Mika splintered his cane against the doorframe, and Emily assumed he objected only to her final accusation.

"You'll find no mercy here," she snarled, heaving the heavy bag into the hallway. She dropped it there and slapped him hard. "I would have given anything to know my child and you took that from me!" She struck him until her palms burned. Breathless, she managed, "At least now I've found Shannon, and I'll be damned if she won't have everything that's rightfully hers. Come after me, Mika Leeds, and I'll direct you to hell!" She turned on her heel and, without looking back, she told Lucy goodbye, propelled the bag down the long marbled staircase, and exited through the main door.

TWENTY-EIGHT

Jack Marsh enjoyed the banking business, mostly because it allowed him to play God. He particularly savored those times when folks would stoop to begging, and he would allow it to continue until it bored him, at which time he'd instruct his assistants to evict men, women, and their offspring, squashing their dreams and quite possibly survival itself. They were nearly always people he'd known since childhood but such ridiculous sentiment he left to lesser men. And with a stroke of his pen, regardless of sweltering heat or sub-zero temperatures, churchgoers and those never seeking absolution found themselves homeless.

Jack grinned when he noticed Ebenezer Pratt at a teller's window. He waved him in and thought him nothing but a spineless, pathetic coward. He'd often wondered how the man could hold his head up in town, but then Jack was certain Ebenezer would never volunteer information surrounding their previous agreement. Jack stretched a sinister grin and said, "Your note's about paid up, Ebenezer." He wasn't surprised when Pratt quickly closed the door behind him. "Come in for another loan, have you?" Jack didn't wait for him to answer. "That land of yours could sustain a couple hundred more head," he taunted. "Now, some folks might consider yours a risky investment, but we both know you've invaluable collateral, isn't that right, Pratt?" Jack felt the skin around his eyes crinkle when Pratt managed a glare.

"Won't be necessary, Mr. Marsh," Ebenezer said, staring at his feet. "Just come by with my monthly."

"How's that girl of yours?"

Ebenezer tossed his hat from one hand to the other, and turned toward the door. "Good day, Mr. Marsh."

"You say hello now to the missus and to young Callie, especially. How old is she now, about sixteen?"

Pratt's posture stiffened. He threw his hat on his head, flung the door open, and sprinted across the lobby.

Jack's laugh thundered throughout the building causing many of the bank's patrons to glance toward his office. He reflected on one of his favorite memories, kicked back in his chair, laced his fingers behind his head, and smiled a smug smile. At least he had fulfilled his end of the bargain, a one-thousand dollar loan and the return of fifteen-year-old Callie Pratt before dawn.

* * * *

Later that morning, Jonas Rutherford shuffled his feet, took a few deep breaths, and finally knocked on Jack Marsh's door. He waited for Jack to motion him towards a chair before he stepped inside.

"Am I to assume you've acted on my proposal?" Jack asked, tapping his pen's quill against a meticulously manicured beard.

"Yes sir," Jonas muttered and Jack relished the man's humiliation. "Ain't proud of it," Jonas said, locking eyes with Jack, "but I got eleven mouths to feed."

"Get to it," Jack ordered. "But first close the damn door."

When Jonas returned to his chair, he said, "I asked around and found out she left town, so I went by her place. From the look of things, she ain't left for good."

"You think I'm about to coin your palm with that worthless stock, you've another thing coming!"

Jonas raised his right hand. "Now, hold on, I did some diggin' and found this Nigra says his family once been Mika Leeds' slaves."

Jack snarled. "Lengthy prattle sets my head to throbbing. Say your piece!"

"He stole away one night a few months after the war ended, on account Mika Leeds..."

"I don't need a town history lesson, Rutherford," Jack growled. "We all know Mika Leeds didn't much give a tinker's damn what ole Abe wrote into law or acknowledge it was the Yanks won the war. You call that news?"

"He says Mika Leeds near killed his wife one night years before any a that, then threw her out. He said he nearly lost his wind when he seen her one day, after all those years, when he happened by the finery shop."

Jack stood, easily reached across the wide oak desk, and grabbed Jonas by the collar. "Why would someone loyal to this woman loosen his lip for the likes of you?"

Jonas reached up and gingerly pried Jack's hand away. "Told the Nigra, I be a real close acquaintance of Mrs. Cook's and that she be in search of her ma. He was anxious to be of assistance on account of Victoria Leeds being such a kind, charitable woman, and always doin' for the slaves."

"Is that so?" Jack asked, only pretending fascination. "That might interest me to no end if I was writing a column for the society page!" Jack stormed around the desk and towered menacingly over Rutherford.

"Victoria Leeds and that shop owner, Emily Dunsmire, are one and the same," Jonas added quickly.

Jack reached in his pocket, produced a few coins, and tossed them in Jonas' lap. "You'll get the remainder if and when this pans out. Now, get out of my sight."

TWENTY-NINE

Shannon removed the old hat, wiped her brow, cursed the hot sun, and smiled over her shoulder at Zach. "Reckon it's time to get you in out of this heat." She brushed the dirt from her clothes without taking her eyes off her son, wanting nothing more than to commit such precious actions to memory. Stretching forward as far as his round belly allowed, he grasped tiny handfuls of warm moist soil and showered it overhead, before sticking a fistful into his mouth. Grimacing and spewing the dark earth, he seemed surprised by the unpleasant taste. His bright blue eyes pleading she assist him, she ran a finger along the inside of his mouth, dislodged the remaining dirt, and wrestled a partially dismembered earthworm from his tiny fist. "Someday it'll all be yours, Zach," Shannon whispered, "every inch of it. Your mama's gonna see to that!"

Deciding a bath was in order, she took him toward the creek, enjoying the breeze and the whooshing sound from the tree limbs overhead. The pin oaks were her favorite, though the paw-paw trees when the mayflowers were in bloom were a close second. The woods were much cooler than the fields, and she stopped at the foot of a large walnut tree to point out a very determined woodpecker. Zach caught sight of the bird, its speckled breast a beautiful contrast to the brilliant red atop his head, and he began to fuss while extending his tiny hand skyward. "You can't hold him, Zach," Shannon explained and immediately regretted the bird watching.

At the creek's edge, she sat Zach on the bank, removed his clothes, and then shed all but her bloomers. Carrying her baby in slowly, Shannon waded out to the middle and embraced the coolness of the water. She heard a rider closing in and cursed silently. Zach sensed her displeasure and began to cry again. Witnessing a man's silhouette in the thickets, she lowered a good part of herself below the surface.

Luke saw her and felt sure she wouldn't welcome company but led Thunder to the water's edge anyway, even though his horse had drank plenty before leaving Plains Paradise. "Thought I heard somebody out here," he said grinning. "Just come by to water my horse."

"Wipe that smirk off your face this instant, Luke Richards, and kindly turn the other way."

Luke plucked her clothing from a scrawny tree branch. "Polite thing would be to bring these to yuh, I suppose."

"You step one foot in here and I swear..."

"On second thought," Luke said, pointing beyond her, "never had much regard for them slimy creatures. If it be me, I'd get to shore right quick."

Shannon glimpsed behind her and spotted the water moccasin. She shrieked, held Zach above her head, and quickly waded toward the bank. "A gentleman would avert his eyes!" she barked ahead.

Luke scanned his surroundings. "There don't seem to be one of them about."

"You're wicked, Luke Richards! Just as wicked as they come."

"I'm not the one out here buck-naked and on the good Lord's day."

"Fool, it's not Sunday!"

"Well, that makes it perfectly respectable, then," Luke teased and began to unbutton his shirt. "Could sure use a cool dunkin' myself."

"Don't you dare free a single button, you mudsill." Luke's laugh warmed her soul though she pretended annoyance.

"Couldn't help but notice you're gettin' a might pink, ma'am," Luke said, tossing her the old plaid shirt once William's.

"Mark my words," Shannon said through clenched teeth, "this is something I'll never forget!"

"Nor I, Mrs. Cook," he crooned. Luke stretched out his hand, but she refused to take it. "Not a time to be proud. That snake's gainin' ground fast."

Shannon reluctantly took his hand, quickly transferring Zach to cover her exposed breasts.

Luke stared until he became uncomfortable. "Not much to them bloomers. Don't know why you women bother." Luke wrestled Zach from her and started up the embankment, stealing an occasional glance over his shoulder.

"Suppose if it were up to men like you, we'd walk around in nothing at all," Shannon blasted. "Now, kindly give me my son and be on your way!"

"Just givin' a lady an opportunity to dress herself proper. Top half of you seems mighty cold."

Shannon glanced down at her shirt and threw an arm across erect nipples. "You are surely getting on my bad side."

Luke whistled low and handed her Zach. "From what I've seen, Mrs. Cook, you ain't got one."

"Good day, Mr. Richards!"

"It surely is."

THIRTY

Jack sipped his coffee slowly and found he didn't enjoy it nearly as much without a thimbleful of brandy mixed in. He took out his gold pocket watch and confirmed the hour he had to pass before the train arrived. He had noticed Emily before. She was one of the few women he gave a second glance. A little too old for his liking, but she was beautiful with vibrant red hair, full hips, and an ample bosom. Of course, with all that to commit to memory, he couldn't be expected to remember the color of her eyes. He thought about her exceptionally fair skin, a rare find in Leeds, a town with few Irish immigrants and, for the first time, he thought Jonas Rutherford's declaration might be correct.

It was Emily's demeanor, which ultimately convinced him. He knew people. That was his job. He knew when they had something to hide and she did. Jack smiled. He liked a challenge, though he suspected she wouldn't be much of one. After all, he was an expert in getting even the most cunning of men to reveal their innermost secrets.

He heard the whistle from the train as it signaled its approach. From the second story window, he watched the wind carry the dust, the train kicked up, into the street outside Ruby's saloon. He inhaled and was able to smell the steam from the locomotive over the rank odor of his whore's cheap perfume.

Jack checked his reflection in the looking glass and ran the whore's comb through his thick black hair. Admiring the sheen, he knew, among other things, he did not have his mama to thank for it. Jack focused on his dark eyes and felt a twinge of both torment and amusement. No wonder so many refused to look into them for long. He splashed water over harshly angulated cheekbones and licked tiny droplets from thin, nearly invisible lips. Smirking at his reflection, Jack angrily recalled his mother's numerous affronts, the scathing criticism nearly always occurred in public. She had been right about one thing, his physical qualities repelled most everyone he'd ever met. But he soon discovered such monstrous homeliness worked in his favor and he relied heavily on the intimidation it provided him. By the time he was twenty, he knew her prediction was accurate; no woman would ever have the tenacity to look beyond his outward appearance. Jack glanced at the whore now stirring in bed and grimaced.

Belle opened her eyes as he turned the knob to leave and bolted upright. "Aren't you forgettin' somethin', Jack!"

After a bottle of whiskey, he could barely endure her less-than-perfect form, teeth, and painted face. Sober, she sickened him. "You should be throwing me silver," he told her snarling. He effortlessly ducked the vase she hurled, plucked a piece of the broken glass from the floor, and pressed it to her throat. "How fortunate for you I have more urgent business."

Jack snickered as he neared the station, the townspeople nearly tripping over one another to get out of his way. He watched the passengers disembark one by one, and soon realized why she was the last. She struggled with the bulging bags, one in particular, and wrestled them away from the conductor and more than one male passenger anxious to assist once she reached the platform. Jack jumped up beside her and snatched the heavier of the two. "Allow me," he said, firmly gripping the bag in one hand, her arm in the other. When her eyes met his, he knew he owed Jonas compensation.

Emily bristled. "Kindly take your hands off me and return my bag."

Jack felt his nostrils flare. "Whatever do you have in this bag, dear lady? If I didn't know better, I'd figure you for a train robber."

"And I wouldn't figure you for a man fancied humor, Mr. Marsh!"

Jack exaggerated a smile and sensed her confidence plummet. He loosened his grip and shoved her backwards before relinquishing the bag. He started toward the bank and suddenly whirled to face her, his abrupt movement as calculated as it was threatening. "Oh, and should you visit Mrs. Cook in the near future, please remind her that her time is dwindling."

Her scowl only inspired him.

"I hear the Sheriff's mistakenly given her hope Governor Bradley will intercede and allow her petty installments, but mark my word the governor will quickly realize such a notion would set a very unwise precedent. Good day, ma'am."

When Jack returned to the bank, he ordered his clerk bring him water. "Where'd you get this, from the horse trough?" he barked. "Bring me some that's cold or seek a position elsewhere!" He threw the goblet, missing Travis by millimeters. He crossed the room, threw open the window, and considered visiting the Chinaman's den. His desire for a pipe full overwhelming, he grudgingly lumbered toward the door to his office and slammed it shut.

Moments later, Emily burst in with Parker on her heels. Jack signaled him away and relished Emily stiffen when the clerk closed the door behind him. "What'd I do to deserve such a wonderful surprise?" Jack asked, clasping his hands together and snaking his eyes over the entire length of her body.

Emily shivered but was surprised when her voice quaked. "The reason for my visit isn't social, I assure you, Mr. Marsh. I've just come to inquire as to the total amount due on the Cook place. Your clerk insisted I talk to you and much to my dismay I might add."

Jack didn't offer her a chair. Releasing his tongue, he ran it methodically over his lower lip, his eyes insidiously trained on her bosom. Satisfied she appeared completely unnerved he tapped a forefinger against his cheek and asked, "Why in the world would nearly a perfect stranger be interested in paying another's deed? We're not talking a pauper's sum here, Mrs. Dunsmire, isn't it?" He didn't wait for a response to either question. He slithered around the desk and loomed over her. "I find this quite irregular and most curious," he taunted, his words blowing hot against her face.

"It's really none of your business, Mr. Marsh," she said,

stepping backwards until she felt the doorknob press against her lower back. "Kindly inform me of the amount due, and I'll be on my way."

Jack laughed. "Banking business is something only men can fully understand, but I'll surely do my best to explain it to you. In simple terms, the bank owns the land." Jack reached behind him, took the deed from his top drawer, and waved it in her face. "And it's not for sale."

"You don't fool me for a minute," Emily fired back, directing the tip of her parasol toward his chest. "You got one thing in mind and that's seeing Shannon Cook out on the street."

"And you don't fool me, Victoria." Jack watched the color drain from her face, grabbed the parasol out of her hand and shoved the tip through the doorframe, barely missing one of her magnificent green eyes.

THIRTY-ONE

Thick smoke hung in the air, but Jack made out a silhouette and realized the trader stood over him anxious to refill his pipe and collect more silver. Jack shook his head and easily wrestled the pipe from the Chinaman. "The pipe's mine," he told him harshly and pounded the pipe against his chest to communicate his inference. "Understand, you miserable slant eye?" Jack didn't swap spit with anyone, which is only one of the many reasons he never kissed his whore. And he always personally supervised her bath. "This town needs more Callies," he said aloud and then filled the air with a shrill, drawn-out howl.

The idea came to him after his last pipe full. Bouncing off a few hitching posts, he eventually arrived back at the bank and instructed Travis to collect Jonas Rutherford. Then he pulled his hat over his eyes, suddenly wanting nothing more than to obsess over his mother's final moments.

When Rutherford crept into his office, Jack tossed the money due him on the desk. "The remainder of the amount agreed on."

Jonas nodded, gathered the coins, and got up to leave.

"You a mind to triple that?"

Jonas took his hand from the doorknob and reluctantly faced Jack again. "Depends."

Jack sniggered. "I thought so. An hour of your time for a week's wages. Enough to put shoes on that gaggle of yours before winter sets in."

Jonas shuffled his feet and squinted distain. "Like I said, depends."

"Tomorrow night you make sure you send that Nigra over to the finery shop. Lead him to believe Mrs. Cook wants him to make absolutely certain Emily Dunsmire and Victoria Leeds are one and the same before things go any further. I'll take care of the rest." Jack could see Jonas was skeptical.

"Expect I'll need to know what 'the rest' involves."

Jack snarled, exposing most of his upper teeth. "It sure as hell doesn't involve you. You want the job or not?"

Jonas somberly nodded.

Jack jabbed a finger toward him. "After all is said and done, no matter what happens, you don't know nothin' about nothin'. If I ever find out anything different, I'll cut you down myself. And then I'll start whittling on that brood of yours."

THIRTY-TWO

The nightmare not only awakened her but Zach. Shannon assumed she must have called out in her sleep. "Hush now," she whispered, stumbling to his crib. Patting his back and softly singing *Seeing Nellie Home*, she thought about the dream. She'd had it many times before and presumed it a faded glimpse at reality. Each time, to her dismay, her mother's face was never well-defined. Just as it always did, the dream began with her mother's screams, Shannon racing down a long staircase in search of her, and Polly in close pursuit pleading she come back. She'd then discover their mother, Victoria, face down on a burgundy and ivory Persian rug, blood matting the hair on the back of her head. Shaking her, Shannon would whimper *Mama* and quiet when her father's harsh words became louder. Cowering as he crossed the room, a slick leather strap in his fisted hand, Shannon's shrill cries would punctuate the ominous silence. Always, Polly would lunge for him and plead he stop. He'd comply and then they would witness him drag their mother through the massive mahogany doors and toss her into the street.

Thinking about Polly, her tears splattered onto Zach's nightshirt. Although she and her older sister had grown apart as the years passed, Polly once made everything bearable. It didn't take Shannon long to learn if she ever needed anything she need simply tell Polly. Their father would have gotten the moon for her. Shannon knew because she'd overheard his exact words. She closed her eyes, remembered exactly what her sister looked like, and a sad smile crossed her lips. Just as quickly, she laughed, because Polly certainly had a way about her. A manipulator, true, but like a magic trick at the fair, even though you know you're being swindled you don't mind because it's fabulously entertaining.

Polly was clearly their father's favorite. Maybe because they were so much alike with raven hair, green eyes, and hell-bent on laying waste to anything that stood in their way. She learned early on that Mika resented anyone Polly gave attention. All Mika's cowhands were also educated on the importance of avoiding the dark-haired beauty. After discovering one in the hayloft with her, Mika ordered him nearly whipped to death and forced both his daughters to watch. Shannon vomited as the strap tore bloody pieces from the young man's back. Polly twirled her curls and almost seemed to enjoy it. Months later, Shannon heard Mika and Polly arguing behind closed parlor doors. The next day, Polly boarded a train and never returned. When their father took to his room and refused to come out, Shannon knew she'd never see her sister again.

Lucy confessed the truth a short time after that. Mika had suspected Polly was with child and didn't want to be, so he sent her to a doctor in St. Louis. *'Somethin' went wrong, Miss Shannon, and poe Miss Polly done up and died'.*

Shannon sat on the edge of the bed and blotted her eyes again. She'd never had the opportunity to tell Polly goodbye. Their father couldn't. She thought about the song she'd sang to Zach and wondered where she'd learned it.

* * * *

"Where you off to, Sheriff?" Deputy Saunders asked.

Jacob realized he was smiling and pursed his lips. "I've some business over to the Cook place. Reckon I'll be back by sunset." Then he counseled himself on a more proper demeanor. After all, he was about to deliver some very somber news. The governor had done a sudden turnaround, and Jacob hoped the decision might work to his advantage. He stood at the window, took the letter from his pocket, and reread it:

Sheriff Conner:

It is with great difficulty that I inform you of my decision regarding The First Bank of Leeds versus the Cook woman. I find it is my responsibility to take into consideration the origination of the note and the circumstances at the time of

same. As the deed is solely in Mr. Cole Cook's name, and he, of his own free will, sold it back to the bank, his wife, Shannon M. Cook, has no legal claim, provided she has not sufficient funds to satisfy the deed at this time.
  Sincerely,
  Governor Robert P. Bradley
  State of Missouri
  6 August 1874

   As Jacob rode out of town, he stopped only long enough to break up a brawl between James and Lawrence Dodson. It seemed the brothers both had feelings for one of Ruby's girls and argued as to which one of them she liked better. Sheriff Conner suggested they spend their hard-earned money elsewhere, go home, and sleep it off, which brought great protesting from not only the girls atop Ruby's balcony but from the crowd expecting some early morning entertainment.
   Jacob didn't have much regard for men who found it necessary to pay for a lady's company, but he did feel the decent women about town were much safer due to the whores. Although a Saturday night often meant no vacancies at the jailhouse, Jacob knew there would be a lot more hangings if not for Ruby's fancy ladies. "Get on home now, the both of you," Jacob demanded again, jumped back on his horse, and felt the urgency build. He was sure once Jack Marsh got wind of the governor's news, he'd beat a path to Shannon Cook if he hadn't already.
   Jacob reined his gelding at the end of Shannon's lane, mopped his forehead dry, laughed uncharacteristically and shook his head. He had seen his share of war, survived a standoff with Johnny Ringo, and Jesse and Frank James, yet this wisp of a woman, so delicate and often soft-spoken, made his hands shake, his belly churn, and usually left him at a loss for words when he needed them most. He rehearsed it all again and didn't hear Luke ride up behind him.
   "Why Sheriff, you look as if yuh just been caught with your hands in the pie."

"Why do you always seem to be about?"

"Last time I checked, Sheriff, this here's a public thoroughfare. Got some business with Mrs. Cook today or is this merely a social call?"

"Privileged information is what it is, Richards!" Jacob barked. "Some reason you need to know my business or Mrs. Cook's for that matter?"

"No particular reason. Just bein' neighborly." Luke tipped his hat, cupped his hand and said in a near whisper, "Don't entertain anything I wouldn't, Sheriff."

"Sonuvabitch," Jacob muttered as Luke rode away. Once past the string of willows and oaks, he saw Shannon settling her baby into the wagon. "Dammit," he whispered. He had hoped for a little small talk, maybe a leisurely walk in the woods. He rode up on her just as she was turning the buckboard about. Tipping his hat, he addressed her proper. "Hope I'm not catchin' you at a bad time, but I've somethin' needs discussin'". He thought she looked more irritated than curious.

"What is it, Sheriff? I'd like to be on my way."

Jacob began to stammer and cursed himself. "Well, this here could take a while. I'd best come back at a more suitable time."

Her sigh cut him deep.

"You've come all the way out here. I expect there's nothing I have to do can't wait till later," Shannon said unconvincingly.

Zach began to fuss, and Jacob suspected her glare wasn't intended for her child. "Lil' tyke seems to disagree. That dog of yours don't seem too happy about it neither," Jacob said, taking a few steps backwards.

"Duke, get on back to the house! He won't hurt you, Sheriff."

Her tone sounded patronizing to him. "Don't think he likes me much... the dog, I mean."

"Reckon he's just doing his job, Sheriff," Shannon impatiently replied. "Don't take it to heart. He does the same to just about everybody." Without thinking, she added, "The exception being Luke Richards. Ole Duke and Zach both seem to really take to that one." She noticed that seemed to anger him and quickly changed the subject. "No sense in standing out here all day in the hot sun. Let's go on inside."

While she tended to Zach, Jacob silently rehearsed his proposal and constantly wiped his palms across his back pockets. "Nice place you got here, Mrs. Cook."

"I'm hoping to keep it, Sheriff. Is that what brings you out here?"

Jacob swallowed hard. He had hoped to ease into it. He brushed his hat against his thighs and stared at the floor. "This kinda thing ain't easy for me." Jacob laughed nervously. "Matter-of-fact, never done it before."

"Sheriff, what in the world are you rattling on about?"

Jacob raked his fingers through his hair and shuffled his feet. "Dadgum it, ain't women supposed to sense these things?" he asked aloud.

On a sigh, she told him, "I'm not much a one for parlor games so I wish to Joseph you would just say what's on your mind."

The words, jumbled and stuck in his throat, finally came out and in a much more condensed version than he'd intended. "Mrs. Cook, it might be in your best interest to become my wife."

Her surprise stared holes through him.

"I know this probably is comin' at you like a whirlwind but, like I said, this ain't easy for me."

Shannon began to stammer. "Why, Sheriff, I don't rightly know what to say...

You're a handsome enough fella, kind, intelligent, respectful, and about as brave as any man I've met, but I... don't even know you."

Jacob cleared his throat and felt the sweat slide down his back. "Be obliged if you'd let me start again."

Marrying for love, Shannon thought, hadn't turned out magnificently. But she didn't need a man and certainly wouldn't settle for Jacob Conner. Shaking her head, she told him, "I'm sorry, Sheriff, but my mind couldn't be farther from an altar."

Jacob whipped his hat across his thighs, disappointment ravishing his eyes. "Reckon I just proposed marriage, you can call me Jacob."

"Alright then, Jacob."

"Please, Mrs. Cook... Shannon, let me say my piece." Jacob stared at his feet again and shoved his hands in his pockets. "Not much good at sugar-coating bad news."

"And I'm not much good at having it thrown at me slow so for heaven's sake say your piece!"

"Governor Bradley's made a decision in the bank's favor."

Shannon's knees buckled and she sat down. Jacob thought he heard her mumble, "Whatever am I going to do now?"

He gnawed his bottom lip. Then he took a few steps closer. "I got a real nice place just south of town. Lots of room for the boy to run when he's old enough, even room for that dog of yours. Got a house I built myself, a pond out back, and a barn. The whole shebang." Jacob dropped on one knee. "I could make you happy, Shannon. I know I could."

"But I'm still married, Jacob, even though my husband's gone and ran off. Guess I don't have to tell you that in the eyes of the law marrying another wouldn't be legal."

Jacob smiled and awkwardly squeezed her hand. "I looked into that and a lawyer friend of mine says since your husband's run off there's nothin' to it. He can draw up the papers and your marriage can be dissolved in no time at all, just like it never happened."

Shannon pulled away and paced a trail in front of the fireplace. "I appreciate the offer, Jacob, I do. But I'm not ready."

Jacob dropped his head and eventually spoke. "Where will you go?"

Shannon leaned against the fireplace and said, "I don't have the faintest notion."

THIRTY-THREE

Shannon needed someone to talk to and immediately thought of Emily. She persuaded Sara to abandon the pasture grass, gathered Zach up, and started for town. She didn't want to think about Jacob Conner's proposal and focused on her land stretched out as far as the eye could see. She slowed Sara once alongside the largest honeysuckle bush and again as they neared the row of apple trees spilling the last of the season's bounty. She knew she was about to lose it all but discouraged the tears streaming down her cheeks.

She kept Sara at a slow trot down the lane. The last thing she wanted was to catch up to Jacob. As it turned out, that was unlikely. Her horse fought the reins at nearly every turn, preferring to leisurely nibble on fallen apples. "Reckon you don't mind the affect those apples have on your constitution, girl, but it's me and Zach have to ride behind you!" Shannon prodded the horse again. "Get up, Sara! Don't much like smelling like a stable floor by the time I get to town," she growled, shifting her frustration surrounding the deed to the horse.

Sara bared her teeth and continued to nip at the reins. Each time Shannon voiced a command, the mare responded with a snort. Shannon reached behind her for the crop, leaned forward, and slapped Sara on her backside. With newfound inspiration, the horse broke into a trot, causing Zach to startle. Shannon pulled back on the reins several times before Sara finally found a more agreeable pace. Without warning, the horse reared up, stressing the yoke and jostling the wagon.

"Whoa! Down girl!" Shannon cried and fought to gain control. Unsuccessful, she cradled Zach tightly and jumped from the wagon. Wanting to break free from her four-wheeled constraint, Sara continued to buck. Placing Zach a safe enough distance away, Shannon approached the horse cautiously and spoke in a soothing tone. Sara reared up again, this time coming down hard, and finally alerted Shannon to the eminent danger. Though the horse had successfully trampled the rattlesnake, Sara was no calmer and continued her attempt at escape. Shannon grabbed the reins again, stroked Sara's mane, and the frenzied quality soon left her eyes.

Young William had set his horse in the direction of the commotion. His horse's speed unchecked, he arrived over the hillside quickly, taking Shannon by surprise. Realizing Zach's perilous position, she panicked and screamed. William managed to rein his seasoned mare in time, but Sara spooked and made a break for the barn. Preferring the quickest route, the mare attempted a path between two large pin oaks. Unfortunately, the course was too narrow for the wagon and the front wheels sheared off. The collision echoed through the valley, which only amplified the mare's anxiety. Trapped and terrified, Sara whinnied, kicked, and bucked.

Shannon looked wearily from the wagon wedged between two massive tree trunks to William. She resisted sharing what was really on her mind and simply asked, "Reckon you can calm that horse?" She watched dumbfounded as William soothed the mare within minutes.

Troubled after he'd surveyed the damage, William shook his head and flushed. "I surely didn't mean all this to happen. Thought you might need some help is all. Now look at what I caused."

Shannon didn't say a word and moved Zach a yard in the opposite direction of the barn. "Best move that horse of yours that way," she told him and jerked a thumb behind her. "When you've done that, take these reins while I unhitch Sara." Once freed, Sara scrambled toward the barn.

William stood still as a church mouse.

Shannon realized the extent of his angst, and gave his arm a quick rub before collecting Zach. "That fool horse has some spirit is all and not much sense. Don't be blaming yourself, William."

"What about your wagon?"

Shannon sighed and shrugged her shoulders. "Reckon I'll

leave Sara be a bit, then saddle Zach up front of me, and ride her on into town."

"No ma'am!" William said, unable to shake visions of her and her baby bucked off and flying horseless over a hillside. "Least I can do is exchange your wagon for mine. I got one back home will suit yuh just fine. I'll hitch it up and bring it over directly." William rode off, turning a deaf ear to Shannon's protest.

She was nearly to the house when she heard rickety wagon wheels fighting dirt ruts. "Mercy, Zach. There's no moss growing under that boy's feet!" She glanced over her shoulder, forced a smile, and found it wasted on Luke Richards.

"Heard about your troubles, Mrs. Cook. Since I was headed into town myself, and the boy's still got his round of chores comin' on, reckon I'll be the one takin' you in."

When he smiled, she denied it hurt not to smile back. "No need, Mr. Richards. I'm perfectly capable of making the trip on my own."

"Might be a good idea if you got somebody knows what they're doin' to break that horse's spirit a bit. Gonna get you and the baby hurt real bad one of these days."

Why is it, this man has to go and spoil everything by opening his fool mouth? Shannon felt her eyes narrow. "And I suppose that would be you. Glory be! By all means, let's send a bank robber to repair a vault!"

Luke's laugh roared across the pasture. "What say you hobble all your high and mighty gab and get on in the wagon? I ain't got the day to flitter away."

Zach began to grunt and reach for Luke. Shannon tweaked his behind. "Traitor," she whispered in his ear. "I'm afraid I don't find your demeanor the least bit charming, Mr. Richards, and don't know that I care to be accompanied by the likes of you into town, unchaperoned." Zach continued to frail about and she grudgingly pushed him into Luke's waiting arms. "Go on and take him. I've enough of ornery menfolk for one day, anyway!"

"Sounds like female troubles to me, partner," Luke said to

Zach but kept both eyes on Shannon. "She'll come around. Meantime, lets you and me go see about that other fiery filly."

"You do that! Go on to the barn! And that baby can't understand a word you're saying," she yelled at his back. "You know that, don't you? You look like a fool puppeteer with his mannequin." He ignored her and she stormed toward the house. Stepping up to the porch, she knocked a hip against the rail and caught her skirt on splintered wood. "Well, if that don't beat all! Dammit to hell!" She heard Luke cackle, clenched her fists, tore the door open, and slammed it behind her.

* * * *

Nearly finished mending her dress, Luke surprised her. "You mind knocking, Mr. Richards? I'm not decent."

"Isn't that the God's honest and wouldn't have you any other way, Mrs. Cook," Luke said, the corners of his mustache turning upward.

"Humph! That silver tongue won't work on me." She drew a circle in the air. When he ignored her request for him to turn his back, she told him, "We've had this discussion before. But maybe you're simpleminded!"

Luke came closer instead. "Zach and me brought you a cool drink from the well. Sure helped set the horse's mood right."

"I suspect it wasn't the water but more due to the primitive connection. For pity's sake, turnabout, and I'll accept your ride to town."

Luke ignored her request again, preferring to enjoy the view.

THIRTY-FOUR

Emily slammed the door as the telegraph clerk sarcastically bid her good day. She heard the telegraph office door open again as she scampered down the walk and knew the clerk was watching. *Good! Now, he'll know darn good-and-well I'm headed over to talk to the Sheriff.* The pain began suddenly, forcing her to slow her pace. Cautiously taking a few shallow breaths, she hoped to forgo the medication. She nearly ran into Jacob Conner as they met at his door. "Sheriff, don't know where you're off to, but I've got something to discuss that won't keep."

Jacob could see that she was upset. Her fair skin flushed and tiny beads of sweat threatened a swan dive from her upper lip. The smile that caused the townsfolk to take a liking to her, the menfolk anyway, wouldn't be on display anytime soon. "Always got time for you, Miss Emily. What's on your mind?"

"This whole damn town being run by Jack Marsh is what's on my mind, Sheriff! I don't intend disrespect, but I'm surprised he's not wearing that tin star."

"Now hold on. I can see somethin's got you riled-up, but I am the Sheriff of this town, and there ain't no man leads me around by the nose hairs."

Emily let out a long breath. "I'm sorry, Jacob. You're a good man. But you know as well as I do that snake can get nearly any man in this town to do his bidding, including instructing Mr. Randall not to send my telegram to the Governor. Trying to convince me of some problem with the line or some such foolishness he knew I wouldn't understand! But I know what he's up to, don't think I don't."

"Well, maybe you can tell me because I sure as shoot don't know what in the Sam-hell you're goin' on about." Jacob glanced up one side of the street and down the other. The more notorious busybodies already had their ears turned in the direction of the jail, and recent experience had taught him that

Miss Emily was a force-to-be-reckoned-with, particularly when fired-up over something. "Let's discuss this inside. After you," Jacob said, holding the door.

After Emily unraveled her story, including the truth regarding her relationship to Shannon, Jacob ran his fingers over the top drawer of his desk and considered taking a snort from the whiskey bottle tucked away at the bottom. "So, let me get this straight, Mrs. Cook has no idea?"

"That I'm her mother? No, and for the time being, I plan to keep it that way."

"And you say you have means to satisfy the deed?"

"Every penny."

"Then what's the problem?" Jacob said, feeling the skin pucker between his brows as he considered his chances of Shannon accepting his proposal now nil.

"Just like a man," Emily muttered. "Haven't you been listening? Jack Marsh is the problem!"

"How so exactly?"

"Now, he's saying the deed isn't for sale!"

Jacob hadn't stopped thinking about his marriage proposal to Shannon all afternoon. Certain she'd only let him down easy and had no intention of ever becoming his wife, he considered Emily possibly the catalyst that could change her mind. "The Governor's decided in favor of the bank," he blurted.

"Why am I not surprised?" Emily leapt from the chair and paced between Jacob's desk and the door. "Present company aside, is there any man Jack Marsh doesn't have in his grip?"

Jacob pretended compassion. "Not much can be done once the Governor has spoken. Damn shame. Mrs. Cook's plight has been weighin' on me heavy. I rode out there today..."

Jacob stole a glance at her and noted she stopped pacing.

"Why's that, Sheriff?"

When she interrupted him just as he figured she would, he considered she might very well play right into his hands. He dramatically raked his fingers through his hair. He rubbed his eyes hard and long. Then he said, "To propose marriage," just quietly enough.

"And?"

"She said she weren't ready."

It seemed to him Emily's stare was unusually intense.

"If you're mentioning this, Sheriff, because you want me to influence her decision, I wish you hadn't."

Her words nearly knocked the wind out of him. "I just thought..."

"Marrying a man for convenience is a losing proposition all the way around."

"But she could learn to..."

Emily shook her head and placed her hand over his. "Jacob Conner, a man like you deserves more than a 'maybe someday'."

Jacob swallowed hard. More than a handful of pretty, young things in town were always trying to snare him, and he wanted the only one who wasn't. "Suppose she'll live in town with you?"

Emily laughed. "That girl a mine has too much pride for such a notion. I knew she had it in her, though it was buried deep down thanks to that piece of dung she was married to,"

"What'll she do, then?"

"The fight's only just begun, Sheriff. I WILL see that the Governor hears me out. When he made that ridiculous ruling, surely he had no idea funds were available to satisfy the deed."

Jacob kept quiet. He'd really look the heel if he decided to share the whole truth at this juncture. "Reckon you're right. Certainly is somethin' he would take under advisement. I'll send the telegram myself," he lied and escorted her to the door.

"Sheriff, it'd put my mind at ease if you would keep the money under lock and key here. Obviously, I'm not comfortable putting it in a safety deposit box at The First Bank of Leeds!"

"I'll add it to that Shannon's left in my charge."

THIRTY-FIVE

William rode Midnight over the hill at such a rate of speed even ole Thunder startled and threatened to topple the wagon and its passengers.

"Whoa!" Luke bellowed, thankful his horse responded immediately for a change. "What in heaven's name you think you're doin', boy," he yelled at William, "tryin' to turn this wagon here into a heap, too?"

"No, sir," William muttered embarrassed. "But I need help! That calf of Millie's decided to come today and is givin' poor Millie an awful fight. She's in a real bad way, Luke."

"Probably got itself turned sideways is all, boy." He checked himself and softened his tone. "You done right to come and fetch me. I'll ride back with the boy," he said to Shannon. "That way you can take ole Thunder into town, though I'd advise against it. Probably be nightfall by the time you head back for one; he minds about as well as flies at a church picnic for another."

"No sense in delaying things, Mr. Richards," Shannon said, gesturing toward the Willoughby ranch. "I'll come along. Never know, maybe I'll be of some help."

Luke shook his head and grumbled, "Don't this just beat all." The last thing he needed was some inexperienced female standing around wringing her hands, probably screaming, possibly fainting, all while he tried to wrestle a calf out of a heifer. "Fine, but you make yourself scarce if you get a notion to kiss dirt. Gonna be a might too busy to pick you up off the ground."

Shannon wrenched her head around and glared. "No time for jaw flapping, Mr. Richards!"

Luke found his snarl wasted on the side of her head. "Get on up here, boy, and take the reins and Mrs. Cook wherever she wants to go. I'll be takin' your horse."

Shannon watched Luke disappear over the rise and began

having second thoughts. "You say she's in a real bad way?" she asked William.

"Worst I've ever seen."

Shannon swallowed hard and considered walking home. "Reckon Luke will need your help?"

William looked puzzled. Nodding, he told her, "I gotta be gettin' back."

"Best get a wiggle on then," she muttered reluctantly.

William jumped from the wagon when they arrived. Shannon winced when she saw the cow. Writhing in pain, its shallow breaths occasionally punctuated with high-pitched moans, Shannon reflected on Zach's birth and felt lightheaded.

"Get on over here, boy, and keep her still," Luke bellowed. With his knees planted firmly on the barn's dirt floor, Luke plunged one entire arm inside the heifer. Swiping sweat from his forehead, he yelled, "Dammit! The calf won't budge."

"Seen Grandpa free one once with a rope," William offered anxiously.

"Go fetch one then, boy. And hurry before she bleeds out."

Shannon watched helplessly as Luke grunted and grimaced.

"Set that baby down and get on over here," Luke told her, snatching the rope from William with his free hand. "I've got a hold of the calf. Once I slip this lasso around it, it's gonna take both me and William to pull it free. Meantime, you keep her down."

"Keep her down?" Shannon shrilled. "How in the world do you suggest I accomplish that?"

"Cover her eyes and sit on her if need be. Just keep her still." Shannon sat Zach a few yards outside the barn entrance and then threw her upper body across the cow's neck. Luke nodded to William after pulling his blood-soaked arm and the end of the rope clear. Jumping to his feet and with William directly behind him, both men grimaced and snorted, struggled to stay afoot, and eventually pulled the calf out.

Shannon gasped. "Heavens, it's alive," she murmured and blinked back emotion as the calf took its first clumsy steps.

"We lucked out, boy." Luke said, smacking William across

the shoulders. "Figured we'd end up puttin' this one down, but I think she'll be just fine."

William kneeled, stroked the calf and held it close. "He," the boy corrected.

"You don't say?" Luke said grinning. "They'll be time for your how-you-dos later. We gotta stop this cow's bleedin' or her little one's days are likely numbered after all."

"You mean she could die?" Shannon asked as William dropped beside Luke.

Luke nodded impatiently as his arm disappeared again. Shannon assumed he attempted pressure and asked.

"Well, I ain't just keepin' my arm warm," Luke barked.

"No need to get testy, Mr. Richards."

"An ignorant question deserves a tart reply. How'd you get that baby a yers," Luke asked, "the Montgomery Ward catalog?"

Shannon stifled a giggle. Sometimes his quick wit was as amusing as it was irritating. Because her own wasn't nearly as swift, she decided to leave well enough alone. Zach was no longer willing to sit quietly and turned his attention toward the calf. "Oh, no you don't," Shannon said and intercepted him before he could get any closer. Zach fussed and attempted to squirm out of her arms.

"A little paddle to his behind should put an end to that," Luke put in.

"I'll decide how to discipline my son. Besides, it looks like you're up to your elbows there in your own mess. Just mind your beeswax."

"Have it your way, but in a few years when he's sassin' you, don't come cryin' to me."

Shannon sniggered. "No need to worry yourself over that, Mr. Richards."

"Thought we were past the formalities." He waited for her eyes to meet his and winked. "Suddenly, I've me a hankerin' for an apple pie."

"Humph! And suddenly I have an idea might stop that bleeding... why don't you stick that fat head of yours in!"

THIRTY-SIX

Once Luke was satisfied the newborn calf had gotten enough colostrum, he and William bedded the heifer and her calf down for the night. Then he instructed William to take Shannon home. "I'll finish your chores, boy," he added. "After that, I'm headin' into town for a while." Luke watched until the wagon disappeared over the ridge. He wasn't sure if he was relieved or disappointed that Shannon never once glanced over her shoulder.

* * * *

Finding he needed to wind down, Luke decided to visit Miss Emily first, and then go on to the saloon. Satisfied he saw a light burning inside the finery shop, he hitched Thunder to the post. No sooner had he stepped onto the boardwalk, he noticed the shadow of a man cast on the building next door. Snugging into the storefront, he drew his gun, waited a few minutes, and scraped his body along the structure to the corner. Whoever had been hiding broke into a run, and Luke caught only a glimpse of black clothing.

His knuckles nearly against her door, he heard voices. Luke peered through the sheer curtains and was startled to see a man inside, particularly at that time of night and particularly a nearly seven-foot tall black man with forearms nearly as thick as tree trunks. He observed them for several minutes. By Emily's expression, Luke got the impression she was hearing more than small talk. He decided it best to lie low, keep his ear to the door, and wait. Luke's hand flew to the doorknob when the man's flew to his pocket. Luke relaxed, realizing his only intent was to retrieve a photograph.

"Here be Miss Polly," Luke heard him say, "when she only twelve or so. Her pa just bought 'er first grown horse."

Emily eagerly gripped the photograph. "Why, Elijah!

Wherever did you get this?"

Elijah hung his head. "We knowed id were wrong, Miss Victoria, but yuh knowed as well as me, id was my mama done raised dat child. Like were 'er own, she did. Lawd, forgive 'er, but she took dat picture from Mistuh Mika's thangs and gave id ta me for safekeepin'. Yuh can keep id if yuh wants ta."

Emily shook her head and placed it in his hand. "For me it only brings a world of heartache." Luke watched her clasp Elijah's hand. "All the years I've missed! Dear God!" she cried and fell into his arms.

"Dat was a hateful man, Miss Victoria!" Luke heard him say. "Only good dat was n'im he gave ta dat child. Ah's shoulda done somethin' dat night, Miss Victoria. Weren't nuttin' but a coward."

Emily cupped the Negro's cheek. "Don't say such a thing, Elijah. Goodness! You weren't much more than a boy. Besides, at least now I've found my Shannon. So, you see, there's still time."

Elijah's eyes widened. "Yuh says yuh found Miss Shannon? Ah's confused as can be, Miss Victoria. Mistuh Rutherford be tellin' me dat id Miss Shannon da one doin' da lookin'! Yas'm, ah been thankin' da Lawd for 'im. Cuz if id weren't fer 'im lookin' me up, ah's might never a known fer certain yuh was still drawin' a breath."

"Shannon's been looking for me?" Emily asked and took a step back. "Who is this Mr. Rutherford? I've never heard Shannon speak of him, and I'm fairly certain that I would have."

Elijah placed his hands on his hips and stared at the ceiling. "Ah's done and did id now. Gone 'n pud my big foot in m'mouth. Mistuh Rutherford ain't gonna like dis. Ain't gonna like dis one bit!"

"I still haven't the foggiest of notions," Emily said, her brow puckering.

"Weren't s'pose ta say nuttin' 'bout Miss Shannon," Elijah explained, raking broad, long fingers through curly hair. "Ah's only s'pose ta come here and make sure yuh was Miss Victoria.

Mistuh Rutherford...he tell me dis be a sa'prize fer Miss Shannon."

Emily kissed him on the cheek and reassured him. "Everything's going to be just fine. I won't say another word on it. You go on home now, and I do hope you'll be bringing those youngens of yours into town to see me soon."

"Yas'm. Ah's be bringin' 'em by real soon." Elijah put on his hat and started for the door.

Luke stepped around the corner of the building, built a cigarette, and waited. Finished with his smoke and satisfied her visitor was long gone, he rapped on Emily's door. When she didn't answer, he assumed she had already retired to bed. Dejected, Luke grabbed Thunder's reins, and the horse snorted and bucked. "What in the Sam-hell's got into you? You're as nervous as a whore on a Sunday pew." The Morab suddenly quit pawing the dirt, pitched his ears forward, and stared wide-eyed between the buildings. Out of the corner of his eye, Luke was certain he saw a shadow bolt in the opposite direction, and he sprinted toward the alley for a better look. Finding nothing, he decided it was just schoolboy pranks and went on to Ruby's.

THIRTY-SEVEN

Not ten minutes had passed before Luke regretted his stop. Talk of Miss Emily's visitor had already reached nearly every ear in the Saloon. The first time Luke heard the woman referred to as a *nigra lover*, he slapped his hat against the bar. The second time, he slammed his glass of whiskey down on the counter. The third and final time, he threw its contents into Billy Malone's face. Unfortunately, for Billy, Billy was cocky. No matter how strongly common sense nagged him to be still, he never listened. His next comment, which involved Miss Emily and *big, strong, black bucks in her bed*, cost him dearly. After Luke sent him to the floor, he wiped the blood from his knuckles onto Billy's shirtfront.

"Listen up!" Luke shouted. "Ain't gonna tolerate no more uncouth words about that fine woman. Don't none of you know her well, else you wouldn't be speakin' about her like you are. Now, anybody else got somethin' to say, best say it before I go to gettin' another drink in my hand."

Ruby was prepared to call out her dancing girls in her usual effort to distract a simmering bunch of rowdy cowhands when Sheriff Conner's sudden presence saved her the trouble. He peered over the saloon doors and sarcastically asked where all the quiet was coming from. Ruby swished past several inquisitive hands and took the Sheriff by the arm. She motioned for the piano player to resume and offered Jacob a drink on the house. She started to explain the situation but became very reluctant to voice the exact details when Jacob chose to stand beside Luke at the bar.

"My apologies should you suffer affront, Luke," she began "but that Miss Emily's caused nothin' but trouble in here all night. First was 'cause of all that money she came back to town with and now 'cause she welcomed a nigra man into her store and after closin' time, I might add!" When Luke glared, she lowered her eyes and began to stammer. "I know what you're thinkin' and heaven knows I ain't got no right to judge, but that woman's socializin' has been a pain in my backside the whole night long. My nerves are shot!"

"Maybe folks in this town should mind their own business," Luke said loudly enough for all to hear. He finished his drink and started for the door.

Jacob pivoted and faced him. "That man just comin' to on the floor over there your doin', Luke?"

Luke sucked his teeth and narrowed his eyes. "Well, would you lookey-there! Now I am ashamed of myself, Sheriff. I woulda figured him to be out at least till mornin'. Must be losing my touch."

A hush fell over the saloon.

Jacob considered his options: uphold a law he himself had made and lock Richards up or gain Emily Dunsmire's favor by disregarding the whole sorry event. Although, he would like nothing better than insure Luke's distance from Shannon by throwing his sorry behind in a cell, he had to take into account William Willoughby's welfare. He finished the glass of whiskey in one long swallow and came to a decision. Because he knew Emily would hound him until he set Luke loose, anyway, he was prepared to gamble very few witnesses remembering much of anything come tomorrow morning.

The saloon doors burst open and both Jacob and Luke instinctively drew their guns, simultaneously levering them dead center.

"Holy shit, Sheriff," Deputy Saunders yelled, covering his head and dropping to his knees. "It's me!"

Luke snickered. "Looks like your deputy just soiled his britches."

Jacob released disgust and embarrassment in one long breath. "What's so all-fire important?" he growled.

Saunders mopped fear from his forehead, covered his wet crotch with his hands, and slunk toward the bar. "Mrs. Bettle was walkin' past the Post Office, Sheriff when she heard two gunshots. She reckon they came from there but ain't rightly sure. She says that they coulda come from Miss Emily's Finery

Shop."

Luke was the first one out the door with Jacob on his heels. Many of the men who weren't too drunk to walk attempted to keep up.

After he found the Post Office door undisturbed and the windows intact, Jacob instructed Luke to stand back as he turned the knob to Emily's store but found it locked. Luke pushed Jacob aside and hammered it with both fists.

"Good God!" Jacob shouted. "The woman's probably asleep!"

Standing nearby and wringing her hands, Mrs. Bettle managed to get Jacob's attention.

Luke questioned her first. "You think the shots coulda come from here?"

"I can't be certain," she said, her stout form quivering.

Luke puffed out his cheeks, getting the sense she enjoyed the attention and planned to milk the situation for all it was worth.

"Mercy me, Sheriff," she purred, grabbing Jacob's arm. "I suddenly feel so very faint."

Jacob snorted his opposition but placed an arm around her thick waist to steady her.

Mrs. Bettle sighed dramatically and swiped a hand across her brow. "I was walkin' down the street, so upset that nightfall was upon me. You see, I was in a terrible tizzy to get on toward home, least some ruffian take sight of my womanly form and set his sights on havin' his way with me."

Luke's irritation with her grandstanding grew. But most of the other men, drunk or sober, harmoniously belly laughed. Speechless, Jacob gestured for her to continue.

"It was then I heard gunshots. Two, I'm as sure as I'm standin' right here. Seein' as the Post Office don't look disturbed, I'd be willin' to bet they did come from the finery shop," she told them, pointing a short, stubby, index finger toward Emily's. Then she pressed against Jacob and whispered, "Should you need any more information, Sheriff, Mr. Bettle's a sound sleeper. I'm certain even a late night visit wouldn't disturb his rest."

Jacob released her so quickly she nearly lost her balance. "Won't be any need for that, ma'am."

Luke began turning the night's events over and over in his mind. Convinced something horrible had happened, he pushed Jacob aside and kicked Emily's door in.

Jacob grabbed him. "Who the hell gave you permission to do that?"

Luke pulled his arm free. "You think it's likely all this commotion out here could go unnoticed? It ain't like her to leave her door go unanswered neither. Maybe you've a mind to stand here all day, but I ain't!"

Jacob snarled and poked Luke's chest hard. "Since I am the sheriff, Richards, I'll be goin' in first, if that sits all right with you!" His eyes searched the crowd for Saunders. "Deputy, keep these folks back outa the way!"

Jacob called Emily's name once through the door but got no response. He started toward the stairs leading to her private quarters. "Stay put," he called over his shoulder to Luke.

"Dear God!" Jacob heard Luke mutter and stopped in his tracks.

THIRTY-EIGHT

Luke stumbled to the doorway wondering how he could possibly tell Shannon Emily was dead and if he should make that pain greater by telling her Emily's true identity. He walked far into the wide-open space behind the storefronts. Every ounce of him felt heavy yet empty. He dropped his head to his chest, pressed a thumb and finger to his eyelids, and grieved for one of the finest women he had ever known.

He'd lost his own mother to cholera shortly before his fifth birthday but he still remembered her, oftentimes wishing he didn't. His pa had never been a strong man, and Luke could still see the empty expression on his father's face when he carried her body out of the house and buried it beneath a full moon. Before sunup, awakened by the crackle of his father's flintlock pistol, Luke knew both his parents were gone forever.

He and his older brothers had had no other family to speak of, so neighbors took them in. Luke closed his eyes, easily recalling his mother's golden hair and her dancing gray eyes. But the melodic tone to her voice was his favorite memory, and he hummed several bars of a tune most familiar before he succumbed to melancholy and sank to his knees, catching his tears in his palms. Luke's grief quickly turned to rage the way it always did, and he whistled for Thunder. The horse always seemed to sense his mindset and reported immediately. With majestic strides, the stallion carried Luke quickly toward Shannon's land.

Well outside town, Luke reined Thunder suddenly. What was he thinking? Shannon would be asleep and he thought it unconscionable to wake her with such news. He decided to return to the Willoughby ranch first, check on William and leave him word of his whereabouts, and then ride out to the Cook place where he would camp until morning.

* * * *

Luke led his horse to the creek, then stopped at the barn and grabbed a blanket. He wiped Thunder down and sat at the base of a large oak tree, leaned against it, and closed his eyes. But he soon found he couldn't sleep. He considered going back home and allowing the sheriff to bring Shannon the horrific news. Luke sighed and the stallion snorted in response. He had to tell her. Emily would have wanted it that way. He wasn't one for rehearsing but managed to formulate a few scenarios. Satisfied but no more relaxed, he was just about to nod off when he heard a rider approaching. He assumed it was Jacob. "Blasted fool," he muttered aloud. He led his horse back to the lane and positioned him across it.

Jacob rode up fast. Luke's black stallion nearly invisible in the dark, Conner reined his gelding so furiously the appaloosa nearly bucked him loose. Thunder danced sideways and drove his nose down.

"That crazy horse a yours is preparin' to charge!" Jacob warned hysterically.

"Nah, don't think he's made up his mind yet." Luke decided he'd best make it up for him and gave the bridle a rough jerk. Thunder immediately brought his head up and nipped Luke's forearm.

"I shoulda known I'd find you here, Richards. Be on your way and don't be mistakin' that for a request."

Luke felt his jaw clench. "Seems to me Mrs. Cook would appreciate a sheriff more interested in findin' Emily's killer than makin' his own parlor points."

"Why you sonuvabitch! What in hell you think I've been doin' all night?"

Luke drew in a lungful and slowly exhaled. He could see the sheriff was upset and probably going into a second day without sleep. Despite the fact, they rarely saw eye to eye, he knew Conner was a good man but as stubborn as a mule and that rankled Luke to no end. "Ain't one of your deputies, Sheriff. I had to come and that's that. But ain't neither one of us gonna disturb Mrs. Cook till we're sure she's up and about, and that's not a request neither. No sense in sending her world cockeyed till we have to."

Anger exaggerated every line on his face, and Jacob spit a wad of tobacco. "Reckon it'll wait," he eventually conceded, dismounted, and led his horse toward the creek. When he returned, Luke's horse unnerved his again, and he steered the appaloosa outside kicking range. "Tell you what. Have it your way. Go on, be my guest. Go ahead and tell the lady the awful news. That suits me down to my damn toes." He smiled cunningly at Luke and commanded his horse into a full run back to town.

* * * *

The birds had been singing overhead for hours when Luke realized he couldn't put it off much longer. And a good hour had passed since he'd watched her come outside and gather water from the well. He vaulted onto Thunder but the closer he got to the house, the more he slowed the stallion's pace. Once there, he dismounted, raked his fingers through his hair so many times he lost count, and knocked softly on the door. Normally, he was a stanch believer in the element of surprise, because in that brief timespan there was no room for dishonesty... only real, raw emotion. When she opened the door, hers came to him by way of a soft blush that warmed her cheeks, a sparkle in her eyes, and full lips parting ever so slightly. Her unspoken but obvious feelings for him made his news abundantly more difficult.

Shannon saw the sadness in his eyes. She'd caught a glimpse of it before, but this time he wasn't trying to disguise it. She heard herself swallow and finally asked, "Luke, what is it?"

THIRTY-NINE

"I've come about Miss Emily."

Shannon dropped to her knees and began to sob. Further explanation wasn't necessary. His eyes told the story.

Luke brought her to her feet, tenderly placed his hand at the nape of her neck and pulled her to him.

She felt his heart race, assumed Emily's had finally given out, and asked him.

Luke grasped her shoulders, took a few steps backwards, and shook his head. "She was killed last night."

"Killed?" Shannon shrieked the question as tears streamed down her cheeks. "But who would..."

He led her to the couch. "That ain't the half of it."

Shannon's eyes widened, her face went white, and she waited apprehensively on the edge of the cushion.

"Miss Emily went to St. Louie, maybe you knew that, maybe you didn't."

"No," Shannon said, shaking her head violently. "She only said she had business back east. What does that have to do...?"

"I'm gettin' to that," Luke interrupted softly, taking her hands in his. "She went to your pa's house."

"Why would she..."

"In the hopes of gettin' money or valuables."

Shannon slapped him hard then shoved him away. "Just a cotton-picking-minute, Luke Richards! I won't have you saying such things about Miss Emily!"

"She was your ma," Luke whispered, wrestling her for her hand. "And she wasn't gonna let anyone take your land away from you. No matter her cost," he added, his words trailing off. Luke watched her and sensed she was putting all the pieces together. He felt certain she realized his truth when she turned her back to him. He also knew she cried harder and nothing he said could put an end to it so he waited.

Without facing him, she asked between sobs, "Why didn't

she tell me, Luke?"

"I reckon she was afraid of losin' you forever," he replied sympathetically.

"I don't understand."

"That's what she was afraid of."

She wrenched her head around, a puzzled expression on her face.

"The whys don't much matter now," Luke said, spreading his fingers and pressing his palms downward.

"Did Mika kill her?"

"Who?"

"My father."

"No, 'less he was here in Leeds."

"Who did then?"

"That's somethin' I intend to find out."

* * * *

Luke stood at the window and held Zach while Shannon struggled with her grief. When she hadn't stopped crying nearly four hours later, he considered Doc Murphy. He thought about Amanda and Wyatt and, in the end, decided a doctor would have little to offer. He heard William ride up before Shannon did. Zach cooed and squirmed, apparently recognizing the boy through the glass. Luke cocked his head toward the door and told her, "It's William."

She wiped her eyes again and sniffled by way of acknowledgement.

"I'll just be outside," Luke said and intercepted William on the porch.

"Miss Emily's..."

Luke's eyes cut to the house. "Shush, boy."

"She's dead?" William whispered.

"'Fraid so," Luke told him and fixed his stare on Zach as if the baby could change things.

"What happened?" William asked, still guarding the timbre of his voice.

"Somebody shot her dead last night."

"Golly! Who?"

Luke shrugged his shoulders. "But I got me a pretty good idea."

"What are we gonna do about it?" William asked, fired-up.

"*We* ain't gonna do jack-squat."

"In case you haven't noticed, I'm nearly a man now. I say we go after this feller and string him up."

That was precisely what Luke had in mind, but in due time, and not with a liability tagging along. "That's the Sheriff's job, boy. It's what folks 'round here pay him for. You take heed of that, hear?"

William kicked at the dirt and hid his eyes.

"'Sides, I need you to stay here and look after Mrs. Cook and this one."

"You're goin' after him, ain't you?" William asked accusingly.

"Not that it's any of your concern, but I'm goin' to light me a fire under that sheriff if one ain't burnin' already."

William's eyes narrowed with suspicion. "Best stop over yonder and take Grandpa's carbine with you."

Luke handed him Zach. "If I wanted me a wife, I'd have one a lot better lookin' than you, boy." He mussed William's hair affectionately and whistled for Thunder. "Damn horse got out of that slipknot again."

"When I rode in, I seen him chasin' Mrs. Cook's mare around."

"Miserable sonuva..." Luke censored the rest.

"Want me to fetch him for you?"

"Nah, I could use the walk."

"Maybe he's worn himself out," William said grinning.

"Not likely." Luke winked. "He ain't much older than you."

Luke headed out and thought about Lance again. He planned to send a telegraph to the outfit down Texas-way, but he knew even should Tucker abandon the cattle drive and hightail it back to Missouri, he couldn't possibly arrive in time for Emily's funeral.

FORTY

Thunder fought the reins and attempted to send Luke into every available low branch. Luke considered giving him a couple of hard wallops but experience had taught him it never did much good. By the time he'd reached the Sheriff's, the stallion had cocked his head around more times than Luke cared to count and nearly nipped a hole through the toe of his boot. "Only fresh air yuh'll be breathin' is through a head chute yuh keep this shit up!"

Thunder kicked a rear hoof to the wind, bared his teeth, and snorted. Although fairly certain his horse's temperament was due to nothing but pure stubbornness and raging testosterone, Luke checked his hooves, anyway. The rear shoes were fine. When Luke finally managed to wrestle his steed's right front hoof up to take a look, the horse attempted to shower him with a wall of urine. Luke smacked the Morab's flank hard. "Sometimes, I wonder if that dern Indian gave you to me out of kindness or just plain spite." His irritation mounting when he didn't see Jacob's appaloosa hitched to the rail, Luke heaved the door open and it ricocheted off the wall. To his surprise, neither deputy looked up from their card game. Annoyed, Luke announced himself. "Sheriff in town?"

Both men dropped their cards and scrambled to stand.

"What can I do for you, stranger?" Saunders asked, his voice quaking as he squinted into the sun.

"You blind?" Luke asked and ducked a split-second before Atkinson fired.

The shot awakened a drunken prisoner. "Come on, boys! Let me outa here. You know I'm a scared of thunder."

"Hobble your lip, Isaac! Ain't a cloud in the sky," Saunders barked and hurled a book at the cell.

"Well, if this don't beat all," Luke hissed. "It's me, Luke Richards! Now put that gun away before you kill somebody."

Atkinson managed to get the gun holstered on his third

attempt.

"Here's a tough question for you boys so listen up. Where might the sheriff be?"

"Didn't say," Saunders said, not the least bit insulted. "Reckon he's out lookin' for Miss Emily's killer."

"Got no idea when he'll be back?"

Atkinson surveyed the bullet hole in the wall directly above Jacob's desk. "Not fer I spell, I hope."

Saunders grinned. "Come to think on it, he got himself all clean-shaven and lathered-up so wouldn't surprise me to find him out at the Cook place."

Atkinson stopped snickering when Luke swung a stare.

"Keep up the good work, boys," Luke said snidely and started for the door. He looked for Jacob's horse, as Thunder settled into a reasonable trot down Main Street, and ignored the whores beckoning him from Ruby's balcony. Nearly at the edge of town, he met the sheriff, a rider dragging a Negro behind a nervous Marwari, its curved ears reminding Luke of a headdress, and an angry mob comprised of nearly twenty.

"What do you think you're doin'?" Luke asked, blocking the route.

"Move along, Richards! Ain't your concern," Jacob shouted.

"That's right," a member of the posse hollered, and the crowd began to chant, "Hang the murderin' Nigra."

"The hell it ain't my concern," Luke blasted. "I don't know what this man done, but I do know he's entitled to a trial." Luke got off his horse for a closer inspection. He quickly recognized the prisoner as the man from Emily's shop.

The crowd continued to chant and when they refused to quiet, Jacob emptied both barrels from his shotgun. "Ain't nobody doin' no hangin'," he bellowed. "Not till this man gets him a fair trial. Anybody got anything different in mind, best plug it now or he'll be findin' a noose 'round his own neck!"

Luke planted both feet in front of the appaloosa. "Hold on, Sheriff. I got some news might shed some light on this here."

Jacob released a long breath and wondered if Luke realized

the peril he'd just placed himself in. "Like I said, this Nigra's gonna get a fair trial. You got somethin' to add will help solve Miss Emily's murder, mount up so as I can properly document your two-bits."

"Put the Nigra on my horse." Luke said and thought the Sheriff possibly considered his offer.

"Reckon he's done alright so far. Another hundred feet or so won't kill 'im," Jacob said with some reluctance. He figured anything different would only incite the crowd further.

Luke jumped on his horse and drifted alongside Jacob. "When I done it, it was to a piece of shit that tried to rape a woman after he beat her. I figured that was a hint more Christian than shootin' the bastard. You allowin' that Nigra be drug like a dead animal is just plain wrong."

Jacob winged both nostrils. His squint communicated the rest. He clucked his tongue and pressed the appaloosa clear.

"Best knock before you go through that door a yers, Sheriff," Luke yelled after him.

Jacob's horse came to an abrupt halt, and he whipped his head ninety degrees. "That some kinda threat?"

"More like a warnin'. One of your deputies fancied decoratin' your office with a little lead."

Jacob swiped a shirtsleeve across his forehead and decided not to solicit further details.

Luke's frustration dictated he follow a considerable distance behind. Once in town, he led his horse to the troth. Finding it empty, he took a few gulps from his canteen, pried his horse's mouth open, and dumped in the remainder.

"Mercy me," he heard Jenny Saunders screech to her companions. "I expect now we've seen just about everythin' there is to come out of the bowels of hell right here on Main Street!"

"Not quite ma'am," Luke sneered. "I was just about to relieve myself."

FORTY-ONE

When Luke stepped inside the jailhouse, Jacob was berating his deputies.

"Ah, don't be too hard on them, Sheriff. Folks tell me if the light's just right I bear a slight resemblance to Jesse James."

"This here's jailhouse business, Richards! Sit your ass down and wait till you're addressed."

Luke eyes met Elijah's and he saw a man preparing for the worst. He decided Jacob could educate his deputies another time. "Sheriff, that man you captured ain't guilty of nothin'. In the eyes of God, anyway."

"That right?" Conner said, snarling. "We got a witness puts him at Emily's directly before we found her dead. That's what we call some pretty damn convincin' circumstantial evidence 'round here."

"And I'm tellin' you, you got a witness," Luke paused, hitching a thumb toward himself, "that seen him go. And leavin' Emily alive and well."

"Who you suppose is responsible then? Tell me that."

"Somebody else was lurkin' outside the buildin' next to hers. Maybe that so-called witness a yers."

"Oh, somebody was lurkin' was they... besides you?"

"That's right," Luke said. "I come to call on Miss Emily but saw her and the Nigra talkin', so I stayed outside and waited. That's how I know, sure as I'm standin' right here, somebody else was around."

Jacob took his hat off and ran his fingers thoughtfully along the entire brim twice.

Luke gnawed his upper lip, his steel gray eyes threatening conflict. "That witness a yours a secret witness, Sheriff? He even exist?"

The sheriff sank his teeth mercilessly into his fountain pen. "No business a yours for the time being. I don't suppose you know the nature of that conversation?" he asked, jerking a thumb toward the cell Elijah occupied.

"Couldn't hear much, but I got the impression it was personal and, more important, friendly." Luke didn't intend to offer more, not yet.

"Now, you see that mob out there. It's growin'. For that Nigra's sake, somebody best come up with some credible answers real quick-like. Even if I send a telegram to the Marshal, it's gonna take some time for him to send reinforcements. Reckon by nightfall I won't be able to hold 'em back."

"That'd make it all nice and tidy for you, wouldn't it, Sheriff? Any man will do, 'specially some poor Nigra whose people are too scared and outnumbered to fight for 'im."

Jacob dropped the pen and clacked both palms hard on his desk. "This here reeks of bullshit, Richards! I think so and so will that mob."

Luke vaulted to a standing position. "You callin' me a liar?"

"No, more of an opportunist," Jacob said as he rose from his desk to create some distance from Luke and update a headcount on the mob.

Luke clenched his fists, popped out of the chair, and obstructed Jacob's intentions. "Care to explain yourself, Sheriff, or would you rather take that badge and those guns off and meet me outside?"

Jacob closed the small gap between them, jabbed a finger toward Luke, and tapered his eyes. "You want an explanation? Here it is! I think when you saw I'd rounded up Emily's killer you couldn't risk me lookin' the hero in Mrs. Cook's eyes so you made the whole sorry lot up."

Luke sucked his teeth and wondered how many days old Judge Carlson would give him if he knocked Jacob to the ground. He thought about William and decided not to gamble on it. "Surely will interest you to know, Sheriff, I don't much care what kind of impression *I* make on Shannon Cook or if I make one at all for that matter. Unlike you, I ain't lookin' for a wife or a warm body to share my bed at night."

"Take a walk, Richards! Take it now."

"You mark my words," Luke said, flicking Jacob's badge, "you got the wrong man. How's Shannon Cook gonna like you allowin' an innocent man hang?"

Jacob crossed to the door, heaved it open, and motioned Luke through.

Luke staked his ground. "You might wanna give that there a whole lot of contemplation."

* * * *

Luke took a seat at the bar and savored his first sip of whiskey. Out of the corner of his eye, he watched George McClanahan stagger toward him. Luke bristled when the old man repeatedly attempted to secure one elbow on the counter and failed. He believed the only thing worse than a man who couldn't hold his liquor was a man who spent a lifetime denying it.

"What'd yuh know," McClanahan slurred, "we got ourselves an honest-to-goodness Nigra-lover here."

Luke ignored him and showed him his back.

"Time you went on home to Emma," Luke heard Ruby say as she quickly steered the old man toward the door.

Luke emptied his glass and sidestepped a few inches when she shimmed over, stinking of cheap perfume and cheaper cigars. The only thing worse than a whore, in his opinion, was a whore who made a living off other whores.

She snapped her fingers, got her bartender's attention, and nodded when Irving grabbed a bottle of her finest whiskey. She gave Luke a long glance, her gaze lingering over swollen biceps and broad shoulders, sweeping upward and taking in his dark brown hair and a face tanned and lined by hours in the sun before ultimately fixing on perceptive eyes the color of lead. "Your drinks are on the house," she told him, leaning in and giving him an unsolicited view of her cleavage. "Why is it, we've never had the pleasure of your company upstairs?" she whispered in his ear.

Luke ignored the question but shot her an indifferent squint.

Unscathed, Ruby laughed. "Virile man like you," she purred, tracing the scar on his left forearm, "must be dippin' at another well."

Luke waited for the bartender to finish filling his glass and plucked it from the counter with his left hand, nearly sending her off balance. "Let's just say I'm partial to untainted waters and leave it be."

She flinched when the coins he tossed Irving noisy skidded across the countertop. "Ain't no excuse for rudeness, Luke Richards, even in here."

"Thanks for the hospitality," he announced with thick sarcasm. Raising his empty glass in a mock toast, he moved to a center table.

When the saloon filled to near capacity before the sun set, Luke had newfound respect for Jacob Conner. Apparently, he'd managed to bully the mob into disbanding, although, from what Luke could hear, threats against the prisoner hadn't let up. "That somebody-or-other Rutherford?" he asked Roy McKenzie and gestured to a tottering, small-framed man.

"Jonas Rutherford," Roy corrected. "Looks to be courtin' a dirt nap. He's as full as a tick, I'd say."

Rutherford's head bobbed and weaved, and Luke managed to block his fall before he hit ground. Still conscious, Rutherford pushed him away, insisting he needed no assistance. Luke knew better. The Strate brothers, notorious thieves that they were, lay low at a nearby table, stalking Jonas as mountain lions would an ingenuous young buck in rut. He settled Rutherford back in his chair and before Luke could bring his glass to his lips, Jonas once again tumbled out of it. Luke considered leaving him lie until he began to mumble something about Emily and a Nigra, and decided to take him outside with hope the fresh air might help sober him up.

Because his horse had once again abandoned him, Luke borrowed a canteen from someone else's pack and poured just enough over Rutherford's head to bring him around. Rutherford countered with punches, which missed Luke by a longshot. "Take it easy! Looks to me you're your own worst enemy 'bout now." Luke growled and broke Jonas' fall again. "What'd you say about the Nigra? About Miss Emily?" Unable to decipher his response, Luke decided to accompany him home. Certain Rutherford was incapable of giving him proper direction, Luke slung an arm around the little man's waist, carted him back inside, and gambled on the bartender's knowledge.

"About a quarter mile outside a town," Irving told him and pointed south. "Can't miss it. House looks like a strong wind could bring 'er down. You'll probably see a bunch of youngens runnin' 'round out front, too. The youngest was nearly cut down by Johnston's wagon last week."

"That Belgian his?"

"Old mare looks to have one hoof in the grave?"

Luke nodded.

"That be his."

Luke dismissed sighting the children as plausible means for locating Rutherford's house, although he assumed many allowed their children outdoors despite nightfall rapidly approaching. He had seen many a sunrise before he came of age. Once outside, Luke whistled for Thunder and felt his teeth grind against one another as he waited for his horse to show. Meanwhile, he heaved Jonas atop the Belgian, retrieved rope from Rutherford's pack, wrapped one end around the little man's bloated belly, knotted it, secured the opposite end to his saddle horn, and hoped for the best.

He heard Thunder's whinny echo through town before he caught sight of him and stifled a grin when the Morab slid to a stop beside him, his lower lip quivering in submission. "You're about two steps away from the bone orchard. Sow your oats on your own damn time," Luke snapped, hoisting himself in the saddle. Grabbing Rutherford's Belgian's reins, Luke gave his horse a command, and Thunder conceded to a slower than usual pace out of town.

Luke found the Rutherford place easy enough. Irving was right. It wouldn't take much of a blast out of the north to bring the entire front porch down. And Luke had never seen that many children, aside from possibly the schoolhouse, gathered in one place before. All but the eldest were filthy and, to his amazement, each displayed sincere eagerness as they welcomed their father home. "Where your ma, be?" Luke asked. He sensed a true camaraderie when they chanted her name in nearly perfect harmony. Luke loosened the slipknot and freed Jonas. With one hand grasping the back of his shirt, the other the seat of his pants, he pulled him from his horse. His feet made contact with the ground not as softly as Luke had planned, and he responded immediately.

"How'd I get here?"

"Your horse," Luke said, motioning toward the mare.

"You come with me?"

Luke nodded.

"You were askin' all kinds of questions."

Luke nodded again. "About Miss Emily."

"And that Nigra." Jonas licked his lips and grabbed both sides of his head. "Everythin's spinnin'. You children go now! Go and see about your ma."

Luke guided him to the porch, reaching it once the last of the Rutherford children went inside, and hoped the structure held a bit longer.

Jonas started to speak and then seemed to have second thoughts.

"You seen somethin', ain't you?"

"That Nigra had nothin' to do with that woman dyin'," Jonas eventually admitted.

"You go into town tomorrow and say your piece to the sheriff?"

Rutherford's eyes divulged terror, his gaze darting from Luke to the door. "I do, might not be just me meets her same fate."

Luke took a seat beside him. "A feller's gotta do what's right, no matter. You know who killed her, don't you?"

Jonas shook his head. "I can't be certain."

"But you got an idea?"

Jonas glanced toward the house again. "All I'm sayin' is the

Nigra didn't do it."

"The sheriff's gonna wonder how you're so sure about that."

"That's all I'm sayin'!" he said, emphasizing every word. After that, he thanked Luke for his help and staggered inside.

FORTY-TWO

Luke got back to the Willoughby place shortly after nightfall and found William in the barn. "How Mrs. Cook be?"

William shrugged his shoulders. "She didn't say much, only told me to go on home."

"And I told yuh to stay put and look after the both of 'em."

William grabbed his saddle and pitched it over his horse. "Nancy Ogleby's havin' a barn dance 'cause of it bein' her birthday." William considered telling Luke that Erza Young would also be there, but he knew his cheeks would flush, and Luke would know how he felt about her and tease him to no end.

Luke squinted and jammed his hands against his hips. "So the long and short of it is it don't much matter what I say?"

William took a step back. "Mrs. Cook told me I shouldn't feel obligated."

"And you think that makes it right?"

William hung his head. "Golly, Luke. Johnny Wills and Jesse McClintock get to go. Even Billy Johnston. All I ever do is work."

"Looks to me the time you spent plasterin' that cowlick down woulda been better spent doin' Mrs. Cook's chores. I got plenty to keep me busy 'round here, boy, what with the others on the drive. I can't be stretchin' myself much thinner, so it's you needs to help out over yonder."

William stood stock-still, his eyes wandering to everything but Luke.

"Well, get boy! Pretty, little Nancy will still be there when you've finished. Never knew a woman worth waitin' for wouldn't be doin' just that."

"Yes sir," William grumbled after he'd kicked up more dirt. "It ain't Nancy I'm worried 'bout," he mumbled as he led his horse out.

* * * *

When he realized Mrs. Cook had taken care of everything just like he figured, William tested a quiet thread of profanity but decided he should wish her a goodnight before he took out. He rapped on the door and, getting no response, opened it. Duke lunged for him, planting his enormous paws on William's shoulders. William lost his balance and hit the floor hard.

Shannon heard the commotion and raced downstairs. "My lands! Duke get off the boy." Shannon laughed and helped William to his feet. "I do believe he's been missing you."

"I ain't been gone but a few hours," William told the dog and stroked his fur.

"What brings you here besides the need to be mauled?" Shannon asked.

William looked at her and suddenly Erza Young was the farthest thing from his mind. "You look 'specially beautiful tonight," he blurted and immediately clamped down on his tongue.

"Why, thank you, William," Shannon said blushing. She rolled her eyes and added, "Just washed my hair is all."

William began to sweat and suddenly his skin felt too small. He planned to avoid eye contact if it meant gouging his eyes out. Looking at her nearly always stirred up trouble.

"Why William, are you feelin' poorly?"

"No ma'am. Just the hot night is all."

She placed the back of her hand against his cheek. "You're quivering and burning up to boot. Now you just sit yourself right down there while I fetch you a cool drink."

William traced his cheek blissfully with his fingers, remembering how her skin felt against his. Then he began to squirm. No matter how much he willed his body to stay still it wouldn't. His skin felt on fire and his heart thudded against his chest. He fidgeted a few minutes longer and bolted for the door.

* * * *

Early the next morning, Luke came in from the pasture and found William feeding the chickens. He called out, but the boy didn't seem to hear him. Luke tempered his irritation and mopped the sweat from his brow. "William," he called again. "You ain't ignorin' me, are you, boy?"

William waved half-heartily, and Luke assumed something unexpected had occurred at Nancy Ogleby's the night before. He'd heard the boy come home, but by the time he got up from Samuel's rocking chair, William was already in his room behind a closed door.

Luke approached him and the boy turned his back. "Somethin' troublin' you?"

"I got chores," William told him but scampered toward the house instead.

"Ah, shit," Luke muttered and wrestled with the decision. Should he go about his business or get-to-the-bottom of William's nonsense? He expected to find the boy in the kitchen but didn't. He tried the parlor. No sign of William. He climbed the stairs two at a time, noted William's door closed, and thought whatever was troubling him was possibly much worse than anything he'd imagined. "William," he called through the door. When he didn't respond, Luke knocked and that went unanswered. He opened the door and found William stretched out on the bed facedown. Luke scowled, took off his hat, and watched it sail across the room. "Care to tell me what all the fuss is about?"

William emphatically shook his head and mumbled something into his pillow.

Luke gnawed on his lip. A few minutes later, he collected his hat. "I guess that's that then. 'Sides," he said, stalling at the door, "I can put two and two together. Somethin' either happened last night you didn't count on or somethin' didn't happen that you worked yourself up into hopin' would happen."

"What are you talkin' about?" William shrieked, wrenching

his head from the pillow.

"You tell me."

William remained silent, and Luke assumed any minute the boy would hide his face again.

"Cuz if you don't, I'm just gonna assume Nancy wanted no part in a kissin' game."

"I already done kissed Nancy Ogleby two months ago!" William blasted as if Luke was about the stupidest human being that ever lived.

"Okay, boy, let me get this straight. You were nearly dancin' a jig last night, workin' yourself up real good, goin' on about Nancy Ogleby and her birthday barn dance, and now you look as though the sky's about to fall." Luke sat on the edge of the bed and considered rubbing the boy's shoulders. "Don't forget, ain't been that long ago I had all them urges causin' both my head and my insides to swim."

"Wasn't Nancy I was worked up about," William offered with the same disgusted tone.

"Now we're gettin' somewhere. But since neither one of us has all day, how about you tell me the whole story, just so I'm not left to guess like we were playin' some fancy parlor game."

"Maybe cuz I'd rather not."

Luke sighed loudly and raked his fingers through his hair. "Look, boy. I'm just tryin' to help. Might be wise for you to take advantage of all this wisdom."

William glanced over his shoulder and barely returned Luke's grin. "I didn't go to the dance."

Luke felt his brows meet. "That right? Mind tellin' me where you were?"

"In the barn."

"Now boy, I seen you ride off toward the Cook place with my own eyes."

William nodded. "She'd done her chores, just like I said she would, and I came back and stayed in the barn till I got tired of that dang rooster spurrin' me."

Luke knew better than to laugh. He rubbed his chin, then his mustache instead. "Somethin' happen over there?"

"I don't," he paused.

Luke finished his sentence. "Want to talk about it?"

William nodded sheepishly.

Luke felt a knot form in his stomach and became increasingly concerned about Shannon's welfare. "Is Mrs. Cook alright? Can you tell me that much?" Luke noticed William's cheeks flush and his eyes brighten, and suddenly he had a pretty good idea just how alright William thought Mrs. Cook was.

William jerked upright so abruptly, Luke nearly lost his center. "Why don't you go find out for yourself?" he shouted. "It's you she's sweet on, anyhow! You're just too ignorant to see it!"

Luke filled his lungs to capacity and wished he'd stayed in the pasture. "Oh, I ain't stupid, boy. But that over there at the Cook place is my business. We're talkin' about yours. Now, you gonna tell me just what in Sam-hell went on over there?"

"I made a dang fool outa myself is what!" William managed between sobs. "And now I can never see her dog again or Zach. And I love that dern dog! Everythin's ruined!"

Luke smothered a grin. "She tell you not to come back?"

William shook his head. "I left outa there before she could say much."

"What happened before that?" Luke asked.

William fiddled with a jagged thumbnail.

"Come on, boy. How many times you ask me to work one of 'em jigsaw puzzles? And I always tell you *I got work to do*, which really means I hate those damn things."

William squinted hard and placed his hands on his thighs. "What the heck do puzzles have to do with anythin'?"

"Puttin' the pieces of this mystery here together is 'bout the most cantankerous puzzle I ever did see. So start talkin' or I'll start guessin' again. And if it comes to that, it could get a little bawdy." Luke knew his promise of some lewd insinuations would get the wheels turning and smiled into a cupped palm when William offered him every little detail. "Damn, boy! That's it?" Luke asked and mussed the boy's hair. "Cuz I can promise you that woman has no idea why you took outa there like your pants were on fire."

"They nearly felt like they were," William mumbled.

Luke laughed and when William joined in, he wrestled the boy to the floor.

"Stop, I give!" William yelled after Luke pinned him.

Because the kid was turning a little blue, Luke let him up. "Remember that Mrs. Bettle from town?"

William nodded and scrunched up his nose.

"Next time you feel that hot fire growin' down south, you picture that one without a stitch on. That'll put it out."

It seemed to Luke William's gills went from blue to green.

After Luke helped him to his feet, William told him, "On account of you always helpin' me with this or that, I'll step aside and let you have Mrs. Cook. 'Less you got your heart set on that Mrs. Bettle."

The laughter started up again, and Luke heard Thunder whinny on cue.

FORTY-THREE

Jacob had held onto Emily's contribution in the hope Shannon, faced with nowhere to go, might eventually accept his proposal. But after several nights of fitful sleep, he found the guilt overwhelming. Feeling sure Shannon knew the whole truth by now, he thought it best to ride out to her place and hand over the money. After he proposed one last time. He sank his chin in a palm and wondered if her grief might give him an advantage. He grabbed his hat from the hall-tree and told his deputies he'd be gone a couple hours. Before he closed the door, he sternly suggested they not shoot the place up in the interim.

* * * *

Luke found William in the barn milking the cows. "I'm headed into town for a spell, but I'll be back before sundown."

"Can I come along?"

"Another time. You still got your chores." Luke nearly reconsidered when he saw William's disappointment, but if Rutherford hadn't given the sheriff his statement yet, things could go sour real fast if they hadn't already. "Fair's comin' to town next week. We'll go then," Luke promised.

"Reckon they'll have the bearded lady?" William asked excitedly.

"Believe you're thinkin' of the circus, boy," Luke said. When William's expression soured, he quickly added, "But you never can tell."

* * * *

Luke passed the sheriff on his way to town.

"Luke," Jacob greeted abrasively.

"Hold up, Sheriff."

Jacob turned his horse about, positioned it a safe enough distance from Luke's, and assumed a hard stare.

"Jonas Rutherford been in to see you?"

Jacob shook his head and decided not to tip his hand. "Why would he?"

"Sonuvabitch promised me he would. He's got particulars about the night Emily was killed."

Luke thought Jacob seemed suspicious.

"What kind of particulars?"

Luke shrugged his shoulders. "All he'd say is the man you're holdin' didn't do it. I was hopin' you could get more out of him cuz I think he knows who's responsible."

When Jacob didn't answer, Luke looked toward town. "Hope this ain't your way of tellin' me the mob got what they wanted."

Jacob continued his silent interrogation and eventually spoke. "Still got the Nigra locked up if that's what you're gettin' at."

Luke smiled without a suggestion of humor. "And you left him with those jackasses you call deputies?"

Jacob spit and Luke could see his jaw flinch. "How'd you come by this tidbit, Richards? And you aware a lot of folks think Rutherford's an odd stick?"

"Seemed to me to have his wits about him. 'Sides, doubt if anybody with half a brain would let fly somethin' like that least it was truth. Not like he volunteered it neither. Took near a bottle of whiskey to unshackle some of that torment."

Jacob threw his head back and Luke thought he rolled his eyes. "You tellin' me he was soaked when he offered that scuttlebutt?"

Luke felt his face grow hot. "More sober than Judge Carlson's ever been, by night's end, anyway."

"Then we got us a real problem. Jonas Rutherford took it upon himself to meet his maker last night."

FORTY-FOUR

When Luke reached the Rutherford homestead, he noted windows covered in dark fabric, the parlor door laid open to the outside, and not one child frolicked about the yard. Luke slunk into the modest room, his eyes shifting from the crumbling plaster to the cobbled-together-wooden coffin situated in the center. Luella Rutherford sat beside it and gave Luke a split-second glance. Her eyes were red and vacant, her soul appropriately lost to yesterday. Only then did he notice all eleven Rutherford children seated in a perfect circle just outside the somber room, each dressed in Sunday best with head bowed, the exception being the baby who slept peacefully in an older sibling's arms.

Luke saw a shadow fall across the floor, and he turned to see Preacher McCabe enter. Luke nodded a greeting and clasped the man's hand warmly, silently communicating his eternal gratitude to the pastor who had once saved him from his own damnation. The preacher opened his Bible and began reading from the scriptures. When he finished, he stooped, took Luella Rutherford's hands in his and spoke in a confidential tone. Luella remained lifeless but, to Luke, seemed to exhibit some hope after that. He wondered if anyone other than himself and Preacher McCabe had come by to pay their respects. He glanced about the room, and when he didn't see the typical obligatory fodder, he doubted it. His eyes followed the preacher as he left the room to comfort the children. He hesitated but eventually took up uneasy space beside Rutherford's widow. "Mrs. Rutherford," he began, in a soft tone, "if there's any way I can be of assistance." He paused. His words sounded hollow even to his own ears because he knew nothing would make her world spin again.

Luella managed a pitiful smile but she wouldn't look him directly in the eyes, safeguarding what little composure she had left he guessed. "Jonas and me seen every sunrise together for near twenty-six years." She shook her head, blinked hard as many times, and Luke knew she was losing the battle. He nodded sympathetically and pressed her hand. Her eyes narrowed and her voice dropped nearly to a whisper. "We had no secrets, so I know the reason for his torment," she said, glancing over her shoulder toward the children. "My Jonas believed it was Jack Marsh that killed that woman."

Luke recognized rage behind her words. She dropped her head in her hands, her shoulders shaking, and Luke assumed their conversation ended. He caught Preacher McCabe's gaze and the Pastor closed the curtain between them. Then Luke took her in his arms.

When Luella could, she told him: "He said as God was his witness he didn't know it was gonna come to that." She reached into the coffin, took a neatly folded paper from Jonas' jacket pocket. "Says as much right here. You take that on to the sheriff."

Jacob nearly convinced himself his visit wasn't purely a selfish act. After all, he hadn't had the opportunity to express his sympathy regarding Emily's death. Knowing most would have done it sooner only increased his guilt. He saw the sorrel as he neared the bend along the tree break, the quarter-horse's chestnut color gleaming in the sunlight. He tried to assign the horse to its owner but didn't remember seeing it before. He decided Shannon must be in the company of a well-wisher and planned to stay put until her visitor left. He waited impatiently beneath a large oak, the smaller limbs twisting and creaking in accordance with the intensity of the wind's gusts. He turned his nose to the sky and wondered if Leeds was in for a late-afternoon storm. When the winds quieted, he felt sure he'd heard a woman's scream. He listened closely and knew he heard a baby's wails.

Breaking the appaloosa into a full run, Jacob abandoned the saddle as soon as he neared the porch. Two-fisted, he drummed the door. Getting no response, he rammed it open. He saw the dog first and thought it dead. Shannon stood a few feet to the other side, blood trickling from her nose to a small puddle already pooling on the oak planks, her eyes manically darting from Jacob to the door. His mind raced as he attempted to make sense of the situation. Realizing he hadn't heard the sound of the door strike the wall after he flung it open, he went for his gun. Before he could skin the Colt Peace Maker, the door swung closed.

FORTY-FIVE

Jacob heard Shannon's screams shortly after the lead blew a hole through his middle. She slumped beside him, tentatively examining the entrance wound from the Winchester '73. He motioned her closer, his words whispered and clipped. "Something. From. Miss. Emily. My. Pocket."

Shannon nodded, cradled his head, and witnessed his last breath a few minutes later. Then she closed Jacob's eyes for the last time and lunged for Cole. "You bastard!" she shrieked, her fingernails leaving wicked tracks from his cheekbone to jaw.

Cole kicked her backwards, and her head struck a table edge. Yanking her by her hair to a standing position, he tossed her onto Jacob's body. "He share your bed?" Cole raised his voice somehow louder, "Did he?"

Shannon shook her head defiantly.

He raised the gun again. "Don't much believe you. I guess it's only fittin' you share one in the afterlife." Shannon sprung in the opposite direction a split-second before Cole put a bullet hole directly between the sheriff's dead eyes. Then he began searching Jacob's pockets. "Well, will you look at this here, an engagement ring!" Cole grinned and stuffed the diamond-studded gold band in his pocket. "He sure got more than he bargained for, now didn't he?"

Shannon bit her lip, her gaze hovering from Jacob's face to Cole.

"Let's see what other treasures he got hidden." Cole patted Jacob's body down and, finding something of interest, he retrieved an envelope and ripped it open. "Whew-wee, the sheriff here is just full of surprises!" Dancing a jig, Cole went outside to count the money.

Shannon hurried to retrieve her son, saw Duke was coming to, and caught a glimpse of her bloody reflection in the curio cabinet. She picked up her screaming infant and noted his right arm was swollen, bruised, and limp. Swaddling him, she set him back down, seized one of Jacob's guns, calmly walked to the door and fired once into the back of Cole's head. He dropped to the ground, his newly acquired bounty wafting across the lane toward lush crops.

Shannon's movements became mechanical. She gathered a quilt from the trunk and covered Jacob's body. She quickly assessed her dog and hoped Doc Murphy could mend a wicked head wound. She pried a small loose board from the porch railing, tore a length from her petticoat, secured Zach's injured arm to the makeshift splint, and then coaxed her dog into the wagon and settled her son in. As Sara obediently trotted down the lane, Shannon noted the winds had calmed, and her mother's gift lay nestled among tassels of corn.

* * * *

Kate Reeds sat at the head of the table, which was customary, her head bent as she lent her hands to the quilt. "Damn!" she cursed after missing her mark with the needle. She glanced up from the table, her hard stare immediately silencing the group's chuckles.

"What in heaven's name is tormentin' you today?" Clarissa Mayfield bravely inquired.

Kate shrugged her shoulders, hesitated, and heard herself say, "Reckon it's that Cook woman." She shook her head, her tongue clicking against her upper palate. "Poor thing."

A collective gasp filled the room.

"Did you just say *poor thing*?" Clarissa asked, rolling her eyes and fanning her bosom.

"You heard right. Think about your Betsy and how it'd be to have you disappear one night, show up years later, and then be shot dead just when she gets to feelin' a kinship."

"What in God's world are you talkin' about?"

"Emily Dunsmire and Victoria Leeds be one and the same." Kate's hand flew to her cheek as she waited for the harmonious exclamations to end. "I'm surprised not a one of us noted the resemblance."

Jenny Saunders burst in. Winded, she raised a finger communicating a need to catch her breath. "Just wait till you see what I seen with my own two eyes!"

"Just spill it before you burst," Kate snapped.

"It's that Cook woman! She come to town with blood all over her and her baby screamin' like a banshee."

Kate was the first to the window. "Poor dear, what's befell her now?"

"It's Shannon Cook I'm talkin' about!" Jenny said, her mentor's sympathy eliciting surprise.

"I'm a lot a things, Jenny Saunders, but deaf ain't one of 'em. Where you been anyway? Weren't it you who suggested we present this quilt to the town at the fair? And yet it's been the rest a us workin' our fingers stiff to finish on time."

Jenny nodded and followed-up with a *yes, ma'am*, and it wasn't just because Kate was the mayor's wife.

"Well, sit your sorry behind down and get to it," Kate barked, gesturing to the empty chair. Then she scurried across the rutty street toward Doc Murphy's.

* * * *

Luke reluctantly set the bottle off to the side, though he was tempted to consume the entire thing. He'd still been grieving over Emily's demise and suddenly his angst was compounded by Jonas Rutherford's suicide. No matter how much he tried to deny it, he felt some responsibility for the little man's turn of events. Unfortunately, the note Jonas' widow had given him was nothing more than speculation. All it helped to prove was Jack Marsh hired Rutherford to snare Elijah into going to Emily's that night. That by itself didn't prove Jack's involvement in the actual murder. But Luke thought his testimony combined with the Rutherford letter should cast enough doubt on Elijah's involvement to free him, despite town prejudice.

Irving took the bottle and refilled his glass. "Thought you could use another. On the house."

Luke raised a palm, communicating he'd had enough.

Irving leaned in after scanning the saloon, bridging the distance between them. "Been somebody in here askin' a whole lot of questions about you and what business you had with Jonas Rutherford the other night."

"You don't say. Who that be?"

Irving glanced over both shoulders again. "The same mean sonuvabitch should find out I told you be puttin' a hole through my head."

"Let me make it easy for you then. You nod if I hit pay dirt. Jack Marsh."

Irving's mouth flew open, surprise registering in his eyes.

"I figured Jack to be a smarter man. Why would he question you?" Luke asked suspiciously. "You're kinda exposed here with all these folks about."

"Got himself liquored up, that's why. Took Belle Flanagan upstairs and near beat her to death when she couldn't tell him everythin' he wanted to know." Irving jutted an index finger in Luke's face. "A real man don't lay hands on a woman. Not like that."

"Tryin' to get yourself in her favor? That why you givin' him up?"

Irving smacked a bar towel against the counter. "Think what yuh want. Just a friendly warnin' is all. 'Cause a man would do that to a woman he's laid with," Irving paused, arching his brows to emphasis his point, "would do a lot worse to someone he didn't give a hoot or holler for."

"Appreciate it," Luke said and raised his glass.

"And I think it's kinda funny Rutherford winds up dead the very next day," Irving added.

"Weren't nothin' funny about it."

"Didn't mean no offense, Luke. But don't be sheddin' too many tears for ole Jonas. It's a known fact he did mosta Jack's dirty work for him; if Jack wanted somebody's land, Jonas would make sure crops failed. If by the grace of God that didn't work, he'd make threats toward Joshua Johnston and he wouldn't buy the landowner's harvest."

"That so?"

"Yes sir. And I reckon I don't have to tell yuh about his ties to cattle rustlers. Who yuh think played middleman? Marsh owns near half this county and owes most of it to Jonas Rutherford's dirty hands."

Luke thought he already knew the answer but asked anyway. "And them who wouldn't sell their land?"

Irving pressed rigid palms against the bar and stared at the floor. "Bone orchard's filled with 'em." Then he slapped the bar towel against the counter again and tended to the other customers.

Less than ten minutes after, Deputy Saunders burst through both doors. "The sheriff's been killed!"

"Ah, shit," Luke heard himself say, surprised by the heavy sadness sweeping over him.

"Good heavens!" Ruby shrieked from the back of the saloon. "What on earth?"

"Cole Cook shot him dead."

"What?" Ruby cried. "When'd he come back?"

"Don't know the particulars. Mrs. Cook's still givin' her account to Deputy Atkinson."

"Well," Ruby said indignantly and jammed a hand against her hip. "You goin' after him or you just gonna stand around here all day playin' the town crier?"

"Been spared the trouble. Shannon Cook shot her husband dead."

Luke grabbed his hat and nearly knocked Saunders down on his way through the doors. Immediately noticing the crowd gathered outside Doc Murphy's, he was relieved when he saw Shannon and surprised Kate Reeds had her arms wrapped around her. He crossed the street and, as he grew near, he could see that dried blood stamped Shannon's forehead.

"And your baby?" he heard Kate ask.

Shannon looked toward Murphy's. "He's resting now that Doc set his arm straight." Her eyes wandered to the jail and the grief she'd stored up for Jacob nearly overwhelmed her.

"Oh, my," Kate said behind her hand. "And Cole done that

to his own child?"

"He did and paid the price," Shannon said coolly. She turned her back on Kate Reeds. She wasn't ready to forgive or forget her previous unkindness. "For those of you who don't already know, Miss Emily's gonna be buried on my land come tomorrow morning." Shannon cleared her throat and tried to collect herself. "My mother was a fine woman and those that wish to pay their respects are welcome."

Kate's eyes swept the crowd insolently. "We'd all be honored," she answered for them.

* * * *

Long before the sun slid behind Johnston's General Store, the entire town knew the reason for Kate's lament. Tales of Mika Leeds and his cruelty were the conversation of the evening whether it was upstairs at the bawdyhouse or on any porch stoop within miles.

Cecilia Atkinson had clear recollection of the day Mika Leeds had come to town and rode *hell-bent,* according to her, towards the bank. Her brother, Christopher, lame and unable to move very quickly, found himself in harm's way. Mika had been able to stop his horse from crushing the boy but quickly turned his horse about and proceeded to whip young Christopher to the ground.

It was Elijah, who had shared many more tales of Mika Leeds' cruelty with Sheriff Conner. Because Jacob's deputies thrived on circulating jailhouse gossip, it wasn't long before nearly everyone in town knew Mika Leeds tortured his wife and threw her out. Most had also been privy to gossip surrounding the lifelong malice Shannon Cook had become accustomed. The majority of the townswomen put their petty jealousies aside, vowing to embrace Shannon Cook at the nearest opportunity. All were convinced Cole Cook got what he deserved.

Kate and Orville Reeds were the first to set out toward Shannon's land the next morning. Like a posse, eleven lone riders and nine creaking buckboards followed their buggy.

FORTY-SIX

It must have been Luke that decided Cole Cook had no place beneath the ground he'd abandoned, but Shannon couldn't be sure. She did know that Cole had received a pauper's crate, an unmarked grave just on the outskirts of town, and that the gravedigger was the only one to pay his respects if you could call it that. Because Jacob's funeral involved much more care and planning, it would take place at week's end.

Shannon blotted her tears with the handkerchief her mother had given her. Finding she couldn't bear to watch Emily's casket lowered into the ground, she averted her eyes. As the mourners prepared to disband, her gaze met Luke's. Suddenly realizing what Emily had meant to him, Shannon immediately turned away.

If Kate Reeds' change of heart surprised Shannon, the reaction from the rest of the women of Leeds astonished her. Each offered condolences while drawing her near, some even brushing lips against her cheek.

"If you ever need anythin', anythin' a'tall... ", Kate spoke for the others, her open-ended statement understood as she clasped Shannon's hands.

"Much obliged for your kindness," Shannon murmured and nodded goodbye to them all. She stood at the top of her lane for some time and watched her guests disappear from sight. She turned when she heard Zach's giggle, felt a smile form on her face, and hurried across the rutty path. Scooping her baby up and holding him close, she told William, "I'm much obliged to you for watching after him."

William nodded and she readily embraced the boy who had lost so much himself. Zach fussed and reached for William. Shannon reluctantly surrendered her baby, eyed her surroundings from the porch to the corral to the valley leading toward *Plains Paradise* and saw no sign of Luke Richards or his horse. Feeling both relief and disappointment, she suddenly sought distraction.

"I'll just be a moment," she told William, deciding to pick wildflowers for Emily's grave. Armed with a bouquet of wild primrose, foxglove, ironweed, asters, daisies, and black-eyed Susan, she trudged three-quarters of the steep hill before she saw Luke sitting alongside the rich mound of earth, hat in one hand, fingers of the other pressing his eyelids hard. "Oh," Shannon murmured, placing the flowers quickly at the head of the grave. "I didn't realize..."

Luke turned away but raised a hand in acknowledgement. Finding his grief transparent and contagious, she bolted, urgently seeking the seclusion of the woods. A gentle breeze in the air stirred the tree branches and the gentle rustling of the leaves brought her some solace. Shannon walked for some time, then double-backed, eventually finding herself in a far corner of the west pasture. Sitting high on a hill, she could see the house's stone chimney, the wide winding creek, and Sara nuzzling her colt. Breathing in the scents of honeysuckle and the humble aroma of wild rosebushes, she watched the squirrels play their game of tag within the small walnut grove to the north. Because of her mother's love, the land would forever belong to her and to Zach and she began to sob uncontrollably.

Shannon heard a rider and knew from his horse's snorts it was Luke. She blotted her eyes and asked, "What are you doing here?" When he didn't answer, she looked up.

Without a word, Luke leaned over his horse and extended his hands. She hesitated but eventually grabbed hold. He effortlessly pulled her from the ground and seated her in front of him. He held her for some time, his face nestled against the nape of her neck, his breathing warm and rhythmical.

"I should get back," she finally whispered.

"Good intentions," he told her, his words blowing softly against her neck. Then his lips traversed her bare skin from the nape of her neck to the crook of her shoulders, before her lips eagerly met his.

Luke drifted his horse closer to the woods edge and slid off the stallion backwards. Pulling her tenderly from the saddle, he kissed the tears from her sunburned cheeks, took the hairpin from her hair and ran his fingers through the long, loose curls as they fell. Without letting her go, he slipped a blanket from his pack, pitched it haphazardly on the pasture floor and, caressing the nape of her neck, drew her body against his. His lips lingered over hers while he eased her backwards onto the blanket, and he began to undress her slowly and methodically.

Hours later a full moon illuminated the hillside, teasing the woods with muted light, long before either Luke or Shannon was ready to let the other go.

FORTY-SEVEN

Shannon awoke the next morning and stretched her arms overhead. She smiled happily at the ceiling and wondered for a moment if she had dreamed it all. She sighed jubilantly, and Duke seemed to perceive the sound as an invitation of sorts. Pouncing on the bed, he loomed over her and drooled. Then he licked her face, and when she'd had enough of that, he nuzzled his wet nose through her tousled hair. Shannon laughed and rubbed his ears. But her thoughts quickly returned to Luke.

A new dawn revealed in-depth consequences, and she threw a forearm over her eyes. She had given her body freely. Her heart was another story. She thought about her life with Cole, her dependence on him, his dominance over her every action, her every breath, and she froze. Just as she decided to avoid Luke Richards whenever possible, Duke began to whine, his eyes seemed to plead she reconsider.

* * * *

Luke stayed in bed longer than usual, his fingers clasped behind his head, Shannon Cook's imprint on all of his senses. He remembered every inch of her, every soft and wonderful detail. But the dawn with its capacity to make men see truth so conveniently misplaced in the cover of dark caused Luke to suddenly wrench himself upright and fix haunted eyes on the photograph of his wife and child. He broke as he'd done countless times before and wondered if he was doomed to carry such overpowering grief to his grave. Now, more than ever, he was determined to forget Shannon Cook.

Getting her off his mind wasn't easy, and Luke trudged to the washbowl and submerged his face. Brutally scratching the stubble on his cheek, he managed to wrench his thoughts to Emily's killer. With Jacob Conner dead, Elijah's fate fell entirely on his shoulders. Luke decided he'd reveal Rutherford's letter to the mayor and his suspicions, demand a federal marshal if necessary, and enlist immediate judicial counsel.

William whistled happily after calling Luke to breakfast. Had God finally answered his prayers? He was certain a spark existed between Luke and Shannon, but last night when Luke returned with buttons buttoned where they ought not be and pasture grass scattered through Shannon's hair, he'd bet his bottom dollar that spark had developed into a full-blown bonfire. Now all he needed was confirmation. Convinced Luke wouldn't tell him much, he decided to pay Shannon a visit. "Luke, breakfast is atop the stove. I'm headed out to do chores," he yelled up the long staircase. He listened closely, thought he heard Luke grumble something, grabbed his hat and let the screen door swing tightly closed on its own.

William took the shorter route over the hill that connected Plains Paradise to Shannon's land rather than the road, which wound laboriously around to her lane. He commanded his horse, Midnight, into a full gallop and soon spotted Zach under a makeshift umbrella. William snickered and wondered what poor creature the baby held in his tiny but deadly grasp this time. As he propelled his spirited gelding down the steep hill, he saw Shannon already at work hoeing between rows of golden sweet corn. "Lord, almighty!" he crooned softly and thought Luke Richards the luckiest man alive. "Mornin', Mrs. Cook... Shannon," he said, dropping from his horse.

"William," she acknowledged, looking past him. "I was hoping that was only you."

William didn't think she looked all that hopeful about much of anything, which confused him and prompted him to second-guess himself.

She stepped out from between the rows and finally graced him with a slight smile. "That your horse?" she asked, appearing only courteously interested.

"Yes ma'am," he said over a sigh. He knew small talk when he heard it and that wasn't what he came for. "It's the one I've been goin' on about," he said, not bothering to summon up any exuberance himself.

"Certainly is a fine…"

"Arabian," William finished, tempted to roll his eyes.

"You have him here yesterday?"

William nodded westerly. He was getting nowhere.

"I guess I didn't notice much of anything yesterday," she explained.

William smiled sympathetically and thought about kicking his own rude self. "Had 'im for a while." He didn't see the need to remind her she'd seen Midnight a few times before that.

"He looks a little wild, you know spirited."

"Yes ma'am!"

Shannon laughed at his enthusiasm. "And that's a good thing?"

"It sure can be, don't yuh think?" He thought she looked flustered and suddenly considered she might mistake his comment for what he guessed transpired the night before. "Didn't mean nothin' by it."

"Some things best forgotten," she replied curtly.

"Honest ma'am, didn't intend no vulgarity," he stammered, surprised by the tears threatening to spill out his eyes.

Shannon softened, wondering what right she had to consider the boy part of her new resolve. "It's getting mighty warm out here already. Why don't you come inside and visit a while?"

William shrugged his shoulders.

She took a few steps toward him and touched his elbow. "That truly is a fine looking horse!"

William brightened. "I been wantin' one like this my whole life."

Shannon laughed and elbowed him softly in the ribs. "Well, that certainly is a while then."

"Wanna ride him?"

Surprised, Shannon gasped and immediately shook her head. "Never been on a creature like that. I'd probably fly right off his backside."

"Nah," William said laughing. "Just gotta get a good grip is all. And show 'im who's boss."

"Perhaps another time."

William shuffled his feet. He wanted answers. He gulped so loudly Midnight pitched his ears forward. "I know it ain't none of my concern, but I reckon I don't understand how you and Luke was so happy last night yet this mornin'..."

Shannon arched her brows. "What about this morning? Mr. Richards have something to share?"

William shook his head. "No, but it ain't like him to keep to his bed this late in the day."

"Hmm," he knew he heard Shannon mutter.

"It's just I was hopin'"

"That Luke and I would fall in love?" Shannon interrupted.

William blushed. "I reckon."

Shannon took his hands. "Grieving can play tricks on the mind, William. Can make a person do things they normally wouldn't. You understand?"

He understood he was treading on very delicate territory and that maybe he should have pried Luke for the sensitive details. "I best go see after 'im. Make sure he's not sick or somethin'." He noticed she wrung her hands, and it seemed to him that Shannon was more worried about Luke than she let on.

"Probably a right smart thing to do. Now, you let me know if you're ever in need of anything." She turned and started for the house. "That goes for Mr. Richards, too," she called over her shoulder a little less hospitably.

William swung a leg over Midnight and decided to take the long way back. Shannon's words had definitely put a whole new complexion on things. He allowed the gelding a full run down the lane and nearly collided with another rider rapidly shortening his distance. William reined his steed quickly, the Arabian's long neck craning nearly ninety degrees, and he stared dumbfounded at the most terrifying man he'd ever met.

FORTY-EIGHT

The rider, likewise, reined his horse, an imposing buckskin stallion, and spit the longest string of original profanity William had ever heard. Jack hadn't anticipated a witness. Not that it mattered. Now was not the time. When the day did come, he planned to implicate Luke Richards in Shannon Cook's death just as he had ensnared the Negro in Victoria's. This day was all about the money he hadn't recovered when he'd ransacked Victoria's shop before he'd killed her. "What's your hurry, boy, and who you be?"

"William. William Willoughby," he stuttered.

"You kin to those murdered a short-while back?"

William nodded. Jack smirked and William thought he sure had an uncanny way of expressing sympathy. "You got business with Mrs. Cook?" William asked, branding a good description of Jack to mind.

"That's right, boy," he said, crowding the Arabian, "my business."

William cowered and suddenly felt ashamed, though he was nearly certain a grown man would have done the same. He backed Midnight a good foot and wondered if it was enough. "Ain't seen you around here before, mister."

Jack threw his head back and roared. "You mean to tell me, you don't know who I am."

William shook his head and wished Luke there.

"Near everybody that knows their maker knows Jack Marsh! Where you been, underground with the night varmints?"

William felt his eyes turn to stone. "No, Iowa. When my ma and pa died I come to live with my Grandma and Grandpa."

Jack tapped a spur to the stallion's flank and the horse moved on the Arabian so unexpectedly William was nearly bucked off. "I believe it was my dear departed cousin killed those kin of yours if I'm not mistaken. Be on your way, boy, and don't look back if you got some sense."

William only pretended to ride out. He let Jack Marsh get several paces ahead, circled back, and hid behind the dense tree line. It wasn't long after, he heard Shannon yell, and he spurred Midnight toward the house. Within five yards of the front porch, he heard her tell Jack to get off her land and saw she had the carbine ready to back up her request.

Jack heard William ride up and had him in his sights before William could even consider what he'd look like with a hole through his head.

"Put it down, Jack!" William witnessed Shannon order in a voice he wouldn't have recognized, otherwise. "Do it! Or I'll blow your fool head clean off!"

William froze and kept his eyes on the muscular devil. To his surprise, Jack didn't so much as blink at her threat and seemed more amused than nervous.

Shannon took a step towards him and cocked the hammer. "And if you don't think I won't, there's an unmarked grave just outside of town might change your sorry opinion."

Marsh dropped from his horse and menacingly clubbed his right foot hard on the first porch step. "What's his business here?" he asked, jutting a thumb in William's direction.

"Leave him out of this."

"Just a simple question."

"Then none of yours would be my answer."

Before William could blink, Marsh lurched forward, grabbed the Sharps by the barrel and tossed it across the porch. "Got some men coming by tomorrow to see you off this land. No need for packing up anything except that bastard's seed, since everything but belongs to the bank."

Shannon waited until he threw a leg over his saddle. "Guess you haven't heard about the new telegraph office over in Fenwick."

William watched Marsh's thin lips practically disappear and his posture stiffen.

"The governor probably knows the truth by now, knows I have every red cent due on that deed. And now there's nothing you can do to get me off my land."

"Well, we'll just see about that," Jack hissed.

"You'll probably find his writ on your desk by morning, maybe a federal marshal inside the bank to enforce it, too."

He turned to face her and she watched his brutal eyes harden. "So much can happen in such a short span of time. Just ask the boy here."

Shannon's eyes darted from the stallion to the Arabian. Jack whipped his moody beast into a full charge before William could move, get a good grip on his reins, or dig his heels deep into the stirrups. The Arabian, in his hasty retreat, spun sideways, throwing William in the opposite direction of the spin. Nearly missing the well pump handle on his impromptu landing, William suffered a split to his lower lip from an inconveniently located rock. Only slightly dazed, he touched a finger to his lip, grimaced, and watched the devil brutally spur the buckskin and disappear over the hill. Then he asked about his horse.

"Sit still, William!" Shannon said, looking him over. When he continued to fidget, she told him, "Look yonder!"

William settled once he saw the Arabian returning, but his words caught in his throat when he spoke. "I thought he'd surely kill my horse. You should stay clear of him."

"I'll do just that once this business is over."

"If it were me, I'd start right this very minute."

"Let me get something for that lip," Shannon fussed.

William shook his head. "It only hurts when you touch it."

Shannon chuckled and withdrew her hand. "If you're up to it, I'd appreciate you staying with Zach while I go into town and pay off the deed. The time's up tomorrow and I won't give that no-account any excuse for pushing me off my land."

William shook his head. "I best get Luke."

"You best not," Shannon said firmly. "I'm not afraid of Jack Marsh."

"You should be," William said, grabbing her forearm. "That's a bad man to cross if ever I seen one."

* * * *

"Luke!" William called, tossing the reins to the wind and vaulting from his horse once he reached home. He searched the house first, then the barn, and finally the bunkhouse.

"What's got your tail feathers up?" Lance asked and set his cup down.

"When'd you get back and where's Luke?"

"Well, howdy-do to you, too! Got in a couple of hours ago, thanks for askin'. Luke said he was goin' into town and then out to meet the others collectin' the rest of 'em cattle ole Red had hidden in Fenwick."

"Thought Red told the sheriff wasn't but fifteen."

Lance wrinkled up his nose and grunted. "You ever bet money a rattler been treaded on wouldn't bite?"

"Course not."

Lance stared intently and William sensed by the Foreman's expression, this required some logic on his part. "Reckon you mean ole Red's no more than a snake and can't be trusted."

"Amen," Lance said, ruffling William's hair. "Now, what'd yuh want Luke for and in such an almighty hurry?"

"It's Mrs. Cook. She traded some harsh words with some right dangerous lookin' sort name a Marsh, Jack Marsh said he was."

William thought Lance took on a whole new interest.

"She did, did she? What about?"

"Keepin' her land is what."

"He still fiddlin' to that tune?" Luke asked as his spurs clanked across the bunkhouse floor.

William nodded as if his neck was on springs. "Yes, sir, and Mrs. Cook ain't sense enough to accommodate him with the proper dose a fear."

"The men gone on to Fenwick, already?" Luke asked Lance.

William couldn't say for sure if Lance nodded. But he was certain Luke and Lance had shared a grin over Mrs. Cook's trouble. "Ain't nothin' funny 'bout it! She's got her mind set on ridin' into town alone and makin' trouble."

Lance let out a low whistle and winked at Luke. "Now don't she always. You plannin' on sittin' this one out?"

William watched Luke's hand fly to his forehead and then slide over both eyes and down his cheeks. He got the impression Luke wished himself both invisible and deaf.

Lance grew serious and hunched his shoulders, his elbows staking a heavy claim on the long table. "Emily paid a right heavy price for that land." The formidable former gunfighter suddenly lowered his head, and William's eyes widened. He'd never seen the stone-cold foreman express that kind of emotion.

Luke elbowed William to get his attention and gestured outside. Lance's feelings for Emily were sonnet caliber, and Luke could see he struggled to keep his grief bottled-up. Once outdoors, he cornered William. "When's she headed out?"

"Straight away from the sound a things."

"Ah, shit!" Luke said, whipping himself in a circle.

William made the mistake of touching his lip, and Luke came in for a closer look. "What happen there?"

"T'aint nothin'," William muttered.

"Jack Marsh put a hand to you?"

"Just spooked my horse is all and I took a fall." William saw the rage trespass Luke's eyes and wished he'd kept his mouth shut.

FORTY-NINE

Luke sat mounted in a grove of sycamores waiting for Shannon to pass. When she did and didn't discover him, he puffed his cheeks and wondered how she would manage alone in such unsettled territory. He laid back an ill-equipped posse's length, her buckboard making so much racket he whistled *Home on the Range* without fear of discovery. Once near the outskirts, she brought the rickety mess to a complete halt and stepped down, the baby in one arm, a parcel of some kind in the other. Curious, but not wanting to give away his position, he stayed put, took the LeMaire binoculars from his saddlebag, and trained them on her activity. "Well, I'll be," he whispered as he watched her lay a bouquet of wildflowers on a grave he assumed was her husband's. She lingered there and he suspected she prayed, which, from all he'd heard about Cole Cook, was a shameful waste of time.

Luke soon grew impatient but wasn't surprised she apparently believed the piece of shit required a Sunday sermon. He dropped his stallion's reins, encouraged his horse to graze, and gnawed on a piece of jerky he'd also pulled from his pack. Even after she climbed up and took the reins, he leisurely finished his holdings. It wasn't as if he didn't know where she was heading.

Once in town, he hitched his horse in front of the barbershop. To his surprise instead of going inside the bank once hitching the mare, she crossed the road toward him with a determined and, admittedly, somewhat off-putting gait.

"Haven't seen hide nor hair of you since that night we spent under the stars and now you're tracking me like a hungry coyote!"

Luke gaped surprise, scanned their surroundings, and noticed the finer ladies of Leeds snickering behind gloved hands. Shannon seemed oblivious. "Calm down, Stormy-Sue, the boy asked me to look after yuh. Woulda come himself if I hadn't."

"Bless that boy for his worry, but I surely don't need your help, Luke Richards. All I need from you I already got and I expect, to your credit, that'll last me a good while."

A smattering of gloved applause and louder giggling reached Luke's ears. He eventually managed to close his mouth and soon wished he'd kept it that way.

"Well, you have nothing to say?" she taunted.

"Reckon you have me at a disadvantage, Mrs. Cook. 'Bout now all I'm seein' is them stars," Luke said grinning. "And I'm startin' to feel a little like a hungry coyote."

Shannon pointed toward Ruby's bawdyhouse. "All the rabbits you want can be found right over yonder!"

Luke's grin grew. "But this particular coyote is just that."

"I believe I've had enough of your Saturday-night-talk. Now skedaddle and leave me be."

Luke feigned disappointment. "Not exactly charitable to wait till a feller's brandin' iron is sizzlin' then throw water on it, Mrs. Cook."

Shannon laughed deceitfully. "Take your own advice, Mr. Richards, preferably to the next county."

Luke tipped his hat sarcastically, but she'd already turned her back. "What could she possibly be doin' now?" he whispered when Shannon disappeared into Doc Murphy's office. When she came out without Zach, he had his answer. He watched her, despite his own objection to doing just that, and admitted she cut a fine figure, unusual yet stimulating, in jeans, boots, and the flannel shirt William had donated. It was a good thing he had come to town to observe her because any other task would have made for a wasted trip.

First, he heard Kate Reeds unique and brash voice rise. A blink later, he saw Shannon sail through the front door of the bank, landing solidly against the boardwalk on her backside. Before she could get up, Jack Marsh pulled her roughly to her feet and shoved something down her shirtfront. Rage blurred much of what transpired immediately after and Luke set his feet in motion.

Kate Reeds tackled Jack like a wolverine to an antelope, and Luke didn't need her words to trickle downstream secondhand to know what she'd said. The mayor, her husband, often relied on this peculiar and unattractive quality when a megaphone was in short supply during a town meeting. "She's got what's due, now give her, her paper!" she repeated.

Jack shook all two-hundred pounds off like a bird would a mite. Luke had never known Kate to bow under the heaviest of obstacles. He wasn't surprised when she went for him again. This time she had help, and he decided it safe to sit back and enjoy the show. Until Jack went for his gun. Luke drew both Peacemakers as he tore down the boardwalk, the storefronts hugging his backside in proper succession. Jack in his sights, Luke returned his guns to leather when Jack simply shook all four women off, retreated inside the bank, and pulled the shade.

"See this here," Shannon boomed to the crowd and waved a wad of treasury notes through the air. "I got every bit due on my deed, this day, the sixteenth of August 1874! I ask you all to bear witness."

The crowd chanted agreement and waited for Kate to speak. "Jack Marsh thinks he owns this town and maybe he does because he suffocated his own mother, he did, and did he find himself at the end of a hangman's noose?"

"No!" The crowd chanted.

"Some say he bullied Jonas Rutherford into an early grave and did he lose a night's sleep?"

Again, the mob crooned dissention, surged, and moved on the bank. The door opened and Travis Parker flew out. His voice and hands shook with equal trepidation, but he managed an acceptable decibel. "Now folks, this here's federal property. Anyone of you make an advance, we got every right to defend it till the marshals arrive." Travis glanced toward the bank and then told Kate privately, "That man is the devil's own. You don't do what I say he's promised me the first bullet."

"You best remind that mudsill nob that my husband is the mayor, and he's already called for a federal marshal to see about that poor hornswoggled Nigra! Mark my word Jack Marsh is gonna swing from the gallows before many more sunrises!" she said, poking a solid finger to Travis' vest before addressing the crowd. "Let's all go home! By sundown tomorrow, the only plan will've hatched is ours."

A few male stragglers, anxious to stake a reputation, chanted their disagreement but soon dismantled, most preferring the saloon.

"Don't you worry none, child," Kate told Shannon. "Must be near half-hundred eyes can testify your case if it comes to it. I'll make certain Abel sends word to the governor and advises him of Jack's tomfoolery."

Shannon thanked her and the four other women still milling about.

"Luke don't give up easy," Clarissa Mayfield said, nodding north.

The others began to giggle, and Shannon's gaze followed their collective one outside Doc Murphy's.

"Fool," Shannon muttered, though she was relieved he'd remained behind as she thought it best to give him her dowry for safekeeping.

Clarissa saddled up close. "That true? You and Luke..."

"My life isn't a sideshow," Shannon interrupted. "You insist on the particulars, you'll have to ask him."

"Humph! I thought we were friends."

When Shannon realized Clarissa's sincerity, she reconsidered. "It's fair to say my lips haven't worn a bigger smile before or since," she volunteered.

"And here we were thinkin' he was quite the gentleman, a real thoroughbred," Kate teased.

"Oh, he's a real thoroughbred," Shannon smiled shamelessly, "just not in the traditional sense."

Cackling ensued and Shannon regretted the whole sorry disclosure.

Jenny Saunders appeared confused. "You sayin' he's NOT a gentleman?"

Shannon grinned. "That's exactly what I'm saying."

FIFTY

Lucy served Mika breakfast and shared no words with him, as was their custom. She often wondered why she had remained but knew the answer. In the beginning, she had no choice, despite the Emancipation Proclamation; Mika Leeds lived by his own laws. Though he had softened considerably over the years, particularly since the death of his beloved daughter, Polly, and wouldn't stand in her way, she was just too damn old and tired, and smart enough to know what little promise even this new world held for an elderly Negro woman. She tended to Mika's shirt, wiping the spilt coffee from it and then his chin, the stroke wreaking havoc on the majority of his facial nerves. She had witnessed his pride, like most of his functions, dwindle little by little and somehow in that degrading process she had come to care about him.

"Humph, humph," she thought aloud, remembering the talk among the help. Most considered Mistuh Mika 'almost human now'. She wiped the oatmeal away, too, and the lingering gratitude in his eyes didn't go unnoticed. She looked away, determined he never sense her pity. It was obvious his health had further declined since Victoria's visit. "Yuh gots ta eat, Mistuh!" she told him when he intentionally dropped the spoon in his bowl.

Mika shook his head and brushed his palm across her hand. He startled when one of the maids burst into the room.

"Celey!" Lucy chastised. "Yuh knows better den bargin' in a room, scarin' the daylights outa a soul!" The young maid's voice hit its upper octaves, and Lucy couldn't understand a word she'd said. "Mercy, child! Wud yuh prattlin' on 'bout? Rein in some dat shindy! Lawdy, dat be da longest string a pure foolishness ah's ever did hear come outa one mouth."

"Word come, Miss Lucy. Word!" Celey squealed, dancing from one foot to the other.

"Wud word dat be, child? And ah's warnin' yuh, id best be

from sweet Jesus 'imself, steada yuh disturbin' Mistuh's table wid some simpleton's twaddle!"

"Miss Victoria! She been killed out in Leeds, Miss Lucy! As sure as I be standin' here, she been murdered!"

Mika clutched his chest, his skin turning a duskier tone than even his normal. Lucy knelt at his side. With both hands slicing the air rampantly, she screamed, "Fetch da doctor, hear, child? Fetch 'im quick!"

Mika forced a hand in the air and shook his head. He pushed off the table and stood. Bewildered and unable to persuade him to sit back down, Lucy followed him to the master suite.

"Dat be horrible news! Jus horrible, Mistuh Mika!" she said, steadying him along the way.

He put a surprisingly strong hand on her shoulder, and she knew to listen carefully. Although his stunted English was becoming increasingly easier for her to decipher, it still presented a challenge. When he finished, she could feel her eyes widen, and keeping her opinion to herself was no longer an option.

"Id a fool's journey, dat wud id be, train or no train! Humph! Leeds town, is id? Doze people prob'ly got a bounty on yer head. And don't be cuttin' me a look like ah's don't knows m'place neither," she warned, wagging a finger. "Da good Lawd knows ah's speaks da truth. 'Em people got right reason ta yearn fer yer ol feet ta twitch da opposite end a rope. Dey prob'ly won't even cut yer sorry carcass down neither. Jus let id bake out dere in dat nasty ol sun till id shrivels up like Injun corn."

Mika grunted a few loud words, and Lucy grudgingly began packing his bags. When she finished, she whispered somberly, "Ah's git Jeramiah ta fetch da carriage." She started toward the door with the bags and turned back. "Mistuh Mika, please stay put! T'aint nuttin' in dis ol wor'd gonna brang Miss Victoria back." She waited for some kind of reply but didn't get one. "Ain't yuh gonna say nuttin'? Ah's been wid yuh all dese years and nuttin'?"

Mika took a key from his vest, prolonging his touch as he

pressed it to her palm. Then she thought he told her if he didn't return to take it to the bank.

Several times, she fought the impulse to run after him and try to convince him of the danger he'd face. But she knew when he made up his mind there was no changing it. He refused to allow some of the bigger men to go along, and when she told him goodbye she knew it would be for good. She stood at the window and watched the carriage leave the grounds. Brushing a tear from her eye, she whispered, "Mistuh Mika, yuh been dead fer a long time now. Yer body jus don't got sense anuf ta knows id."

FIFTY-ONE

Certain Shannon was no longer in jeopardy, Luke decided to wet his whistle and boost his disposition. Moments after he arrived in the saloon and took his first sip, Shannon charged the winged doors and asked to speak to him outside. He wasn't the only man that nearly choked on his whiskey.

"Awe ma'am, you can't come in here," Irving enlightened her after catching a glass he'd nearly dropped.

Shannon smirked. "Well, unless I'm some kind of mirage I believe I've done just that." Then with a hand on each hip, she stared Luke down. "Either come outside, Luke Richards, or we can rub elbows at the bar. It don't make no never mind to me."

Luke felt his scalp tighten. "Don't put that bottle away," he told Irving, "and, dependin' on her flash, one might not be enough."

Once outside, he grabbed her by the arm and led her into a narrow alley. " "Let loose of me," she yelled, breaking away. "What's the matter? You don't cotton to being followed around like a wanted man or a prized pig?"

"I told you I only done it for William."

"Guess that's the God's truth. Didn't see you even twitch when Jack Marsh threw me in the street."

"You don't need no man lookin' after you, remember? 'Sides, that reckonin' come as a total surprise to you? There's only one way to deal with the likes of Jack Marsh." Luke stationed his hands at his hips and loomed over her. "Ain't no reasonin' with a man like that, particularly with your shared history."

"What'd you know about it?" Shannon shook her head in disgust. "This town's plumb full of nothing but tittle-tattle!"

"Know enough to know you're playin' with dynamite and you don't have the good sense to know it. And look at you in those britches! Who do yuh think yuh are, Calamity Jane? Next thing we know you'll be uprootin' that baby a yers and joinin'

Bill Hickok's Wild West show!"

Shannon snarled and rubbed her arm. "Jack Marsh don't seem to be the only one with a short fuse. Put a hand on me again, Luke Richards, and you'll dearly pay."

Luke held his hands up in surrender and backed away. "What's so all-fired important?"

"Hold this for me," she said, pushing an envelope toward him. "Inside's everything due on my land."

He took the envelope, raised a pant leg, and packed it in his boot scabbard. Then he turned to leave. "Gonna be gettin' on night soon," he said over his shoulder, and she sensed a true sadness in his tone. "You best be headed back."

Shannon touched his elbow, and when he faced her, the decadent look in his eyes made her blood simmer. Would it be so wrong to spend time with such a man because she desired it, not because her existence depended on it? "Bound to be a beautiful night," she said, moving on him, stretching up onto her toes, and fisting his vest for support. "Nice breeze," she whispered in his ear, "probably lots of stars out," she added, purposely blowing the words slow and soft against his lips. "Especially up on that hill."

Luke swallowed hard and could feel sweat drops form on his forehead. His hands damp, his heart racing, his mouth was suddenly too dry to respond, his willpower no match for a woman like Shannon Cook.

FIFTY-TWO

"You know the boy's gonna be expectin' me to make an honest woman outa you now," Luke teased come sunup, tenderly raking his hand over her naked body.

"'I expect he will," Shannon whispered, turning in to him.

Luke pulled his head back, looked into her eyes, and arched his brows.

"Don't worry yourself none. I'm surely not planning on throwing a lasso over you, Luke Richards. Your company now and again suits me just fine."

Luke flipped over onto his back. "Expect you'll ever change your mind?" he asked, staring at the ceiling.

Shannon hesitated, puzzled by his reaction. "I think things are right as a trivet just as they are."

"I'll tell the boy you turned me down then."

"You'll do no such thing!" Shannon squealed and jumped on top of him.

Luke grinned and pulled her down until her lips met his. "I'll tell him, to you I'm nothin' but a fast trick or a bull driven from the chute, rode hard, and put away wet."

"Consider me bucked then," Shannon said, laughing and sliding clear. He grabbed for her, but she jumped out of his reach. "William's sure to have his hands full before long, unless the boy can grow teats," she explained. "Zach should be howling any minute now."

Luke lunged for her again. "I know how he feels."

* * * *

By the time, Shannon made breakfast for William, Luke, and the few ranch hands not already out on the range and tidied up the Willoughby home, it was nearly noon. She loaded Zach in the buckboard and glanced about for Luke.

"He went into town," William said, his grin revealing nearly every tooth. "Marshal's supposed to come today," the boy told her, suddenly rearranging the dirt with his toe and pouting. "A course he wouldn't let me tag along."

Shannon arched a brow. "I never heard Dixie-doodle about any of that."

"On account of that Nigra," William offered. "Luke don't wanna see him hang."

Shannon felt her eyes glaze over and thought about Emily. "Nor me. That man's as straight as an arrow."

"Yuh know'd him?"

Shannon nodded. "He worked for my father," she said, her eyes sweeping the ground. She stopped there, unwilling to share memories surrounding the numerous whippings Elijah endured at the hands of Mika's Foreman, and usually more for sport than punishment. "I'd best be on my way," she said instead and forced the corners of her mouth into a smile.

William positioned himself in front of Sara and grinned as if he'd just cheated the devil. "Reckon Zach'll be over later?"

Shannon's eyes narrowed playfully. She ignored his inquiry and set out for home.

* * * *

"Mr. Richards," Kate shouted, catching Luke outside the sheriff's office. Winded, she wagged a finger and attempted to catch her breath. "Marshal's been here already and told that dimwitted new sheriff to set the Nigra loose."

Luke whistled his amazement, figuring a judge the only one to make such a weighty decision.

"Said there weren't enough evidence and gave Saunders the dickens for holdin' 'im this long. Mentioned somethin' about times a changin' and he best be prepared."

"What about Marsh?"

"Marshal went after him. Searched the bank. Even the Chinaman's den. Travis said he lit out shortly after the bank opened. Jack's whore said he was cursin' when he seen the marshal come in town. Beat her somethin' awful before he took out."

"He got any kin 'round these parts?"

Kate shook her head. "It's like I told the marshal, only kin we know'd about was his mother and that no-account cousin yuh kilt."

"You happen to mention Red Morton to the marshal?"

"As sure as I'm standin' here!"

Luke nodded and chewed thoughtfully on his bottom lip. "Jack'd be a fool to stick around Leeds," he thought aloud, "a bigger fool to head over Texas-way."

"That he would. I seen the marshal stop at the telegraph office and it don't take a lot of imagination to figure he was requestin' more expert guns, prob'ly Texas Rangers and an Injun scout too."

"Sheriff in?"

Kate chortled and puffed out her cheeks. "That's part of my reason for waylayin' you, Luke. Abel agrees with the resta the town it's high-time for a change. He's got Saunders in his office as we speak and that other nitwit, too. Abel's gonna offer you the job. Nearly the whole town's behind you," she added hopeful.

Luke shook his head and trained resentful eyes on her. "You consider that an honor, you'd be the only one a us. That's a death sentence is what it is."

Kate took a step toward him and puffed out her chest. "You look here, Luke Richards! This town lost an honest man when we put Jacob Conner in the ground..." She stopped there. Luke had made his point.

"I'll think on it," he eventually offered, tipped his hat, and stepped into the street.

FIFTY-THREE

Luke considered the offer, and just about the time he'd made up his mind to reject it, he considered it again, even though he'd managed to keep a low profile since the Cheyenne's involvement in the Bozeman war and preferred to keep it that way. The conflict and tension growing stronger between the tribe and the white men who continued to desecrate the Cheyenne's sacred hunting grounds, Luke had been prepared to fight alongside his Indian brothers. Chief Red Cloud, however, had other ideas; fearing for Luke's safety, the chief suggested he leave Wyoming and never return. Having developed a strong and eternal bond with the Tsitsistas, Luke was hurt but more angered by the unfair treatment of the Cheyenne. From that point on, Luke developed a dislike both for the army and lawmen in general, and emptied his six-shooter anytime he happened upon renegade soldiers raiding a sanctioned Indian village without provocation.

By the time Luke had reached Missouri, he'd developed both his keen marksmanship and a turncoat reputation. With the United States Army forever trying to put a name to his face, he decided to hide out in Missouri's unsettled territory. Finding himself affected by kindhearted Samuel and Mary Willoughby and their promise of steady work, he thought it time to, once again, put down roots.

Jacob Conner had adjusted Luke's attitude, too, to an immense degree and, after much debate, he decided to carry on Conner's tradition. Lance Tucker also played a role in his decision. Luke had kept his suspicions about Jack Marsh's involvement in Emily's murder under wraps, because he knew if Lance found out there would be no stopping him. Lance had confided in him, once their friendship grew, that Texas had a bounty on his head for a man he'd killed in self-defense. Gunplay with a politically connected man like Jack Marsh would surely get Tucker hanged. But a sheriff apprehending a suspected murderer dead or alive would hardly warrant scrutiny.

His mind made up, he arrived at the Mayor's office and accepted the appointment. The ceremony was brief, quiet, and unappreciated by Sheriff Saunders... until the pursuit of Jack Marsh came up.

Mayor Reeds rubbed his baldhead and kept his eyes on the floor. "I prob'ly shoulda brought this to light before I swore you in," Abel said sheepishly. "That marshal, who come to town this morning's, just been found. Shot dead not five miles north a here."

"Who found 'im?"

"Don't see what difference that makes, Luke."

"Don't know why it would be a secret."

"Red Morton," the mayor reluctantly replied.

Luke arched both brows and stared at the mayor hard.

"Now, I know what you're thinkin', Luke. Red's always been in cahoots with Marsh. But he swears that's why he came in, 'cause he figured fingers would be pointin' his way."

"He thinks Marsh did it?" Luke asked. "You think Marsh did it?"

"What other possible reason would anyone have for gunnin' down a federal marshal?" Abel chuckled. "It's not as if we have the likes of Billy the Kid 'round these parts."

"Where's Red now?"

"Hold up at Ruby's. He figures Marsh will be expectin' him to gun for him if need be, and he wants no part of it."

Luke laughed. "Draws the line at cattle rustlin', does he?"

"There be all degrees of sinners, I reckon."

"He got any idea where Jack might be headed?"

"No, accordin' to him. And I believe him. Marsh was born and raised here, ain't never left to my knowledge. No one knows what he might be thinkin'. Personally, I don't think he'll cross too many states. My guess is he'll head north, maybe Iowa."

"Any word on the telegraph the marshal sent?"

Abel Reeds shook his head. "We're on our own for the time

being. You wanna wait for reinforcements?"

Luke spread his hand, a thumb and forefinger raking his face from temples to chin. "A lot of ground to cover if he's had that kind of head start. Don't reckon there's much chance of gettin' a posse together?"

Abel blew out a bellyful of air. "For Jack Marsh? Not likely."

"Well, no sense in sittin' 'round here. I'll do some scoutin' before sundown and see you in the mornin'."

"Alright, Luke... I mean, Sheriff." Abel smiled warmly and extended his hand.

FIFTY-FOUR

Luke rode north until night came on, then double-backed. He hadn't seen any fresh tracks and thought daylight would greatly benefit further investigation. Nearly at the Willoughby's and having come in due south of Shannon's land, he completed his nightly sentinel, covering Plains Paradise's two-hundred-acre circumferences within an hour, and chose to call it a night.

"It just a coincidence you finally ride in after I done all the chores?" William teased from the porch.

Luke smiled. "'Em boys aren't back from Okie yet?"

William jumped from the porch. "You know darn good and well they ain't," he said and attempted to stroke Thunder's mane. Luke's horse snorted a warning and William jumped back.

"Boy, you know better than that."

"What's wrong with that horse a yers, anyway?" William asked, his cheeks flushing embarrassment.

Luke grinned. "He's mighty particular I reckon."

"I think he's just plumb mean like you," William teased.

"That's right," Luke agreed, dropped from his horse, and ruffled the boy's hair. "Got grub served up?"

William rolled his eyes. "Stew, leftover from last night. That suit you?"

Luke wrinkled his nose and brushed his tongue across his palate. "That mess is still ranklin' my insides."

"We could go into town," William suggested excitedly.

Luke shook his head. "I'll be goin' in there soon enough."

"Why's that?"

"I was gonna wait and let Lance in on the news first but reckon I'm a little more partial to you anyhow." Luke waited. "Well, aren't you gonna ask?"

William grinned. "I'm still thinkin' on my rankin'."

* * * *

Jack crept on her as she lay sleeping, the floor creaking a warning with nearly each of his steps. He had decided to club her dog to death rather than risk alerting her with his gun's discharge. But never encountering the animal and assuming it left out to hunt, Jack smiled smugly and took his time studying every inch of her. Focusing on every deviant detail surrounding his long-awaited fantasy, the excitement quickly got the best of him, and he leaped onto the bed, straddled her, and simultaneously placed a sweaty oppressive palm over her mouth.

Shannon's eyes sprang open and she attempted to focus. Only one man had a hand of such scale. Only one man's scent brought such malevolence to mind, and she managed to sink in a few teeth.

Impervious, Jack hissed, "That's right, it's me." He wrestled her hands overhead, tying one then the other to the bedposts with a thin leather strap. Each time she tried to shove a knee into his groin he slapped her hard. Without another word, he ripped her nightclothes off, tearing bits of her flesh away in the process.

Shannon fought him hard, kicking and writhing beneath him. Pushing her kneecap from his groin, he promised this, his last threat, would be her final warning. Forced to breathe only his hot breath she wrenched her head sideways.

"Chances are after this, if I were to let you live, you'd be following me around like a love-sick hound dog." Tracking one side of her face with his tongue, he entered her hard and drove her head into the headboard. She screamed beneath his hand, and her pain only excited him more.

The fourth time her head ricocheted off the headboard, her screams abated, and she bit his chest so violently he withdrew. He fisted her, widening a gash in her lower lip. Then he described in detail what would happen to Zach should she continue to resist. She immediately obeyed and attempted to erase the visual of coyotes fighting over her baby's limbs.

Despite her compliance, Jack continued to beat her, his nightlong ritual of whipping and rape ending only for short intervals, either long enough for Shannon to regain consciousness or him to fill his lungs with opiate. Each time she blacked out, he drenched her with water from the pitcher at her bedside.

By the time dawn arrived, his body could no longer fulfill his mind's fancy. Certain he'd heard her take her last breath, Jack spat on her face, now barely recognizable, and watched the excrement slowly worm its way down her cut and disfigured cheek to the torn, blood-soaked bedding. He considered wiping the gore from his body, but walked to the window instead and admired himself in the morning light. Once dressed, he took one more look at her and laughed satisfaction. Then he closed his eyes and, drawing in a long contented breath, he committed this, his greatest gratification, to memory. He paused at the crib and considered suffocating her whimpering infant. Jack lingered there for several minutes, feeling neither compassion nor malice, and painfully recalled fragments from his childhood. Soon after, he left the room whistling.

One foot nearly in a stirrup, he heard rustling behind the house. He assumed it was the dog returning. Not wanting to waste a bullet, he quickly mounted the buckskin, whisked the Winchester from its scabbard, and planned to deliver a deadly blow with the butt should the opportunity arise.

FIFTY-FIVE

Mika Leeds rode the borrowed horse; a timid and cautious filly, within twenty feet of the house, tugged at the gold chain looped around his belt, and produced a tarnished pocket watch. He struggled with the worn clasp but eventually managed to open it. Staring intently at the woman's photograph inside, he mumbled, "Victoria" and fixed his wet eyes on the full moon.

As he drew closer to the house, he realized he had heard a baby's cries. He listened and when the child's wails weren't addressed, his white shaggy brows puckered, and he dismounted as quickly as he could. He struggled with the holster but eventually managed to pluck the old Colt Walker free. "Cook," he yelled when he encountered a man around front on horseback. "Where you off to and where's my daughter?" he demanded, his inquiry garbled.

Jack laughed and lit his pipe. Mimicking Mika's diction until it bored him, he said, "We-ell, if it is-e-e-ent old man Leeds as I live and breathe."

Mika's gape evidenced his surprise and he squinted past the small flame. "Marsh?"

"Spit that out just fine, now didn't you?"

"That blood?" Mika managed, gesturing toward Jack's hand. When Jack didn't answer, Mika trembled and attempted to jerk the old 44-caliber upward.

Jack chuckled. "Now what you gonna do with that old man?"

"Something I should have done long ago," Jack thought he heard him say.

Jack grasped the pipe hard with his left hand, a disclosure that would have given Mika Leeds the upper hand at an earlier point in his life. Jack levered the Winchester, his single blast gutting then launching Mika Leeds backwards a good yard.

* * * *

Luke couldn't sleep. This new opportunity offered him a financial security he'd never known. Although he could still work the range as well as the younger men, there were nights he laid awake switching positions to ease more than one ache or pain. Not so long ago, he'd come to the conclusion his was an occupation not guaranteed an older man.

His unexpected good fortune drastically changed his perspective. No longer could he excuse his reluctance to marry due to means. He'd finally come to grips with his great loss, realizing now that loving another was no more a betrayal to Amanda than utilizing a viable limb following the objectionable removal of another. His mind made up, he smiled and hoped he could persuade Shannon.

Shortly after dawn, he surrendered to the notion sleep wasn't to be his. Before he had both boots on, he heard a dog's bark. Luke grumbled the distance from bedside to window and was surprised when he saw Duke. "What the hell," he offered to no one in particular.

"Luke," William called from his room. "You hear that?"

Luke considered asking the kid if he'd ever known him to be deaf. Instead, he replied, "It's Shannon Cook's bloodhound."

"You sure? 'Cause the Walters have one looks just like it."

"I'm sure boy!" Luke snapped. Various scenarios flooded his sleep-deprived brain and all of them scared the hell out of him. He quickly pulled on his shirt and heard William clomp down the stairs.

"Somethin's got into 'im, Luke," he heard William yell beneath his window. "Just look at 'im. He won't stop and he's got a hold of my pant leg but good!"

Luke tore down the stairs and sailed out the door. He called Duke, and the dog immediately shadowed him. "I'm headed over there!" he told William and whistled for his horse. Immediately, he heard Thunder's hooves crushing ground.

"Ain't you even gonna saddle 'im?" William called through the stallion's dust.

Forcing his fascination with Luke's horsemanship aside,

William scrambled to saddle Midnight and rode out after him.

* * * *

By the time he arrived, Luke was carrying Shannon from the house. "Get the buckboard, boy, and hurry!"

William gaped and nearly vomited. He had never seen so much blood on anyone left to draw a breath. He thought he also knew why Luke had draped the bloodstained quilt over her.

"Now, William!"

William forced bile down. "But what about Zach?"

"He's fine for the time bein'. Now, go!"

William considered Thunder and muttered "Oh, hell no!" Aside from the fact, he thought the horse a cantankerous pain in the backside the stallion bore no tack. He sprang atop Midnight instead, tapped a toe to the Arabian's flank, and galloped toward the barn.

After many attempts to revive Shannon failed, Luke pressed his face to the quilt and prayed, for once in his young life, the kid would be swift. He teetered a few times and just as he considered seating himself on the porch step, he heard the buckboard's rickety advance. "You fetch Zach while I settle her in and be quick!" Luke demanded and noticed the boy's face was as white as down.

William quickened his pace toward the house but called over his shoulder, "There's an old dead man over yonder."

FIFTY-SIX

"Keep her still if she comes around," Luke anxiously told William after encouraging Midnight into a steady but aggressive canter. "And keep a tight grip on that baby."

"He's hungry, Luke. He won't stop cryin'."

Luke searched his pocket and found a strip of jerky. "Take this," he said, shoving it over his shoulder, "but don't let him get a hold on it."

"How's he gonna eat it then?"

"They invite you back to the schoolhouse next year, boy?"

"Yeah," William said and wondered what that had to do with it.

"How's Mrs. Cook doin'?"

"Looks the same. Ain't opened her eyes."

Luke pressed William's horse harder. "She breathin'?"

"I think so."

"What kinda answer is that!"

"Yes! Yes, she's breathin'."

"That dead man, what'd he look like?"

"He was real old. Had white hair and…"

"And what?"

"A big hole through his innards."

"Regret you had to see that."

"No more than me," William said and Luke knew he was thinking about Samuel and Mary. "You think the Injuns killed that man and did all this to Mrs. Cook?"

The identity of the dead man no longer on his mind, Luke's nostrils flared, but he bit his tongue. Even though the boy's perceptions were a result of prejudiced accounts by ignorant men, he still had an overwhelming desire to educate him. "No more than I reckon this horse can sprout wings like Pegasus."

"That horse weren't real, not like Injuns."

"There a particular reason you got your mind set on Indians bein' responsible?" Luke asked, feeling his anger rekindle.

"Reckon yer right," William reconsidered. "Injuns woulda burnt everythin' to the ground and either kilt Zach or took 'im."

"Mrs. Cook even so much as twitched?" Luke prodded, needing an abrupt subject change as much as an update.

"No."

"Baby still gnawin' on that jerky?"

"Yes sir! He's having a grand time with it. I was thinkin' on it, and Jessica's Aunt Clarissa just had her a baby this summer. Reckon she wouldn't mind takin' on Zach, here."

Luke tightened his grip on the reins and wished the boy would shut his yap. Apparently, the kid thought Shannon as good as dead. Figuring no response would encourage more prattle from the boy, he pondered further oration. Not in time.

"No sir, bet she wouldn't mind at all. She's got 'em out mosta the time anyway, least that's what Jessica's brother says. One of 'em flappin' in the wind whilst her baby suckles the other."

Surprised and nearly amused, Luke thought the boy might be onto something. With the best of luck, he anticipated Shannon still faced a lengthy recovery. "Flappin' in the wind is it?"

"Yep, flappin' it be, when it ain't peekin' outa her pinafore lookin' all pitiful and lonely. Yes sir, two teats; one baby. Just makes sense."

"Tell you what, boy. When we get to town, you go fetch this Aunt Clarissa and ask her."

William grew quiet, and Luke wished he could see his face. A few minutes later with a tone as serious as an undertaker's, he told Luke, "Reckon I'll take Zach with me, least she think I'm up to a trick." William hadn't taken his eyes off Shannon the entire time. He'd put his ear to her heart repeatedly, even managed to repeat the *Lord's Prayer* silently while occupying Luke. He'd done his best to distract the man he'd come to think of as his father. He'd nearly ran out of clever things to say and was relieved when they reached town. He leaned over and softly kissed Shannon's head. Then he said another prayer.

Luke stood and heaved the reins over the hitching post once outside Doc Murphy's office. He jumped over the seat, into the buckboard, and carefully collected Shannon as he secured the quilt.

William, on his heels and bouncing Zach, threw the door to Doc Murphy's open and stepped aside.

"Good God!" Doc exclaimed and motioned toward a back room. "Take that baby outside," he told William.

Luke carried her down the short, dark hallway and laid her on a table. He didn't see a lot of optimism in Doc's eyes after he'd examined her.

"Best go for now, Luke," Doc said. "I'll have my report when I have it."

Luke hesitated and Doc eased him out the door. William wasn't in the outer office. Luke took a chair, put his head between his knees, and part of him wished he'd kept his distance from Shannon all along as he'd intended.

Kate Reeds burst in and Luke attempted to quell her curiosity with minimal details. "And you got no idea who done it?" she asked, her eyes searching his with amplified intensity.

Luke had his suspicions and the sarcastic tone to her voice suggested she did, too. "Reckon our thoughts run in accordance."

"Texas Rangers ain't comin', Luke. No federal marshals neither. Abel says that outlaw John Wesley Hardin...you prob'ly heard of that ornery critter-kilt a deputy sheriff over to Brown County, down Texas-way, a couple months back. No surprise they consider our little fuss here in Leeds just that."

"I'll be headin' out once..." Luke stopped there and gestured toward the back room.

"A course," Kate said, cupping his hand.

"Seen anything of William?"

Kate laughed. "He had a rather interestin' proposition for Clarissa Mayfield."

Luke hung his head and felt his crows feet tingle.

"Quite an enterprisin' young man, he is. Gets 'im an eyeful and sees to that hungry youngen in one fell swoop."

Luke chuckled. "He ain't no gal-boy that's for certain."

Kate laughed and suddenly launched upright when Doc Murphy came from the back room, the stiff white cloth in his hands a sharp contrast to the crimson splotches covering his apron. "She'll live but she'll need some watchin' over."

Luke started for the narrow hallway.

Doc stopped him. "She needs her rest. If you're so inclined you can come by later."

Luke hesitated, determined feet still poised for the back room. "You tellin' me the God's honest?"

"I am," Doc said. "She's been through the mill. Leave her to her rest."

Kate slung an arm around Luke's waist. "You and William stay on with me and Abel. We got plenty a room and Abel says I surely know my way 'round the cook stove."

Luke ran his hands the entire circumference of his hat's brim. "Much obliged, Mrs. Reeds, but we got chores."

"Yer sheriff now," Kate reminded him.

"Still got chores."

"Then after. Supper'll hold just fine."

Luke thought about being just a few hundred yards from Shannon as opposed to miles. "Yes ma'am, we'd be honored. I best round up them boys."

"Leave the baby be. Me and Clarissa will see to 'im."

FIFTY-SEVEN

Luke had decided hours before, for the boy's sake, that he'd load the body in the buckboard when the time came. Ordinarily, he'd have no qualms about slinging the poor old bastard across Thunder's hindquarters and hauling him to town that way.

"Want me to put up yer horse?" William asked once they'd finished the chores.

"And find nothin' of that barn but a heap of sticks when we git back?"

William chuckled. "Reckon yer right. But won't he tag along?"

"You see 'im?" Luke didn't wait for him to answer. "He's long gone, boy. Must be a mare in season not fer off."

William blushed and mumbled, "Can't rightly blame 'im."

The boy sat up front with Luke, turning his head every now and then to glance at the covered body. He didn't say another word until they'd nearly reached town.

"You thinkin' on somethin'?" Luke asked him once he steered the horse onto Main Street.

"When you see Mrs. Cook, it be alright with you if I come along?"

"Don't see why not, as long as the Doc don't give us grief."

Luke reined Midnight when they reached the undertaker's. It didn't take long to put a name to the body. "Well if that don't beat all," the lanky, nearly toothless, odd fellow said aloud. "Never thought I'd see Mika Leeds step foot in this town ere again. Shame he's played out. A lot of folks woulda rather seen him swing."

* * * *

After supper, Kate echoed the undertaker's remarks. "Mika Leeds Jayhawked many a farmer's coin," she explained, "among other things".

Luke chuckled low over her word choice. Luke had never favored allegiance to either the union or confederacy during the war. However, regardless of Luke's lack of alignment with the Confederate Bushwhackers, Lance had successfully persuaded him to respect their conviction and passion for revenge.

He excused himself and sensed William on his heels before he reached the front door. Having already stabled Midnight, they walked from the edge of town to Doc's. Luke rapped lightly on the door, relieved a light still burned.

"Come in," Doc said, sweeping the door to the wall. "She's doin' well, all things considered. A little groggy, but she's been askin' for her boy."

Luke's hand flew to his forehead. He hadn't thought to bring Zach. Of course, she'd want to see him most of all.

Doc apparently read his thoughts. "She's too weak to be wrestlin' that youngster. Give it a few days."

"But don't she need to," Luke was at a loss for words.

"She's no longer lactating, if that's what you're gettin' at." Doc moved closer and spoke to Luke confidentially. "And I doubt she ever will again, if you get my meanin'."

"You tell her that?" Luke asked, feeling both rage and pity surge through him.

"That's not somethin' she needs to hear right now, but if she asks, I'll apprise her. Go on in, William, but don't be too long." When William disappeared through the doorway, Murphy dragged Luke outside. "It was Marsh, which don't come as no surprise. You familiar with his attack sometime back?"

"I heard enough," Luke said and felt his jaw tighten.

"Only reason Jack kept his nose clean this long where Shannon Cook's concerned is on account of her husband, though a lot of us figured Jack woulda gunned him down long ago."

Luke clenched his fists tighter and an angry rash ravished his face.

"Stay out here and cool off," Murphy suggested. "I'll go fetch us a bottle."

Luke's eyes routinely scanned the boardwalk and fixed on the bank. Doc returned and poured them both a drink.

* * * *

Inside, William managed to engage Shannon in a little small talk. Because her eyes wandered to Luke's the minute he stepped into the room and remained there long after he sat by her bedside, William decided it was time for him to say goodnight.

Shannon nodded and managed a slight smile. She started to speak and grimaced. Luke assumed her mind was on Zach, and he assured her he was in good hands. The revenge he intended to seek for her while liberating the town of Leeds he kept to himself.

"That's long enough," Doc warned, peering around the door jam. "You need your rest, young lady."

Luke leaned over her bedside and kissed her forehead. "I'll see you come mornin',"

She nodded weakly and was asleep before he cleared the door.

FIFTY-EIGHT

Hearing the shots just as the sun came up, Luke's eyes sprang to awareness. He slid his feet into his boots and checked both gun cylinders, innately. As Kate's fists pummeled his door, he directed gun barrels toward the ceiling, rolled his wrists, and clicked both cylinders shut. His gun belt hanging businesslike, he was already at the door before she knocked again.

"Jack's whore's outside," she told him, stringing every sentence together without drawing a breath. "Says he's holdup at Ruby's. Cut off one of the other whore's ears, he did," Kate cried hysterically, "and old man Jamison took the girl on to Doc's."

Abel spoke from behind her. "She says he killed Red Morton and the Chinaman both. He's in a mad state, the likes she's never seen. He's got 'im a bagful of money to boot! Killin' folks is one thing—"

"But takin' money outa yer pockets is the final straw, that it?" Luke interrupted sarcastically and pinned on the star.

"Now hold on, Richards!" Abel said before Kate pushed him aside.

"I'm afraid he'll go after Shannon if he knows she's still alive," Kate blubbered. "Maybe come after that baby a hers too," she shrieked, grabbing hold of Luke's arm.

"Only place he's goin' is the bone orchard," Luke seethed and brushed past them.

Luke thought it no wonder he hadn't found any tracks. Marsh had never left town. Belly crawling once he reached the saloon doors, he peered underneath attempting to get a fix on Jack's exact location. Failing, he rolled out of view and got to his feet. His backside hugging the brick structure, he stepped sideways, covertly pushed one door slightly askew, and stole a quick glance. He immediately spotted Irving at the bar and brought his finger to his lips. Judging from the commotion near a back corner, he assumed Jack's siege successfully continued from there. Irving eyes darted in that direction, verifying Luke's assumption.

Luke dropped to his knees and rolled under the winged doors. Then he stationed himself along the bar's brass kick rail. From there, he crawled along the base of the large mahogany structure to the end, disappointed when his view of Marsh remained limited. He'd have to rely on Irving's eyes.

Ruby and another woman noticed Luke's entrance, and Ruby eyes persuaded the young whore not give away his presence.

Jack saw the subtle exchange and fired randomly, shattering the saloon's window in five quick shots. "That you, Richards?" he bellowed in a bizarre baritone after which a woman's scream sliced through the eerie quiet. Before Luke could formulate a plan, Jack tossed a bloody finger toward the bar and demanded Luke show.

Instead, Luke stayed still and staked his position. A chorus of terrified screams suddenly sounded and a human heart, still beating, landed with a sickening thud near the corner of the bar.

"I got more where that came from!" Jack roared. "Come out, come out wherever you are!"

Luke immediately revised his strategy and propelled his body toward the opposite end. From there he could easily see Ruby but, once again, could only guess Jack's exact position. Before he could signal objection, Ruby grabbed her famed buffalo gun, 'Old Reliable', which she kept hidden behind the player piano, and stormed Jack's corner. "You got one bullet left by my count, you miserable son-of-a-bitch," she told Jack. "Care to wager odds which one a our guns'll make the bigger impression?"

Ruby reminded Jack of his mother. And strangling the cruel old hag while she thrashed about beneath him hadn't healed the deep-rooted emotional wounds. He grinned, one he'd practiced long and hard in the mirror, and placed the gun on the table. "You got me dead to rights," he told Ruby. "Got but the one bullet and I'm saving it for someone special."

Ruby dropped the Sharp's rifle to her side, her eyes fixed on his gun hand. Jack surreptitiously drew the dagger from the sheath within his boot and skillfully hurled it into her heart.

Luke had already revealed his position, gambling Ruby's advance to be just the distraction he needed. Rattled as he witnessed Ruby struggle for her last breath, Luke hesitated and missed his shot, his single opportunity. Jack's bullet penetrated his kneecap and Luke went down hard. Jack claimed Ruby's rifle and checked the chamber. Then he strolled over to Luke, kicked his gun out of reach, and plucked the other from his holster. Smiling over him, he ripped the star from Luke's vest and told the barkeep to bring him a bottle.

Irving's gaze fleetingly settled on Luke, and Luke read his intentions. Even should Irving successfully manage to break the bottle over Jack's head, unless he knocked him out somebody would die. Luke shook his head, nearly indiscernibly, and hoped Irving wasn't a fool.

Jack took the whiskey bottle from the barkeep and uncorked it. Straddling Luke, he said, "Let's have us a little man-to-man talk. Truth be told, I've never been one to hold my tongue on private matters, banking business being the exception. And I do believe I got some information regarding Shannon Cook might be of interest." Jack's manic laugh echoed off the walls. His eyes scanned the room and he yelled, "Now, those of you with a flair for more refined conversation best cover your ears." He held Luke's dead stare and told him, "Because there's nothing refined about what I did to her."

As Jack vividly described every detail, Luke's rage nearly superseded rational judgment. He waited for Jack to raise the bottle again, shot his upper body forward, head-butted him hard, and then wrestled him for the gun. Irving vaulted over the bar, but, by that time, Jack had secured the weapon and used the butt to shatter Luke's cheekbone. Jack retreated a few paces, exaggerated his aim, and told Luke to prepare to die.

A shotgun blast punched the air, the percussion rocking bottles off shelves. Jack's head exploded and the shooter collapsed in the doorway.

Old man Jamison peered cautiously over the saloon doors, then rushed in. "She heard that jezebel I took over to Doc's flappin' her jaw, and there was no stoppin' her," he breathlessly explained to anyone listening. "Took hold of my gun, she did, and off she went."

The acrid smell of gunpowder still hanging in the air, Irving swiped at his eyes. "Help me get him clear," he told Jamison, and they rolled Jack's body off Luke. "Stay with 'im. I'll go fetch the doc."

Luke's eyes probed the room for the shooter. Suddenly realizing Shannon's involvement, he used the wall for support and shimmed himself upright. Old man Jamison assisted him, and Luke hobbled frantically toward her. He plopped down on his backside and pulled her into his arms. Her body lifeless, he shook her while he anxiously called her name. When she opened her eyes, he buried his face in her hair and whispered, "Thank God!" Then he asked her, "What can I do?"

"You can make an honest woman outa me for starters, Luke Richards," Shannon whispered back.

ABOUT THE AUTHOR

A novelist for many years, *Shannon's Land* is definitely a departure from *Write Off*, the first of Woodling's Detective Michael Malone series, and her two young adult novels, *Slices* and *The Turning*. Although the author once considered psychological and political thrillers her niche, she is contemplating a sequel to this western.